M

Mala stared at the man, hard, as her heart freefell straight to her pelvis.

And her brain warped back twenty years to a time when nobody knew that Spruce Lake High's senior class president had a secret crush on a bad-ass kid whose ice-chip blue eyes regularly sent chills of forbidden promises down her spine, even though he never—not once—returned her smile.

A boy with sinfully thick, caramel-brown hair and the sharply defined, beard-shadowed face of a man; a boy whose lean, muscled body had filled out his worn, fitted jeans and T-shirts like nobody's business, whose direct, disquieting gaze spoke of innocence lost but not regretted. He had appeared out of nowhere, a month into their senior year, only to vanish six weeks before graduation. Mala hadn't seen him since.

Until today.

Dear Reader,

A new year has begun, so why not celebrate with six exciting new titles from Silhouette Intimate Moments? *What a Man's Gotta Do* is the newest from Karen Templeton, reuniting the one-time good girl, now a single mom, with the former bad boy who always made her heart pound, even though he never once sent a smile her way. Until now.

Kylie Brant introduces THE TREMAINE TRADITION with *Alias Smith and Jones,* an exciting novel about two people hiding everything about themselves—except the way they feel about each other. There's still TROUBLE IN EDEN in Virginia Kantra's *All a Man Can Ask,* in which an undercover assignment leads (predictably) to danger and (*un*predictably) to love. By now you know that the WINGMEN WARRIORS flash means you're about to experience top-notch military romance, courtesy of Catherine Mann. *Under Siege,* a marriage-of-inconvenience tale, won't disappoint. Who wouldn't like *A Kiss in the Dark* from a handsome hero? So run—don't walk—to pick up the book of the same name by rising star Jenna Mills. Finally, enjoy the winter chill—and the cozy cuddling that drives it away—in *Northern Exposure,* by Debra Lee Brown, who sends her heroine to Alaska to find love.

And, of course, we'll be back next month with six more of the best and most exciting romances around, so be sure not to miss a single one.

Enjoy!

Leslie J. Wainger
Executive Senior Editor

Please address questions and book requests to:
Silhouette Reader Service
U.S.: 3010 Walden Ave., P.O. Box 1325, Buffalo, NY 14269
Canadian: P.O. Box 609, Fort Erie, Ont. L2A 5X3

KAREN TEMPLETON
What a Man's Gotta Do

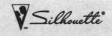

INTIMATE MOMENTS™

Published by Silhouette Books

America's Publisher of Contemporary Romance

 SILHOUETTE BOOKS

ISBN 0-373-27265-0

WHAT A MAN'S GOTTA DO

Copyright © 2003 by Karen Templeton Berger

This edition published by arrangement with Harlequin Books S.A.

Visit Silhouette at www.eHarlequin.com

Printed in U.S.A.

Books by Karen Templeton

KAREN TEMPLETON,

a Waldenbooks bestselling author, is the mother of five sons and living proof that romance and dirty diapers are not mutually exclusive terms. An Easterner transplanted to Albuquerque, New Mexico, she spends far too much time trying to coax her garden to yield roses and produce something resembling a lawn, all the while fantasizing about a weekend alone with her husband. Or at least an uninterrupted conversation.

This RITA® Award-nominated author loves to hear from readers, who may reach her by writing c/o Silhouette Books, 300 E. 42nd St., New York, NY 10017, or online at www.karentempleton.com.

Dedication
To my mother—known these days as Grandma Kay—
who has steadfastly supported whatever harebrained
thing I've ever wanted to do. A mother five times
over myself, I now understand just how much courage
that sometimes took.

Acknowledgments
To Roger Huder, not only for his crash scene rescue team
expertise, but because he also gamely helped me find a
way to place my hero in the middle of things. And to
Marilyn Pappano, who read an early draft of the scene in
question and didn't say, "You've got to be kidding."
Many thanks!

In memory of
Kathy McCormick, M.D., my steadfast advisor on all
things medical for several years. You will always be
remembered for your patience, generosity and kindness.

Chapter 1

Eddie King never had understood what it was about him that seemed to shake people up. Not that the pregnant lady frowning at his résumé on the other side of the cluttered, pockmarked desk seemed particularly shook up, exactly. But Eddie was hard-pressed not to notice that Galen Farentino hadn't yet quite looked him straight in the eye, either, even though she was the one doing the hiring.

He supposed a lot of people thought he was a bit on the eccentric side, if not at least worth keeping one eye on. For one thing, old Levi's and cowboy boots didn't fit most folks' expectations of what a five-star-quality chef was supposed to look like. Then when you factored in his refusal to get riled up about much, his preference for keeping to himself, the way he kept flitting from job to job after all these years…hell, in somebody else's shoes, he'd probably keep one eye on him, too.

Eddie linked his hands over his stomach, thinking how much the cramped office tucked behind the restaurant kitchen still looked pretty much like it had two decades ago. His peripheral vision caught the photo on one corner of the desk, a wedding shot of his prospective employer and some huge, dark-haired man in a tux. One of the man's arms possessively encircled his bride's waist, while the other supported a tiny blond girl on his hip. All three of 'em wore sappy grins.

Eddie glanced away, like the picture hurt his eyes.

He idly scratched his prickly cheek, thinking he needed a shave, bad, after that long drive from Florida. It was crazy, coming all the way up here when this job wasn't even in the bag yet. And why he'd been led to come back to Spruce Lake, he'd never know. Molly and Jervis had both passed away years ago, so it wasn't like he had any real ties to the place. And anyway, Eddie usually steered clear of small towns, much preferring the anonymity of the big city. But that ad in the trade rag on his former boss's desk had just kinda leapt out at him, and since the thought of spending the winter someplace where they actually *had* winter was not altogether unattractive, he'd figured what the hell. Since it'd been years since he'd applied for a job he hadn't gotten, he wasn't too worried about getting this one. And if he didn't? No big deal. He'd just move on.

He was real used to moving on.

"Your references are very impressive, Mr. King," the red-head now said, more to his résumé than to him. He guessed her to be around his age, but she mustn't've been in Spruce Lake back then, since he didn't recognize her. Then she looked up, reluctantly almost, her face not much darker than that white turtleneck sweater she had on underneath her denim maternity jumper. She'd said on the phone that both her doctor and her husband had ordered her to go easy for the remainder of her pregnancy, and that she then intended to take at least six, possibly eight, weeks maternity leave after that. So the job would last four, five months at the outside. Which suited Eddie fine.

As if reading his mind, she said, "I couldn't help but notice you've worked in—" she glanced again at the résumé, then back at him "—eight different states in nine years."

"Yes, ma'am, that's true."

Her head tilted. "Yet every reference I contacted said they were sorry to see you go. In fact, the owner of *La Greque* in

New Orleans told me he offered you quite a handsome salary to stay on.''

''He sure did.'' Galen's eyebrows lifted, encouraging an explanation. Eddie shifted in the same seventies-era molded plastic chair his butt had warmed during more than one lecture all those years ago. ''They were all temporary jobs, ma'am. Fill-ins, just like this one. Which is the way I like it, seeings as I don't like getting tied down to one kind of cooking for too long.''

The phone rang, cutting off further interrogation. Galen mouthed a ''sorry'' and took the call. Eddie crossed his ankle at the knee in the don't-give-a-damn pose that Al Jackson, Eddie's septuagenarian boss back when this had still been the Spruce Lake Diner, had seen straight through. An odd, rusty emotion whimpered way in the back of Eddie's brain; he frowned slightly at the scuffed heel of his boot, concentrating instead on the early season snow snicking arrhythmically against the office's tiny, high-set window. He hadn't mentioned his former ties to the place to his prospective employer—what would be the point?—but now that he was here, this odd, unsettled feeling kept nagging at him, like maybe there were answers here to questions he'd never bothered to ask before. Never wanted to.

Galen hung up the phone, picked up a pen and started twiddling with it. Her plain gold wedding band glinted in the flat light. ''If I hire you, can I trust you won't leave me high and dry?''

He kept his gaze steady, almost sighing in exasperation as a telltale blush swept up the woman's cheeks. All he was doing was looking at her, for God's sake. And if it was one thing Al had drummed into him, it was that if you want respect—if you want folks to take you seriously—you had to look them in the eye when you talked to them, a philosophy only reinforced by four years in the Marines. ''I may not be in the market for anything permanent, ma'am, but I don't leave people in the lurch. I'll stay as long as you need me to.''

After a moment, she apparently decided to believe him. ''Glad to hear it,'' she said, then awkwardly pushed herself up from her chair. Eddie stood as well, ducking underneath the still too-small door frame as he followed the woman back out into the immaculate kitchen, where a half-dozen assistants were preparing for the evening rush. The restaurant/pizzeria had taken over the building next door as well, making *Galen's* twice the size of the original diner, but the kitchen didn't look much different than it had. Oh, some of the equipment had been updated—a bigger, fancier stove, a pair of new Sub-Zero refrigerators—but otherwise, it, too, was just like he remembered. A shudder of déjà vu traipsed up his spine; it was right here that an old man had cared enough to show a displaced Southern boy with a two-ton chip on his shoulder how to channel all that resentment into making apple pie and hamburgers and beef stew and real milk shakes.

To do something with his life, instead of bitchin' about it.

He realized Galen was looking at him, her smile slightly apologetic. "You know, we don't have to do this right now," she said. "I mean, you probably want to find someplace to stay first, get settled in?"

Eddie shoved back his open denim jacket to hook his thumbs in his pockets. "Already did that, as a matter of fact. Got a room in a motel right outside of town. Figure I'll look for a furnished apartment or something, once you hire me." When she didn't take the bait, he added, "I can cook in my sleep, ma'am. So now's as good a time as any."

"Well, if you're sure…"

"I'm sure."

"Okay, then. Well, we agreed on three dishes, right? Your choice, except that one of them needs to pretty standard—red spaghetti sauce, lasagna, ravioli, something like that. I don't care about the others, as long as they're Italian. If they pass muster—"

"They will."

"—if they pass muster," Galen repeated, "you can start tomorrow."

Eddie stuck out his hand, quickly shook Galen's. "Deal," he said, then shrugged off his jacket, shoved up his sweater sleeves and slipped into the only world he trusted.

* * *

This morning, it had been nearly sixty and sunny. Now, at four-thirty, it was barely above freezing, and had been spitting snow for two hours already. And Mala Koleski, whose thirty-seven-year-old body's themostat didn't take kindly to sudden temperature changes, was freezing her hiney off. She wished.

"Come on, guys," she said through chattering teeth as she hustled the kids down her mother's ice-glazed walk and into Whitey, her ten-year-old Ford Escort, blinking against the tiny snow pellets needling her face. She usually tried to meet the school bus herself in the afternoons—a definite advantage to working from home—but it had taken her far longer than she'd expected to unearth last month's receivables from the garden center's new computer program after one of their employees decided to be "helpful." So now she was running late. And freezing to death. And grateful she'd gotten away from her mother's before the woman could scrutinize her for signs of physical and emotional decay.

"I need to stop at the restaurant for a sec," she said, yanking open the back door, "then we've got to get home or else there's gonna be a couple nekkid Pilgrims in the school play tonight. For God's sake, Carrie—button your coat!"

"I'm not cold," her seven-year-old daughter announced through a toothless gap as Mala practically shoved them both into the back seat.

"Why can't I sit up front?" Lucas whined.

"B-because it's not safe," she said to Lucas, clutching her sweater-coat to her chest. Her nipples were so rigid, they stung. "Carrie. Now. Button up."

Underneath a froth of snow-kissed, coppery curls, a pair of big blue eyes blinked back at her. "No."

"Fine. Freeze." Mala slammed shut the door and scurried around to the driver's side, hurtling herself behind the wheel. Yes, she knew the child would moan about how cold she was in five minutes, but tough. Mala had more pressing things to occupy her pretty little head about. Like finishing up those damn costumes. Thawing out her nipples. Figuring out how to finance Christmas without putting it on plastic. Again. Finding a new tenant for the upstairs apartment before the first big heating bill came. One who maybe wouldn't just up and leave, stiffing her for two months' back rent—

"Mama?" Lucas said behind her. "I gots to pee."

"Hold it until we get to *Galen's*, 'kay?" She gingerly steered the car onto Main Street, tucking one side of her hopelessly straight pageboy behind her ear. The bright red hair, the kids had clearly gotten from their father, but Carrie's curls were a total mystery.

The car's rear end shimmied a couple inches to the right; silently cursing, Mala carefully steered with the skid, pulled out of it. New tires—ones with actual treads—had just officially been promoted to the top of the priority list. Tires she might've had already if that jerk hadn't—

"I'm gonna wet my pants!"

"Do and you die," Carrie, ever the diplomat, cooly replied.

"Carrie," Mala said in her Warning Voice, despite feeling pretty much the same way. "Two more blocks, Luc—cross your legs or something."

Lucas started to whimper; Carrie started in about wussy, crybaby brothers, and Mala turned on the windshield wipers, thinking of all the joy Scott had missed by walking out of their lives three years ago. Okay, so maybe Mala had given him a push, but still.

She eased the car through a four-way stop, then glided into a parking space in the alley behind the restaurant, casting a brief but appreciative glance at the snow-speckled, pepper-red Camaro parked a few feet in front of her. Lucas was out of the car before she'd turned off the engine, hauling his bony little butt toward the propped open kitchen door.

"Lucas! Don't run—!"

"I told him to go before we left Grandma's," Her Supreme Highness intoned from the back seat, "but would he listen to me? Noooo—"

Splat! went the kid on the icy asphalt.

With a sigh, Mala hauled herself out of the car and toward the heap of now-sobbing-child lying facedown in the alley, her flat-soled boots slipping mercilessly in the quickly accumulating snow. Considering Lucas had on at least four layers of clothes, she doubted he was hurt, but she'd long since learned that the decibel level of his screams was in direct and inverse proportion to the seriousness of the injury. A stranger, however—like the tall man now darting out of the restaurant's kitchen door, snowflakes clutching his thick, wavy hair and heavy sweater like crystalized burrs—might well think the child had been set upon by ravening wolves.

"You okay, kid?" the man asked as Mala reached them both. In fact, he'd already helped the child to his feet, thereby proving that nothing was broken, although you sure wouldn't have known that from the Lucy Ricardo wail emanating from her son's throat.

"Yes, I'm sure he's fine," Mala said in the guy's general direction as she squatted down in front of her howling son. "Lucas! Luc, for heaven's sake…" She tried to keep her teeth from knocking as she dusted dry snow from the child's face and spiky hair. At least his glasses hadn't fallen off, for once. "It's okay, sweetie—"

"I falled dooooown!"

Mala tilted the child's face toward the light spearing from the partially open door. Nope. No blood. Out of the corner of her eye, she noticed Carrie's approach, the child's expression even more serious than usual underneath the fake-fur rimmed hood of her coat. Which was done up, surprise, surprise.

"Mama told you not to run, dork-face," she began, but there was genuine concern threaded through the otherwise imperious tones. Her daughter could be a pain in the patoot at times, but she was a protective pain in the patoot. Especially toward her younger brother, and especially since Scott's vanishing act. Just ask Josh Morgan, the third-grader who'd gotten Carrie's loaded backpack in the groin last year when he'd reduced her son to tears by calling him "Lucas Mucus." Still, the smart-mouth comment earned her Mala's glare. Carrie sighed. "Is he hurt?"

"Other than his pride, uh-uh," Mala said, straightening Lucas's wire-rimmed glasses and planting a quick kiss on his cold little lips before allowing herself the luxury of breathing in the warm, garlic-laced air beckoning from the noisy kitchen. Her stomach rumbled; she'd skipped lunch, and the thought of the canned chili she'd planned for tonight's dinner made her very depressed.

Lucas glanced up at the man standing silently a few feet away—oh, right, an audience—then back at Mala. "I wet my pants," he whispered on a sob, and she got more depressed. Especially when Carrie groaned.

"It's okay, sweetie," Mala whispered back, skimming tears off the mortified little face. "There's dry clothes in the trunk." With all the stuff she carted around in that trunk, she could outfit an emergency storm shelter for a month.

She finally hoisted herself upright, fighting the urge to groan as her joints popped—that extra twenty pounds she was still lugging around from Lucas's pregnancy wasn't doing her any favors—trying to get a good look at the man who'd come to Lucas's rescue. Except, between his skulking in the shadows in the darkening alley, as if not quite sure what to make of her kids—an understandable reaction—and the snow pinging into her eyes, all she got was a vague impression of angles and clefts and lashes no man should be allowed to have, dammit.

Along with a subsidiary impression that those angles and clefts and long lashes were somehow familiar.

"Thanks," she said, guiding the still whimpering Lucas toward the door.

The man nodded, muttering "S'okay" in a soft, Southern accent.

Ding! Ding! Ding!

Mala whipped around so fast she nearly knocked Carrie over. Oblivious to her daughter's affronted "Mama!" she stared at the man, hard, as her heart free-fell straight to her pelvis and her brain warped back twenty years to a time when she could still get into jeans that didn't have elastic at the waist, a time when nobody knew that Spruce Lake High's Senior Class President had a secret crush on a bad-ass kid whose ice-chip blue eyes regularly sent chills of forbidden promises down her spine, even though he never—not once—returned her smile.

A boy with sinfully thick, caramel-brown hair and the sharply defined, beard-shadowed face of a man; a boy whose lean, muscled body had filled out his worn, fitted jeans and

T-shirts like nobody's business, whose direct, disquieting gaze spoke of innocence lost but not regretted. He showed up at school every day, yet never spoke to anyone, never carried around any books, neither got involved in any activities nor caused any trouble. Not that Mala knew of, at least. He had appeared out of nowhere, a month into their senior year, only to vanish six weeks before graduation. Mala hadn't seen him since.

Until today.

She stood there, hugging herself against the cold, barely aware of Lucas's entreaties to get inside as she let Eddie King once again ensnare her gaze in his.

Then it dropped, unerringly and unapologetically, to her breasts, and she thought, *Hold the phone—somebody noticed.* Damn, she'd just about forgotten what it felt like to have a man look at her with a little *Hmmm* in his expression. God knew, Scott sure hadn't. Not once she'd gotten pregnant with Lucas, at least. Yeah, yeah, so she was a feminist turncoat. Tough. Rushes of sexual awareness didn't often happen to single mothers with two kids and too many pounds plastered to their butts. It was kinda nice, having her nipples tighten for some other reason than being cold.

Even if it was just a passing thing.

At seventeen, she'd been the quintessential good girl, while Eddie King had been the quintessential good girl's fantasy. At thirty-seven, not a whole lot had changed on that score.

But she had. At seventeen, she'd still believed in "one day…" At thirty-seven, that day had come and gone. But not before taking a healthy chunk out of her ample butt on its way out the door.

Eddie had no use for memories. The bad ones—and there were plenty of those—he'd ditched years ago. And the few good ones…well, that'd be like refusing to throw away a pair of shoes you'd outgrown, wouldn't it? No matter how cool they were, if they didn't fit, no sense hanging on to 'em.

Mala Koleski had been a pair of shoes that'd been the wrong

size from the get-go. A pair of shoes he'd never even bothered trying on.

Not that he hadn't been tempted.

In any case, he hadn't thought about her in years. Yet all it took was one chance meeting, a split second's worth of a connection that was startlingly and unmistakably sexual, to haul those memories of her front and center, boy, all shined up and ready for inspection.

Whether he liked it or not.

The kids annihilated the moment, as kids tended to do, and they'd all stumbled back inside, where he and Mala did this dumb so-wow-how-are-you-doing-fine-and-you? number until she'd shepherded her babies into Galen's office and Eddie'd gone back to the stove.

Where the sizzling sausage and peppers now taunted him. Galen had more or less left him to his own devices, and instructed her staff to do the same, even though they'd been helpful enough about showing him where everything was. Still, he could feel them all watching him as they went about their chores, like they were wondering how he was gonna pull this one off. Not from meanness, nothing like that. Just…curious. Probably as much about why he didn't join in their jawin' as about his cooking skills.

Well, if he got the job, they'd figure out that one soon enough. He was into doing his job, period, not getting overly chummy with his co-workers. It wasn't that he had anything against being friendly. And that chip he used to cart around had pretty much disintegrated years ago. He'd tell the occasional joke, put up his two bucks for the football pool or pitch in for somebody's wedding present, stuff like that. He just had no use for getting involved in people's personal lives.

Just like he had no use for anyone getting involved in his.

Eddie grabbed the bottle of wine set to one side, dashed some into the pan, reveling in the fruity steam that billowed up. From the office, he heard Mala's laugh.

Soft. That had been the only word to come to mind the first time he saw her, dashing between classes, surrounded by a half-dozen giggling girlfriends. Everything about her—her full figure, her velvet-smooth voice, even her perfume, which hadn't been overpowering like most of the other girls'—had made him think of being someplace warm and comfortable and…soft. She'd glanced at him, just for a heartbeat, as she whizzed past on her high-heeled sandals, and all the air just whooshed from his lungs at the sight of those vaguely curious green-gold cat's eyes. A smile, genuine and just this side of devilish, erupted between round, dimpled cheeks, but he wasn't completely sure it'd been for him. He remembered standing stock-still in her wake, watching the ends of her dark, gleaming hair twitching across the top of a generous bottom unabashedly displayed in snug designer jeans. An achy sense of longing that he never, ever allowed himself—not then, not now—had damn near knocked him over.

Eddie chuckled to himself as he turned down the heat under the pan. Oh, he'd ached, all right. Hell, his physical reaction at the time had embarrassed the life out of him. While it had been hardly the first time the sight of some girl had gotten him hot, it had definitely been the first time he'd feared for the buttons on his 501's. And while he was way beyond getting embarrassed about things like that these days, he wasn't beyond being startled. Because damned if those buttons weren't being put to the test again.

Her hair might be shorter, and that pretty face attested to the fact that she was a woman in her late thirties. But the eyes still held that note of devilment, and the dimples were still there, and her voice had ripened into a huskiness that both soothed and excited. And she was still soft as a hundred down pillows all piled on top of each other.

And still out of his reach.

Behind him, he heard a minor commotion as Mala apparently ushered the boy through the kitchen to the bathroom in order to change his pants. Mama-mode suited her well, he decided, although he also decided not to think too hard about the man responsible for those kids. The man who got to snuggle up to all that softness every night.

Dimly, he heard the boy start crying again.

He dragged over a bowl of already cooked rigatoni, dumped

out the sausage-pepper mixture. Damn, those kids were something else, weren't they? The girl, especially—whoo-ee. She'd
put the fear of God in King Kong. And the boy—what was up
with the crybaby routine? Kid had to be, what? Five, six? And
still bawling from a tumble in the snow? *Shew,* Eddie couldn't
remember the last time he'd cried. Being the new kid on the
playground every year or two kinda knocks that right out of
you—

"What's that?"

He looked down into a pair of challenging blue eyes underneath an explosion of red curls that didn't look real. Long legs
in white, lacy tights or whatever you called them peeked out
from underneath a purple jumper with flowers all over it, in-
congruously ending in clunky pink-and-silver sneakers. Kid
was skinny, but not fragile. Probably one of those girls who
liked to beat up boys. And did, regularly. "Italian sausage and
peppers. Wanna taste?"

That got a wrinkled nose. "No, thank you. Peppers don't
agree with me."

Cocking one brow, Eddie opened one oven door to remove
the baked ziti. Instantly, the temperature in the kitchen rose
another ten degrees. It wasn't that he didn't like kids, even
though the idea of having any of his own never even made the
playoffs. He just never quite knew what to make of them, was
all. "Who told you that?"

"Nobody *told* me," came the indignant reply. "I get all
burpy when I eat them. What's your name?"

Eddie straightened, set the ziti on the prep table behind them,
then grabbed a towel from the bar on the stove, wiped his
hands. Where the hell was the kid's mother? "Eddie King. And
yours?"

"Caroline Sedgewick, but most people call me Carrie. My
mama's Galen's accountant. That's why we're here, so she can
get some papers or something so she can take them home and
work on our computer. After she finishes our costumes for the
play tonight. Galen's gonna have a baby pretty soon. That's
why her belly's so big. Are you the new cook?"

Figuring the question signaled a break in the onslaught,

Eddie said, "That's what I'm hopin'. You know, you sure got a lot to say for such a little thing."

"I know." Unaffected, the child hiked herself up onto a nearby stool, making something sparkle on the sneakers. "I'm in first grade, but I can read better'n anybody in my class. Better'n some second graders, too. Lucas can't even write his name right yet, and he's only a year younger'n me. But he's a boy. And everybody knows boys are slower'n girls."

"Oh?"

"Uh-huh. Well, 'cept for my uncle Steve, who lives out on a farm. He just got married last summer and we all got to go to the wedding, which was all the way over in Europe because Aunt Sophie's a princess. But I heard Grandma Bev tell Pop-Pop one day when they didn't know I could hear 'em talking that my daddy was dumber than…well, it's a word that rhymes with 'spit' but I'm not supposed to say it." Then she pointed. "What's that around your neck?"

Feeling slightly dizzy—what was that about somebody marrying a princess?—Eddie felt for the chain that was always there, then slipped it out from underneath his sweater. Had to admit, the kid was kinda entertaining. If you were into bossy little girls with egos the size of Canada. And one thing he'd say for someone who talked that much: it made his part in the conversation much easier. "It's a cross. Used to belong to my mama."

Carrie leaned over to inspect it. He half expected her to whip out a jeweler's loop. "It's pretty. How come you have it?"

"My mama gave it to me right before she died, when I was real little. About your age, in fact."

She looked up, her expression melting into what Eddie could only surmise was genuine sympathy, tugging something in his chest he didn't want tugged. "Are you sad? That your mama died?"

"It was a long time ago. Like I said."

"Oh. Where's your daddy?"

With a shrug, he slipped the cross back inside his sweater, his emotions back inside their little box. "I have no idea."

Eddie realized the child was scrutinizing him like she was

trying to decide whether or not to admit him to the club. "My daddy left us when I was four," she said at last, showing a sudden interest in the way the flowers were arranged on her jumper. "We don't know where he is, either—"

"Carrie—for heaven's sake! Stop pestering the poor man!"

Eddie turned around to see Mala, Lucas in tow, jerkily shrugging back into her long tweedy sweater. The two spots of color sitting high on her cheeks kinda clued him in that she'd overheard.

"It's okay," he said, surprised to discover he meant it. At least, for the moment. Not that he wanted to make it a habit, mind, of having heart-to-hearts with little girls.

"Yeah, well…" Downright humming with nervous energy, Mala tugged a strand of electrified hair out of one gold loop earring as she dangled a red-and-black car coat in front of her son. Although she looked good—damn good—she'd put on a few pounds since high school, which she'd done her best to cover up with a baggy ivory sweater over a straight, beige skirt that came nearly to the insteps of her flat-heeled boots. Too bad, 'cause he'd bet she'd look real fine in a pair of those tight jeans like she used to wear. "She can talk your ear off, if you let her. C'mon, Luc…get this on—"

The strain in her voice tore another memory loose, of him and his mother walking down some street, somewhere, his hand tightly clamped in hers as she hurried along, as if trying to outrun her tears. He'd been four, maybe five, afraid to ask his mother why she was crying in case he was somehow at fault.

"I'm real sorry to hear about your husband," he said.

Mala glanced at him, clearly as startled as he was, then away. "S'okay. It's ancient history now. But thanks. I guess. Lucas, *now*. We've got to go—"

"Not until you help me with a taste test!" Galen said as she waddled over to the prep table. She planted her hands on her swollen belly, either ignoring or oblivious to the tension sputtering around her. "Wow, it smells absolutely fantastic!" She picked up a fork from the tray on the end of the table and went after the sausage and peppers. "C'mon, Mal—dig in. You know you want to."

"Galen, really, I'd love to—" Mala wrestled the coat onto the boy, who kept craning his neck to stare at Eddie like he couldn't figure out what he was "—but I'm so far behind now—"

"Oh, my God!" Galen pressed her hand to her chest, her expression downright rapturous, then dug into the ziti. Two seconds of chewing later, she said, "You can start looking for that apartment, because mister, you are *hired!* Mmm, Mal—" she swallowed "—what about yours?"

"What about my what?"

"Your upstairs apartment. Didn't you say you were looking for a tenant?"

The words *bad* and *idea* came roaring out onto the field from opposite sides of Eddie's brain and collided right at the fifty-yard line. It was one thing dealing with tight jeans for fifteen minutes, another thing entirely dealing with the prospect of being permanently—and hopelessly—erect for the next four or five months.

Because that's what living anywhere near this woman would mean. He didn't understand any more now than he did twenty years ago what it was about Mala Koleski that turned him on so much, but the fact was, she did. However, what he did understand was that—even allowing for the mutual consideration of such an eventuality—women with kids were bad news, not unless the idea of *long haul* was at least sitting on the sidelines. Hell, in Eddie's case, they weren't even in the stadium.

And judging from Mala's expression, she apparently thought the idea held about the same appeal as lying naked on hot coals. He wasn't sure whether to be insulted or flattered. Or what to do with the image of her lying naked on anything, which was now stuck to his brain like a piece of Scotch tape you can't shake off. "Oh, uh…eventually, sure," Mala said, then waved her hands. "Wait a minute…what about the apartment over the restaurant?"

"Not available. I promised it to Hannah Braden a few days ago." Galen turned to Eddie, her nose wrinkled. "College kid, wants a little independence, you know how it is."

"Well, my place isn't available, either. I mean, not yet."
Cheeks blazing, Mala knelt down to zip the kid's coat. "It's
not fixed up. The other tenants left it in a real mess and—"

"Oh, get over yourself. What did they do…leave crumbs on
the counter? Besides, you just said yourself you needed to get
someone in there soon."

Shew. That glare Mala was giving Galen could broil steaks.

"Hey, look, it's okay," Eddie interjected before somebody
spontaneously combusted. "Besides, I need to find someplace
furnished—"

"Oh, it is," Galen said, a tiny frown nestling between her
brows, like she was wondering why everybody was making
this so complicated. "And it's just a few blocks away, too."
Then she leaned over and stage-whispered, "And she's a real
pushover. Bet she'd let you have it for next to nothing."

"Galen! Honestly! Would you mind letting me negotiate my
own deals?"

A triumphant smile spread across the redhead's face. "Be
my guest."

Mala opened her mouth, only to immediately shut it again.

A short person tugged on Eddie's sleeve. He looked down
into Lucas's blue eyes, fought the urge to straighten the kid's
glasses. "If you come live with us, I'll let you borrow Mr.
Boffin."

"Lucas, for heaven's sake—he wouldn't be living *with* us!
Just…oh, *rats.*" Mala forked one hand through her hair, which
only added to her frazzled look. Then she said to Galen, "Mind
if we use your office?" turned on her flat heel at Galen's
"Sure" and stomped to the back.

Chapter 2

Eddie followed, shutting the door behind him. Damn, but it was a small office.

"Open the door," Mala said.

He did. It didn't help.

As badly as he'd wanted to see if she was as soft as she'd looked twenty years ago, that was nothing compared with how much he wanted to find out now. And if it'd only been a certain part of his anatomy talking, he probably could've ignored it a lot better than he was doing. But there was something else going on here, something he didn't understand and certainly didn't like. Something that involved wanting to ease those worry lines in her brow and convince her that not all men were idiots even though Eddie wasn't all that sure they weren't.

Especially the ones in this room.

"We don't have to let her bully us, you know," she said, startling a grin out of him.

He slipped his hands in his pockets, wondering if it was just his imagination that Mala seemed to be having a real hard time focusing on his face. "No, I suppose we don't." And here's where he could have said, without any trouble at all, *"And I*

*could just go find someplace else, so why don't we just forget
about it?"* So nobody was more surprised than him to hear
come out of his mouth, "But sounds to me like you got an
apartment that needs a tenant. And it just so happens I need a
place to live. So this could be a mutually advantageous prop-
osition, when you get right down to it."

Mala looked at him, wide-eyed, while he weighed the danger
of getting down to…things and wondered when his mouth and
libido had joined forces against his brain. She crossed her arms.
"Do you smoke?"

"Not anymore."

For a second, she almost looked disappointed. Except then
she half smiled, just enough for him to see the dimples, and
he thought maybe she was about to say something else. Only
she didn't, not right then at least, like her thoughts had tripped
her up. He thought again about this business of him uninten-
tionally rattling women the way he did, and it occurred to him
that this one didn't seem to be quite as rattled as most. At least,
not in the same way. Even as a teenager, she'd had no com-
punction about looking him dead in the eye. And even now,
while he could plainly see something like fear etched in those
faint lines around her mouth, the fear wasn't about him, he
didn't think, as much as it was about herself.

Although, the way he was thinking at the moment, maybe it
should be about him.

And where did he get off guessing what was going on inside
other people's heads? Let alone worrying about it?

Then they both seemed to realize they'd been staring at each
other for some time, which apparently provoked Mala into saying, in a rush, "Okay, here's the deal. It's a small one-bedroom
apartment, separate entrance, on the top floor of my house.
There's a kitchenette and a full bath. Yes, it's furnished, but
we're not talking the Hilton, here. Despite Galen's avowals to
the contrary, the tenants did leave it in a mess, and I haven't
had a chance to clean it yet, so don't come crying to me if the
toilet doesn't sparkle. I normally charge four-fifty a month, plus
utilities, but since you'll be moving into it 'as is,' I'll knock

off two hundred bucks for the first month. It's actually a pretty good deal, considering. And it's close.''

"And you don't want me there.''

"Smart man.''

"So why're you giving me a sales pitch?''

"Because I need the money and prospective tenants aren't exactly lined up around the block.''

Traces of what was left of her perfume wriggled through the cooking smells from the other side of the door. Something pretty, unfussy. Potent. He thought for a moment. Real hard. And not with the part of his anatomy that was.

"In other words, you can't be picky.''

"You got it.''

"I'll need a place for my car.''

"There's a detached garage in the back. You can use it.''

"Well, then, it sounds good to me. As long as—''

"But you have to promise to stay away from the kids.''

Not that he'd planned on adopting the little buzzards, but still. His eyes narrowed. "Since I'm not much of a kid person, that shouldn't be a problem. But what prompted this… condition?''

She let her breath out in a harsh sigh, then pinned him with her gaze again. "I can tell how much the kids already like you.''

That was not what he'd expected her to say. "I don't—''

"Galen told me all about your not ever staying in one place very long. This is nothing personal, believe me…'' She stopped, studied her hands for a moment. "They've been abandoned once already,'' she said softly. "And to be perfectly honest…well, Carrie sees Galen with her husband, and my brother with his new wife, and I can see the wheels turning in her head. That they have a complete family and we don't. Or at least, what she thinks of as 'complete.''' In the split second between sentences, Eddie saw her eyes darken. "What kind of mother would I be, letting them become attached to somebody who's only going to be around for a few months? So if you take the apartment, you have to promise me you won't let them glom on to you.''

He thought that over for a minute then said, God knows why, "That philosophy must make dating kind of hard," and she mumbled something about it not being a problem, and instead of letting it drop, like a smart man might've done, he heard himself say, "You tellin' me you haven't even gone out with anybody since your husband left?"

Her chin shot up, right along with her dander. Not to mention the color in her cheeks.

"I don't see how that's any of your business."

He let out a sigh. "You're right, and I apologize. Guess that's why I've never been much good at conversation. Can't seem to talk to anyone for more'n five minutes without pissin' 'em off. Which is why I suppose I prefer to keep to myself. Less hurt feelings that way."

After a moment, she said, "I don't wound easily, Mr. King. Not anymore, at least. But if you prefer your own company, that's fine with me. I'm only looking for a tenant, not a buddy."

"Which I suppose means you're not gonna answer my question."

Her eyes narrowed. He chuckled. Why, he didn't know, but something about this woman brought out the worst in him. Or the best, depending on how you looked at it. "No, I didn't think so. Okay—you want cash or a money order for the first month's rent?"

"Maybe…you should have a look at the place first?"

"Fair enough. Give me the address. I'll be over tonight."

"151 Mason. Three blocks east, one north. Two story house, white with blue shutters. Can't miss it—the yard looks like a Little Tykes graveyard. Oh, but I won't be there until after eight-thirty. The kids have a thing at school."

"Got it." He straightened up, started toward the door, then turned back. And this time, he saw a protective set to the lady's jaw that he doubted had anything to do with her children.

Eddie considered several things he might say, only to decide anything he might come up with would only land him in a heap of trouble.

* * *

You wouldn't think it would take so long to gather up a duffel bag, check out of a motel, then hit the grocery store for a few essentials, but it was nearly nine by the time Eddie got to Mala's house. Being as her Escort was hogging the driveway, he pulled the Camaro up in front, smirking at the white picket fence bordering the toy-strewn yard. A pair of rangy, almost bare trees fragmented the lukewarm porch light, further littering the snow-dusted lawn with grotesque, undulating shadows. It had cleared up; he got out of the car, hauling in a lungful of sharp, metallic air as he swung open the screaking gate at the foot of the walk.

His boots seemed to make an awful lot of noise as he made his way up to her front door.

Still in the same skirt and sweater she'd been wearing earlier, Mala opened the door before he hit the steps, one finger to her lips. "The kids are asleep," she whispered when he reached the top. Coffee-scented warmth beckoned from inside. "Come on in while I get the keys to the apartment."

He wiped his boots on the doormat, then did as she asked, quietly shutting the door behind him. The old-fashioned entryway was dimly lit, but enough for him to take in the wide staircase hugging one photo-lined wall, the faded Oriental rugs scattered crookedly on the scuffed wooden floor. And Mala. Her feet encased in thick, slouchy socks, she stood with one arm hugging her ribs, the other hand fiddling with a small gold loop in her ear. Caution hovered like a mistreated pup in her light eyes, at odds with the directness, the generosity of spirit that he now realized was what had intrigued him so much all those years ago. A tiny, fierce burst of protectiveness exploded in his chest, scaring the very devil out of him.

"Want some coffee?" she asked. "I just made it."

Eddie caught the automatic "no, thanks" before it hit his mouth. Fact was, a cup of coffee sounded great, and he couldn't think of any reason why he shouldn't take her up on her offer. Except one.

"I bet it's decaf."

"I bet you're wrong."

"Then I guess I don't mind if I do. Black, please."

"Gotcha. Be right back."

She straightened up the crooked rug with the heel of one foot before she went, though.

Other than the muted sound of some TV drama coming from what he assumed was the living room, the house was astonishingly quiet. And on top of the coffee aroma lay a mixture of other scents, of clean laundry and recent baths and woodsmoke. Like what most people meant when they said, "Home."

He grunted, looked around. He'd been in enough hacked-up houses to guess the layout of this one, although this seemed nicer than most. An office, looked like, in what had been the original front parlor to the right; through the wide doorway off to the left, he caught a glimpse of sand-colored wall-to-wall carpet, beige-and-blue plaid upholstered furniture, a warm-toned spinet piano, a brick fireplace, more pictures, more kid stuff. The kitchen would be out in back, most likely an eat-in, and there were probably some add-ons, too, maybe a couple of extra bedrooms or something.

"Here you go." Mala came down the hall, handed him a flowery but sturdy mug of coffee, then plucked a heavy sweater off the coatrack and slipped it on, all the while watching him, her expression still guarded. Waiting for a reaction, he realized, even if she didn't know that's what she was doing. He took a sip, nodded in approval. Relief flooded her features; a stab of irritation shunted through him, that she should care that much what some stranger thought about her coffee.

"It's real good," he said.

"My mother taught me, when I was still little."

Eddie lifted the mug in salute. "But *you* made it."

A smile flashed across her mouth, followed by a low chuckle. "You can really lay it on thick, can't you?"

He angled his head at her. "I'm no better at flattering than I am at conversation, Mala. The coffee's good. So just deal with it."

She blushed, nodded, then slid her feet into a pair of wooden clogs by the door. "The entrance is in the back," she said, yanking open the front door. When he glanced at the stairs right there in the hallway, she simply said, "Blocked off," and left it at that.

And here Mala had thought she was immune to things like slow, sexy smiles and the pungent, spicy scent of fresh-out-of-the-cold males.

Not to mention the sight of soft, worn jeans molding to hard, lean thighs.

Ai-yi-yi.

The thin crust of snow crunched underfoot as she led Eddie wordlessly around to the side, then up the wooden stairs leading to the apartment.

The key stuck.

"It does that when it's humid," she said under her breath, wondering, just as the damn lock finally gave way and the door wratched open, why every other sentence out of her mouth these days seemed to be an apology. She flicked on the living room's overhead light, stepping well out of the range of Eddie's pheromones as he followed her inside. She cringed at the faint tang of old pizza and stale beer still hovering in the air, even though she'd cleaned up the worst of the mess more than a week ago.

"If the lock gets to be too much of a hassle," she said, "let me know. I'll change it out."

His face remained expressionless as he took in the room. She clutched the coffee mug to her chest, hoping the warmth would dissolve the strange knot that had suddenly taken root smack in the center of her rib cage. Her nerves lurched, sending her heart rate into overdrive. "Like I said, it's not the Hilton."

To say the least. Bare, white walls which needed another coat of paint, she noted. Beige industrial grade carpet. Ivory JCPenney drapes over the two large windows. The earthtone tweed sofa and two equally colorless armchairs had been in her parents' den, once upon a time; Mala had scrounged the coffee table, mismatched end tables and black bookcase from yard sales, picked up the plain tan ginger jar lamps at Target. Not shabby—she'd seen shabby, this wasn't it—just basic. And about as personal as a dentist's office.

"Feel free to hang pictures or whatever, make it feel more like home."

No comment. Just the buzz from that sharp blue gaze, silently taking everything in over the rim of the mug as he sipped his coffee. Mala swiped her hair behind her ear.

"Um, kitchen's over there." She pointed to the far end of the room where, behind a Formica-topped bar, the secondhand refrigerator sulked in the shadows. The living room light reflected dully off the grease-caked, glass-paned cabinets: she made a mental note to buy more Windex. Her mother would have a cow if she knew Mala was actually showing someone the place in the condition it was in. "I guess what they must've done was knock out a wall between the master bedroom and one of the smaller ones to make the kitchen area and living room, leaving the bedroom and bath the way they were."

The hair on the backs of her arms stirred. She glanced over, caught Eddie watching her, his gaze steady, unnerving in its opaqueness, much more unnerving in its overt sexual interest. Over a frisson of alarm, she squatted, grimacing at some stain or other on the carpeting. Between his silence and his staring and her nerves, she was about to go nuts.

"Why do you keep looking at me?" she said to the stain.

"Sorry," he said. Mala looked up. He wasn't smiling, exactly, as much as his features had somehow softened. "Didn't realize I was." Then he added, "I just would've thought you'd be used to having men gawking at you."

The slight tinge of humor in his words threatened to rattle her even more, especially because she realized he wasn't making fun of her. She stood, her cheeks burning, then crossed to the empty bookcase, yanking a tissue out of her sweater pocket to wipe down the filthy top shelf.

"Like I said, I haven't had a chance to clean, so it looks a little woebegone at the moment. But it's a nice place when it's fixed up. There's lots of light in here during the day, and everything works. I'm afraid you're at my mercy for heat, since the thermostat's downstairs and I tend to think there's nothing wrong with having to wear a sweater indoors in the middle of winter, but it's automatic, on at six-thirty, off at ten. And the apartment has its own electric meter, so I'll be passing along that bill to you separately—''

His chuckle caught her up short. She turned, her breath hitching in her throat at the sight of the smile crinkling his eyes. If he'd smiled at her like that when they'd been back in school…well, let's just say her virtue might have gone by the side of the road long before it actually did.

"Now I know where your daughter gets it," he said.

"Gets what?"

He held up his hand, miming nonstop talking.

She decided it wasn't worth taking offense. "You should meet my mother," she said, only to silently add, *No, you shouldn't* as she started down the hall. "Bedroom and bath are right down here…"

"What'd he do to you?"

Mala turned, startled. "Who?"

"Your husband."

"What makes you think—"

"You weren't like this before. Nervous, I mean. Like you're about to break."

On second thought, things were a lot better when he *wasn't* talking. "How would you know what I was like? You wouldn't even speak to me back then."

"Don't always have to converse with somebody to know about them. In fact, not talking makes it easier to watch. And listen. See things about folks maybe they can't always see for themselves."

Anger, apprehension, curiosity all spurted through her. "And what is it you think you see about me?"

"I'm not sure. Someone who's lost sight of who she is, maybe."

The gentleness in his voice, more unexpected than the words themselves, brought a sharp, hard lump to her throat. For three years, she'd refused to let herself feel vulnerable. In the space of a few minutes, this man—this stranger—threatened to destroy all her hard work.

Her fingers tightened around the handle of her mug. "Do you make it a habit of going around analyzing people without being asked?"

He shook his head, his expression serious. Genuinely concerned. "No, ma'am. Not at all."

"Then why do I rate?"

"Because it burns my butt to see how much you've changed," he said simply, softly, waving the cup in her direction. "That the girl who didn't seem to have a care in the world now seems like she's taken on all of 'em."

She laughed, although that was the last thing she felt like doing. "I'm twenty years older than I was then. I'm a divorcée with two kids and my own business. I have bills out the wazoo, a car that needs coaxing every morning to get going and parents who worry about me far more than they should be worrying about someone this close to forty. So, yeah, I guess I've got a little more on my plate than worrying about acing my trig exam or how many balloons to order for the senior prom."

"That's not what I'm talking about."

Zing went her heart, thudding and tripping inside her chest. "I told you," she said quietly, desperately, scrabbling away from treacherous ground, "I'm just looking for a tenant. Not a buddy. Or..." She shut her eyes, dragged the unsaid out into the open. "Or anything else."

"Anything else?" he drawled on a slow, knowing grin.

Embarrassment heated her cheeks. Cripes, she was more out of the loop than she thought. "I'm sorry. I have no idea where that came from—"

"It came right from where you thought it came from," he said, his voice low and warm and tired-rough. "From me."

Oh, dear God.

"I can't...I mean, we c-can't—"

"I know that. Which is why I'm not really coming on to you, even though that's how you're no doubt reading it." She frowned, thoroughly confused. He smiled, and her insides went all stupid on her. "What I mean is, I can't help it if I'm sending out 'I'm interested' vibes. I am," he said with a no-big-deal shrug. "But I get what you're saying. And that's fine with me.

I'm not lookin' for anything, either. Not now. Probably not ever. The idea of settling down gives me nightmares, if you want to know the truth. I just don't have whatever it takes to be a family man, I guess. And like you said, the kids…'' He let the sentence trail off. ''But that doesn't mean a few not-very-gentlemanly thoughts haven't crossed my mind in the past few hours. About what things could be like if both of us weren't so dead set on avoiding complications.''

Her ears started to ring. ''You're attracted to me?''

There went that sin-never-looked-so-good smile again. ''Didn't I just say exactly that? Oh, Lord, lady,'' he said on a chuckle. ''For a bright woman, you are sure slow on the uptake about some things, aren't you?''

Apparently so. Well, yes, there'd been that *hmmm* thing back at the restaurant, but she didn't think that was anything personal. So now she stared at her coffee for a good three or four seconds, luxuriating in the idea of being found desirable. Realizing that, if she were smart, she'd tell him the apartment was no longer available. Instead she lifted her eyes and said, ''Thank you, Mr. King.'' *You have just given me reason to live.*

He lifted the mug in salute, his mouth tilted. ''Anytime.''

She definitely caught *that* fast enough. Fighting back yet another blush, she mumbled something about seeing the rest of the apartment and clomped down the short hallway to the back. Eddie followed, slowly, as if he had no use for time.

Mala stopped in front of the white tiled bathroom, which was almost all tub, a wonker of a claw-footed number. A plain white shower curtain hung like a plastic ghost from a ring over its center. Eddie was standing very close to her as they both peered into the room. In fact, if she moved an inch to the right, she could…

…see that the tub had more rings than Saturn.

''And for what it's worth,'' she said, whacking her way through a jungle of hormones to get to the small bedroom, ''there's a walk-in closet. Cedar-lined, no less.''

But she could tell Eddie's gaze had been snagged by the linens—sheets, blankets, pillows, towels—neatly stacked in the center of the fairly new double mattress. He walked over, skimmed one knuckle over the pillow. Mala tried not to shiver.

"I thought maybe you might not have any of your own," she said from the doorway. "You know, since you just got here. And I have extras. Mostly stuff my mother pawned off on me. There's dishes in the cupboards, too, and a couple pans and stuff. But that doesn't mean you get maid service," she added quickly. He twisted around, amusement crackling in his eyes. And she found herself fighting a twinge of disappointment that they'd already explored the outer limits of their relationship five minutes ago. "Washer and dryer are downstairs, in the mudroom. I do laundry on Fridays, usually, but you're welcome to use them any other time."

He studied her for a long moment, then said, "Sounds good to me. Where do I sign?"

She wasn't sure whether to be relieved or scared witless. "Come on back down. The receipt book's in my office."

He shadowed Mala into the office, pulling out his wallet while she rummaged through her desk for her receipt book. He wasn't a particularly big man, not compared with her line-backer brother, or even Galen's husband, Del, but sometimes there's more to a man than his size. In Eddie's case, it was his quiet intensity, she supposed, that seemed to infuse every molecule with his presence. Not to mention every molecule in her body. The book found, she glanced over, clearly saw four hundreds and a fifty in his outstretched hand.

"I said two-fifty for the first month, remember?"

"I know what you said. But you'll find it's real hard to argue with someone who won't argue back."

Irritation singed her last nerve. But at herself, not him. "I'm not a charity case, Mr. King."

"The name's Eddie. And what you are, is stubborn. Didn't I just tell you you'll get nowhere arguin' with me?"

"Why?" she asked, just this side of flummoxed. First the man as good as says he has the hots for her, then he wants to throw away two hundred bucks. This was seriously messing with her entire belief system. "Why on earth would you voluntarily pay more than I asked?"

"I have my reasons," he said. "Now you gonna take your money or not?"

She wrestled with her pride for about two seconds, then took the money. "Thanks."

"See how easy that was?"

A quick glance caught the slight smile teasing that take-me-now mouth. Mala wrote out a receipt, annoyed to discover her hand was shaking, then handed it to him with the keys. "I'll try to get up tomorrow sometime to clean—"

"I can clean my own bathtub," Eddie said, slipping his wallet into his back pocket, then setting his empty coffee mug on the corner of her desk. "You have a nice night, now. I'll see myself out."

Mala sank into her desk chair after he left, only then noticing her answering machine was flashing. She really should get Caller ID one of these days, but right now it was ranked way on the bottom of a depressingly long to-do list. She halfheartedly punched the play button.

A hang up. Just as well, since she didn't think she could conduct a logical conversation right now if she tried.

Eddie stomped up the stairs to the apartment, his forehead knit so tight, he thought it might stay that way. And he wasn't breathing right, either. Doggone it—what *had* he been thinking? In the space of a half hour, he'd managed to break every single rule in his book, number one being, "Don't get involved, bonehead."

He batted open the door—nobody'd bothered to lock it, seeings as he was coming right back up, anyway—and went inside, jerking back the drapes and opening a living room window to air out the place some. Not that he hadn't been in places that'd smelled a far sight worse....

Shoot, it must've embarrassed the life out of Mala, showing him the place in this condition. Women tended to get their drawers in a knot about stuff like that. And this one's drawers, he imagined, thinking back to when he used to watch her scur-

rying from class to class, her arms always loaded with about a
dozen books, had probably been knotted since she was three.

Those eyes of hers…damn, damn, *damn*. Fierce and questioning and scared and so incredibly honest, even behind that
puny veil of control, it knocked him clear into next week.

Hell, Eddie was the last person to think about reassuring
some woman he barely knew that things'd work out. About
reassuring *anybody*. He didn't much believe things did, for the
most part. But he was at least used to dodging the crap life
seemed determined to fling in his path. If Eddie didn't like the
way things were going, he could pretty much just up and walk
away. Mala Koleski, though, wasn't the type of person who
could do that. Not with two kids, especially. He could tell that
right off, and he admired her for it. Which was why Eddie
couldn't help thinking that here was someone who deserved
whatever it was she wanted.

That she needed to know that.

Still, what the Sam Hill had come over him, getting all personal like that? And then, even worse, admitting he was attracted to her? Eddie rammed a hand through his sorry-looking
hair, then just held it there, even though most of his brain cells
had long since left the building. Sweet heavenly days, he'd
never wanted to kiss a woman so bad in his life. And he sure
had never wanted to take one in his arms and tuck her head
against his chest and just…hold her.

He slipped off his jacket, threw it on the sofa, then went on
back to the bedroom to make up the bed. It smelled much better
in here, thank heaven. Like freshly washed linens.

And Mala.

With a groan of frustration, Eddie sank onto the edge of the
bare mattress, scrubbing a hand across his face.

Okay, so he'd admitted his attraction because something told
him it'd been a long time since anyone had let Mala Koleski
Whatever-Her-Married-Name-Was know she *was* attractive.
That a woman didn't have to look like those emaciated Hol-
lywood actresses for a man to get turned on. So he figured she
should know that she was worth a man's time and attention,

doggone it. Even if he couldn't be that man for more than about two minutes.

But that was okay, since he figured hell would freeze over before she'd take him up on his offer, such as it wasn't. Women like her just didn't do that, get involved with strays like him.

A weird, empty kind of feeling swelled inside him, vaguely familiar but definitely unwelcome. He got up, trying to shake it off, but it followed him right into the bathroom like an overloyal puppy.

"Go away," he actually said out loud, but it didn't. He looked over at the sink as he draped the thick, soft towels over the bar next to the john, saw the new bar of soap she'd left out for him.

The emptiness torqued into an sharp, nasty ache.

"You can't," he said to his reflection. "*She* can't."

He yanked open the cupboard door under the sink, found a whole mess of cleaning supplies. Dumping a thick layer of cleanser into the tub, he set to scrubbing it, thinking it'd been a long time since he'd entertained the idea of wanting something he couldn't have.

Chapter 3

The Monday before Thanksgiving, Mala lay in bed, half-asleep, trying to fight off that itchy, icky feeling you get when Something Bad is about to happen.

"Mama! Guess what!"

She burrowed down farther into the pillows. "Unless there's a van outside with balloons all over it," she said, "go away."

"Ma-*ma!*" Like Tigger, Carrie *boing-boinged* up the length of the bed, and it occurred to Mala that the only time her bed shook these days was when small children were jumping on it. Which, while a dispiriting thought, didn't qualify as the Something Bad because that wasn't something that was *going* to happen. It already had. "It's a snow day!"

That, however, definitely made the short list. But after marshalling a few more brain cells, Mala decided that, nope, that wasn't quite it, either.

Not that this wasn't bad enough—if it were true—since that meant, being as the kids were already off for Thanksgiving Thursday and Friday...and Saturday and Sunday...she'd only have two kid-free days to do five days worth of work. Swiping her hair out of her face, Mala hiked herself up on one elbow, trying to get a bead on Carrie's beaming, bobbing face. Her curls were a radiant blur in the almost iridescent glow in the many-windowed, converted porch she used as her bedroom.

"You're kidding, right?"

"Uh-uh. We got like a million feet of snow in the yard! You can go look! I already listened to the radio and they said the Spruce Lake schools were closed! We don't have any scho-ol, we don't have any scho-ol!"

Mala suppressed a groan as she glanced at the clock radio by her bed. Seven-ten. Far too early for so many exclamation points.

In footed, dinosaur-splashed jammies, Lucas unsteadily tromped across the bed, dropping beside Mala with enough force to rattle her teeth. "I'm cold," he said, wriggling underneath the down comforter next to her, his beebee—as he'd christened his baby blanket at eleven months—firmly clutched to his chest.

"It'll warm up in a few minutes," Mala said.

Carrie skootched down on Mala's other side, planting her ice-cold feet on Mala's bare calf.

"Cripes, Carrie!"

"The heat's not on."

Damn. The furnace pilot must've gone out again. That made the second time this week. Not that it was that big a deal to relight it, but she supposed she couldn't put off having somebody come out to give the ancient furnace a look-see any longer. Especially as she had a tenant. A tenant who, bless him, hadn't yet complained about freezing his butt off in the mornings.

A tenant who, bless him, had made himself scarce since the night he moved in.

Except in her dreams.

Lucas snuggled closer, smelling of warm little boy and slightly sour jammies. Ah, yes…reality. As in, kids and clients and recalcitrant furnaces and laundry and meals to fix and mother's and brother's and well-meaning friends' worried looks to dodge. And vague, itchy-icky feelings of impending doom.

Running away sounded *pret*-ty damn attractive, just at the moment.

Just at the moment, she wondered what it would be like to be able to come and go whenever you pleased, not having to answer to anyone, not be tied down to any one place for longer than a few months.

Carrie threw her arm around Mala's middle, leaned over and kissed her on the cheek.

Not having a child—or two—to come get in bed with you on a cold, snowy morning and remind you that you were the center of their universe.

She hugged and kissed first one kid, then the other, then gently swatted Carrie's bottom through the bedclothes. "C'mon, move over—I gotta get up."

"C'n you make pancakes?"

"Maybe. After I get the furnace going." Mala struggled out from underneath the covers, static electricity crackling as she yanked at her flannel nightgown to dislodge it from the bedding. Half hopping, half stumbling, she stuffed her feet into her old shearling slippers as she made her way across the carpet to the window to see just how generous Mother Nature had been.

Yup—she rammed one arm, then the other, into her terry cloth robe, glowering at the vast expanse of white outside her window—it had snowed, alrighty. Not a million feet, but at least one, gauging from the pile of the white stuff on the picnic table. Oh, joy.

It was still flurrying, although the faint blue patches in the distance meant the storm would probably break up before noon. But with this much snow already on the ground, Mala thought on a huge, disgusted yawn, nobody was going anywhere, at least not until some kind person took pity on them and plowed the street. Which could be Christmas, with her luck. Whitey was probably sitting in the nice dry attached garage, chuckling. Man, she'd sell her soul for something with all-wheel drive.

The ceiling creaked slightly under the pressure of Eddie's heavy, deliberate footsteps overhead. She heard the upstairs door slam shut, followed by the sound of boots clomping down the outside stairs. She edged back from the window and watched him plod through the soft snow toward the second garage out back in just his jeans and that denim jacket of his, and she felt her brow furrow in concern that he wasn't dressed warmly enough.

Lord. She was such a mother.

He had the day off—the restaurant was closed on Sundays and Mondays—and she found herself wondering what he'd do, since his Camaro wasn't any more snow-worthy than her sissy little Escort. Not that it was any of her business. She just wondered.

Mala suddenly realized he'd come back out of the garage and was looking in her direction through the light snow, his gaze steady in an otherwise expressionless face. She doubted he could see her, not from that distance and with it still snowing, but it was as if he knew she was standing there.

Heat dancing across her cheeks, Mala backed away, just as a sudden shaft of sunlight turned the flurries into whirling, glittering confetti. And as if in a dream, Eddie began trudging across the yard toward her window, the sparkling flakes settling onto his thick, curly hair and broad shoulders like fairy dust, at such odds with the serious set to his mouth. When he got to within a few feet of the window, he stopped, then mimed shoveling.

Mala raised the window, the brittle cold instantly goosebumping her skin. Lucas crawled out of the bed and wedged himself between her and the windowsill. One little hand arrowed into the soft drift. "Honestly, Lucas—" Mala snatched back his hand, then wrapped him in her enormous robe and hugged him to her stomach, like a mother hen enveloping her chick. "You could just come around to the door, you know," she said to Eddie, her breath a cloud.

His gaze snapped back to her face. "Waste of time, seeing's as you were already standing there. So, you got a snow shovel?"

"You don't have to—"

"I need to dig out my car."

"Oh, of course." She shivered. "Yeah, there's one in the shed."

He turned, glanced at the wooden shed huddled against the back fence, then angled his head back to her. "It locked?"

She shook her head. He nodded, then trooped away.

A half hour later, she was standing in her living room after her shower, staring at the TV and contemplating the possibility of being sucked into the perpetual springtime of Teletubbie-land—but only if one could exterminate the Teletubbies first—when she heard the rhythmic scraping of metal against cement outside and realized she'd been had.

Eddie hadn't exactly planned on shoveling the entire walk when he'd gotten up this morning. After all, he was just the tenant. Wasn't his responsibility. But then he got to thinking about it, and it just seemed like the right thing to do. And since not too many opportunities to do the right thing crossed Eddie's path, he figured he might as well take advantage of it. You know, just in case St. Peter asked him for a list or something down the road.

Didn't hurt that the exertion had the added benefit of taking the edge off his run-amok libido.

It didn't make a lick of sense. There she'd stood, no makeup, her hair every-which-way, wearing some kind of sack with a bigger sack thrown over it, and his blood had gone from frozen to boiling in about ten seconds. And she was just as close to forty as he was, to boot. In fact, in the stark light, he'd even seen a few strands of gray in her dark hair. Yet she opened her mouth, and that morning-gravelly voice of hers spilled out of the window at him, and all he could think was, *whuh.* He'd been trying to put a finger on just what it was about her that turned him inside out for the past half hour—okay, for the past week—but he was no closer now than when he'd started.

The sidewalk was looking pretty good, though.

Eddie straightened, letting his back muscles ease up some, then wiped sweat from his brow with the back of his sleeve before it froze to his forehead. Underneath the denim jacket, he had on three layers of clothes, and now he was overheated.

His breath misted in front of his face as he squinted in the snowfall's glare, taking in Mala's neat little neighborhood, a conglomeration of one- and two-story houses, some frame, some brick, most with porches. Yards were small to average, tidy, liberally dotted with snow-flocked evergreens. Fireplace smoke ghosted from a few chimneys, teasing the almost bare limbs of all the oaks and ashes and maples, slashes of dark gray against the now crystal-blue sky. A few blocks off, a small lake, embedded in a pretty little park, twinkled in the sunlight.

It was a nice town, he supposed. If you liked that sort of thing.

From the back, he heard the kids yelling and laughing; Mala must've just let them out. Eddie went back to work, listening to them whooping it up over his shoveling, trying to ignore the ache of pure, unadulterated envy threatening to crush his heart. Still, it was a good thing Mala was doing, giving them the freedom to be happy in spite of what their daddy had done.

She was a good woman, he thought, almost like it was a revelation. And his thinking that had nothing to do with his breath-stealing sexual attraction to her. It had everything, however, to do with why he needed to stop thinking about sex every time he thought about Mala Koleski.

The front door opened. He bent farther over the shovel, but not before he noticed she was wearing baggy blue sweats over a gray turtleneck. She clunked down the steps in those clogs of hers, something clutched in her hand.

"Here. You might as well use these."

Eddie looked over, noticed her hair was still damp, like she hadn't taken the time to dry it properly. Then he saw the gloves in her hands. Turned away. "Those your husband's?" Down the street, someone else came out of his house, shovel in tow.

"I would've burned them if they had been. No, they're a pair of my father's. He left them here a year ago. We couldn't find them, so he got another pair. Of course, then they turned up. So, anyway…" She pushed them toward him.

They were good gloves. Pigskin, maybe, lined in fur.

He shook his head. "I can't take those."

"Don't be ridiculous. What am I going to do with them?"

When he didn't reply, she added, "Borrow them, then, if I can't dislodge that bug from your butt. But in case you haven't noticed, this is Michigan. In November. It gets cold."

Eddie lifted his gaze. "Says the woman standing out in twenty-degree weather with wet hair."

Stubbornness vied with amusement in those cat's eyes of hers, softened by the breath-cloud soft-focusing her just-washed face.

"Who'd be back inside by now if you'd stop arguing with me."

He took the gloves, put them on. They fit perfectly.

"Thanks," he muttered.

"You're welcome. And thanks for shoveling. I appreciate it."

Eddie grinned. The gloves felt real good, he had to admit. "I take it this isn't one of your favorite chores?"

She smiled back. "You might say that—"

A child's scream blew the moment all to hell. They both turned in time to see Lucas—at least, Eddie thought that's who it was, it was hard to tell with all the clothes the kid had on—barreling through the side gate, bellowing his head off. Carrie followed, her hatless curls fire in the sun, yelling nearly as loudly.

Mala's hands flew up. "Geez, Louise…what *now?*"

"Carrie hit me in the face with a snowball!"

"I did not! It hit your shoulder!"

"There's snow in my eyes!"

"That's 'cause it bounced! But I didn't throw it at your face!" She whirled around to her mother. "I swear!"

"You're *lyin'!* An' it *hurt!*"

Carrie stomped her foot, her rage-red face clashing with her hair. "It did not, crybaby! The snow's too soft to hurt!"

"All right, the both of you," Mala said, her hips strangled by a pair of snowsuited arms, "that's enough. Okay, honey," she said to Lucas, cupping his head as he hung on to her for dear life. "You'll live. But honest to Pete, Carrie, *how* many times have I told you not to throw snowballs at him?"

''He threw one at me first!'' the girl shrieked, her arms flying.

''Did not!''

''Did so!''

''I t-told you to stop and you wouldn't! You jus' kept throwin' 'em and throwin' 'em, an' I ast you to stop!''

Her mouth set, Mala glared at her daughter. ''Carrie…?''

The ensuing silence was filled only by the sound of someone else's shovel rasping against their sidewalk. Then, ''You always take his side! Always!''

In the space of a second, Eddie saw weariness add five years to Mala's face. ''That's not true, Carrie—''

''Yes, it is! He's the baby, he always gets his way! Ow!''

All three faces turned in Eddie's direction, as Carrie wiped the remains of a half-assed snowball from her shoulder, her mouth sagging open in shock as bits of snow dribbled down one cheek. ''Hey! Why'd you do that?''

Eddie leaned on the shovel handle. ''Did that hurt?'' he asked quietly.

''N-no,'' the child said, tears cresting on her lower lids. ''But it wasn't very nice.''

''No, I don't suppose it was, was it?'' he said, then straightened, tapping the shovel on the sidewalk, just once, before he said to Mala, ''You got any salt? I might as well lay some down so this won't freeze up on you all over again tonight.''

''What? Oh, uh…in the shed,'' Mala said, her voice brittle, her eyes glittering. Then after a couple of beats of looking like she was going to pop, she gathered her chicks and hustled them back to the house.

In the sunlight, her drying hair was fire-shot, too.

By the time Mala got back to Eddie, a good twenty minutes later, she was downright bristling. And yes, she knew she was overreacting, but tough beans. At least she was fired up enough to be able to march into the garage and light into him before he had a chance to do that thing with his eyes that threw her so much. ''What the hell's the big idea, throwing snowballs at my kids?''

In the process of putting oil in the Camaro, Eddie raised his head and cocked one eyebrow. "Is this a delayed reaction or what?"

Unfortunately, she'd had a momentary brain cramp about the drawl, which was nearly as bad as the eye thing. Mala raised her chin. "I couldn't say anything in front of them. Then I got tied up on the phone. Well?"

He calmly wiped the end of the funnel with a paper towel. "As I recall," he said, twisting the car's oil cap back on, "it was one snowball, at one kid. And it was soft as cotton, I swear."

"That's not the point. The point is—"

"The point is—" he slammed shut the Camaro's hood "—their bitchin' at each other was obviously about to drive you crazy, it *was* driving me crazy, and that girl of yours needs to learn it's not all about her."

Then he did do the eye thing and her heart knocked against her ribs. Mala crossed her arms, forced herself to stay focused. "So you decided to take matters into your own hands?"

"It worked, didn't it? Although, I have to admit, she's right about one thing. You definitely baby the boy too much."

"Excuse me?" She sucked in a breath, hoping it would keep her voice steady. "He's barely six, for the love of Mike. And what makes you an expert on raising kids?"

"Oh, don't go getting all riled up," Eddie said with a half grin, wiping his hands on a rag. "All I'm saying is you're not doin' the kid any favors by coddling him the way you do."

"And what would you have me do? Smack him every time he cries? Punish him for something he can't help?"

"*Dammit,* woman—" He'd removed his jacket, even though the garage was unheated; now Mala could see every muscle tense underneath a flannel-lined denim shirt hanging partially open over a sparkling white T-shirt. He tossed the rag onto a nearby workbench, then looked back at her, his darkened gaze searing into hers. "Of course not! Okay, so maybe I don't know anything about raising kids, but I sure as hell know how mean they can be. And if Lucas cries as much at school as I hear him when I'm around here, life must be hell for him on the playground.''

Oh, dear God. It wasn't irritation with a whiny kid that had prompted his unsought advice, she suddenly realized, but something far deeper. And far, *far* too complicated for her to deal with right now, if ever. Especially with someone who wouldn't be around, who was more than willing to tell her where she was going wrong but who couldn't be bothered with putting his theories to the test in a real-life situation. She waited a beat, then said, ''You know what you said about keeping to yourself? Maybe this is a good time to remember that—''

''Mama!''

Mala whirled around to the garage opening, hugging herself against the cold. ''What?''

''Grandma called,'' Carrie yelled through the barely cracked open kitchen door. ''She's coming over.''

Just what she needed. Then she looked back at Eddie, whose now shuttered features set off an alarm in her brain that somehow their exchange had shaken him as much as it had her. But hey—who'd started this, anyway? Not only that, but in the week since his return, Mala had learned nothing more about Eddie King than she'd known before. By mutual consent, true—she was no more inclined to pry than he was to divulge— but the point was, since she had no idea what, if any, his sore spots were, she refused to be held accountable for accidentally hitting a bull's-eye or two.

She also refused to apologize for who her children were.

''Look,'' she said, ''I *know* Lucas is overly sensitive. I *know* sometimes Carrie could give Imelda Marcos a run for her money. And God knows there are times when I'm tempted to believe I'm the worst, most ineffectual mother in the universe. But you know what? Lucas is one of the kindest children I've ever known. And as for Carrie…well, at least I can sleep at night knowing that nobody, but *nobody's* ever gonna walk all over my little girl.''

Without waiting for a response, she stomped out of the garage, her arms tightly crossed over her ribs as she plowed across the snowy yard to the house.

Some four hours later, Mala glowered at the computer screen, willing her head to stop throbbing. The day had not gotten any better after the snowball incident. Not for her, at least. Oh, the kids had made up, per usual, which would have been fine except that, since they decided it was too cold to stay outside and the snow was too "mushy" to make a snowman, anyways, they'd been chasing each other around the house for the past three hours, shrieking with laughter at the tops of their extremely healthy lungs. Which meant she'd straightened up the house at least three times, not counting lunch, since she kept expecting her mother to arrive at any minute, which she hadn't yet done. And which meant Mala hadn't gotten an ounce of productive work done the entire day.

Especially as her mind simply would not let go of the Eddie King Quandary. The more she thought about it, the more confused she got. About the way her heart was still doing a boogie and a half at that raw, vulnerable look in his eyes. About the fact that she had to admit, now that sufficient time had passed for her to get over herself, that he'd been right, dammit. Especially about Lucas.

Still, the man had no business sticking in his nose like that. And if he ever did it again, he was gonna find himself looking for a new place to live, boy.

Maybe.

She thought of her shoveled sidewalk and sighed.

God knew, people butted into Mala's life all the time. She was hardly raising her kids alone, not with her parents living barely ten blocks away and her brother and Sophie taking the kids off her hands at least once a week to hang out with their adopted brood of five. But they were family, part of a unit whose members were SuperGlued together; this guy wasn't, and never would be, part of anything. Eddie King was the kind of man who might be dependable, in his own weird way, but there was no getting around the fact that he was still a baggage-laden commitment-phobe who substituted charm for sincerity.

He was also the kind of man who'd spend a good two hours shoveling her sidewalk, her driveway and a fair portion of old Mrs. Arnold's sidewalk next door as well. Without being asked.

Who'd say he wasn't a kid person, yet would care enough to show concern for a little boy's self-esteem, even though he had to know he was taking his life in his hands by confronting said child's mother about the issue.

But who wasn't the least bit afraid to confront said child's mother, either.

And then there was the little sidebar dealie of his being the first man since Scott who made her skin sizzle when she got within ten feet of him.

Her hormones strrrrretched and yawned and said, groggily, "You rang?"

Yeah, well, she knew all about sizzling skin and where that led.

Mala lobbed a pencil across the room, then sank her chin in her palm and stared out the window, watching the sun flash off the icicles suspended from her next-door neighbor's eaves as she admitted to herself that the one hitch in her decision not to put herself through the dating/courting/marriage wringer again was that, contrary to popular belief, she wasn't dead. In fact, if recent physical stirrings could be believed, she was a helluva lot more alive than she'd thought. However, she had far too much sense—

Another roar of shrill laughter shot down the far-too-short hall.

—not to mention children, to let herself be bossed around by a few clueless hormones. Loud and insistent though they might be.

"Ooooh, Lucas—you are gonna be in *so* much trouble!"

Mala shut her eyes and the hormones hobbled back to their cold, airless cell. To the casual observer, the downstairs apartment was more than big enough—besides the living room, there were three bedrooms, two baths, the eat-in kitchen and the office. Today, it seemed about as big as a matchbox. And four times as suffocating.

Something thudded out in the living room. The doorbell rang. The phone rang. Lucas screamed. Carrie remonstrated. Lucas screamed more loudly, the sound escalating as he approached the office, which meant he was ambulatory at least. The phone rang again; Mala picked it up.

"Grandma's here!" came Carrie's yell from down the hall.

"I slipped and bumped my head!" Lucas wailed. "Kiss it!"

"Lucas, shush!" She kissed his head, said "hello?" but got nothing for her trouble except a dial tone.

"Ma-*ma!* Grandma's *here!*"

Her headache escalated to nuclear proportions.

Like a dog burying its bone, Bev Koleski wiped her booted feet about a hundred times on Mala's doormat before stepping inside, chattering to the kids. Mala glanced out at the curb. No car.

"You walked?"

"Well, of course I walked," her mother said as she began shedding layers of clothes—scarf, gloves, knit hat, down coat, cardigan, a second sweater and, at last, the wiped-to-death boots—neatly placing each item on or by the mirrored coatrack next to the front door. Then she tugged down a rust-colored turtleneck that she'd been swearing for ten years must've shrunk in the wash over fearsome, polyester-ized hips. The women in Mala's family were not petite. "Carrie, honey—go put on the kettle for me. Yes, you, too," she added to Lucas, whose ten-second old boo-boo had already been consigned to oblivion, then said to Mala as the kids bunny-hopped down the hall to the kitchen, "You don't think I'm gonna risk gettin' in a car with the streets like this, do you?"

No, of course not. Out of the corner of her eye, Mala spied somebody's wadded up…something draped over the banister. She sidled over, snatched up whatever it was as Bev frowned in the mirror at her somewhat lopsided hairdo, which, thanks to better living through chemistry, had been exactly the same shade of dark brown for thirty years. With a resigned sigh, she swatted at her reflection, then dug in her aircraft carrier–size vinyl purse for a pair of pink terry cloth scuffs, which dropped to the wooden floor, *smack, smack*. Then she squinted at Mala as she shuffled her feet into the slippers.

Oh, Lord. Here it comes.

"You look tired."

"I'm fine, Ma."

"Don't lie to your mother."

"Okay, I have a little headache. It's nothing."

Golden brown eyes softened in sympathy. "Kids making you nuts?"

"Not any more than Steve and I did you. And you lived."

"Barely." Then the eyes narrowed even more. "You doin' okay, money-wise?"

"Yes, Ma. Picked up two new clients this week, in fact. But thanks for the vote of confidence."

"This has nothin' to do with confidence, and don't get smart with me, little girl. I'm not stupid. It's hard, raising two kids on one income. Bad enough you won't let your father and me help out—"

"Ma. Stop."

Bev pursed her lips. "Then why don't you let us at least hire someone to go after the scuzzbag. Wring child support out of him if you have to."

"And I've told you a million times, I don't want Scott's money. He's gone, it's over, and I don't want anything to do with Scott Sedgewick, ever again."

"The kids deserve a father," her mother said.

"Not that one, they don't."

"Oh? You got somebody else lined up for the job?"

Mala laughed, a sound as dry as the heated air inside the house. "Damn, you're good. I didn't even see that one coming."

"Took years of practice. You should take notes."

Yeah, like maybe she should've taken notes on what to look for in a life partner before she let a charming smile and pretty words delude her into thinking, after years of fizzled-out relationships, that Scott had been The One. That he'd fall in love with his children, once he saw them. Managing a smile despite the fact that her heart suddenly felt like three-day-old oatmeal, Mala turned away, starting for the kitchen. Her eyes stung like hell, but damned if she was gonna cry in front of her mother.

She didn't get it, why the pain seemed to be getting sharper, not duller, as time went on.

Especially in the past week. Ever since Eddie King and his damned, vulnerable eyes and his damned, sexy-as-hell drawl and his double-damned good-enough-to-eat body moved in upstairs.

The itchy-ickies started up again.

"Hey—" Her mother snagged her arm and turned her around, then lifted one hand, gently cupped her daughter's cheek. Mala bested her by a couple inches, but the instant she felt that soft, strong touch on her skin, she felt like a little girl again. Except, when she'd been little and innocent and trusting, her mother's touch had always held the promise that, sooner or later, everything would be all right.

"Your father and me, we are so proud of you, baby. You and Steven both. Sometimes, Marty and me just sit at the table and talk about how lucky we were, to get a pair of kids like you two. You know that, don't you?"

Afraid to speak, Mala only nodded.

Bev went on, now skimming Mala's hair away from her face. "The way you take care of these kids all by yourself, run a business on your own… God knows, I don't think I could've done it. But sometimes, we worry about you. That you're lonely, y'know?"

"Ma—"

Bev's hands came up. "Sorry, sorry. I didn't come all the way over here to upset you." She started toward the kitchen. "Anyway," she glanced back over her shoulder, "I figured it probably wouldn't hurt to have someone around to keep the kids out of your hair for a couple of hours, so you could get a little work done. We'll bake cookies or somethin'. Oh, hell— you haven't had a chance to clean the living room in a while, huh?"

Oh, hell, was right. Mala dashed into the living room right behind her mother, snatching up whatever she could from the most recent layer of kid-generated debris before her mother got a chance. She just didn't get it—she and Steve had never dared dump stuff all over the place the way her two did. And it wasn't as if she didn't get after them. It just never seemed to take.

"So. Is he here?"

Slightly out of breath, Mala glanced over at her mother, who was about to vanish behind the free-standing sofa. Oh, crud…now what do you suppose was back there? "He, who?"

"Your new tenant."

"Uh-uh. He went out a couple hours ago."

Like a bat out of hell, actually.

Bev stopped, her arms full of assorted sweaters, books and a two-foot tall inflatable dinosaur. "In this weather?"

"He's a big boy, Ma. He'll manage."

Her mother gave her a look, then swooped behind the sofa. Then Mala heard, "He's real good, let me tell you," followed by her mother's reddened face as she struggled back up.

"Good?"

Bev gave her a "keep up" look. "Yeah, good. As in, cooking. Your father and I were up to *Galen's* Saturday night, figuring we should give it a try, although your father wasn't all that sure he wanted to, since you know how crazy he is about Galen's ravioli. Where do you want these?" she said, holding up a bunch of socks. Mala grabbed them out of her mother's hand. A good half dozen, none of them matching. "Anyway," her mother went on, "I had the lasagna, but I made your father have the grilled tuna, since the doctor told him he needed more fish in his diet, and they were both out of this world. Between you and me, maybe even a little better than Galen's."

"Really?"

"Okay, maybe not better, but just as good. He uses slightly different seasonings or something. But when we told the waitress—it was Hannah Braden that night, you know, Rod and Nancy Braden's girl? I mean, isn't that something, with all that money they have, she doesn't think she's too good to wait tables to earn her own pocket money."

"Ma-aa? Geez."

Bev swatted at her. "So, anyway, when we told her we wanted to thank him personally, she said she was sorry, but he wouldn't come out front for anybody. Can you imagine that?"

Mala bent over the coffee table to clear away the same assorted cups and plates she'd already cleared twice today. "Eddie prefers to keep to himself. That's all."

"Still?"

The thin, annoying whine of the teakettle pierced through the whoosh of the heat pumping through the floor vent. Mala straightened, swiping back a hank of her hair with her wrist. "What do you mean, *still?*"

"*Nana Bev!*"

"I know, honey," Bev called over her shoulder. "And don't you dare touch it—I'll be there in a sec." Then to Mala, "From when he was here before, when you were still in high school. Mind you, I only saw him the one time, but the way he hung back, that stay-away-from-me look on his face…" She shook her head.

"I had no idea you even knew who he was."

"Which just goes to show there's a lot about your old mother you don't know," Bev said. Mala rolled her eyes. "Anyway, he was staying with Molly and Jervis Turner, y'know—"

Yes, that much she knew.

"—and Jervis occasionally did some work for your father, when he got more calls than he could handle. He couldn't handle the complicated stuff, but he was fine when it came to switching out plugs or installing new ceiling fans, things like that. Anyway, this was when I was still going into your father's office a couple days a week to do the books. Jervis came by for his paycheck, and he had Eddie with him. Jervis wasn't much of a talker, either, but he said the boy was staying with them until he finished out school, that his mother had died when the kid was six, and that the kid'd lived with various and assorted relatives down south since then. And that Molly and him might've taken the kid on sooner if anybody'd bothered to ask. Since you never said anything about him, I figured he wasn't part of your group."

Mala forced her knotted hand to relax, then shook her head. "By his own choice," she said, remembering how Eddie had rebuffed everyone's overtures. Not rudely, exactly. But it hadn't taken long for everyone to get the hint. For a while, Mala had regretted not trying harder—even as wrapped up as she'd been in her own hectic life, she'd sensed Eddie's hanging back was actually a challenge, seeing if anyone would care enough to work for his friendship. But he'd scared her, she realized, even then. So she hadn't met his challenge.

He still scared her, she realized.

He was still challenging her, too.

She sucked in a quick little breath, then said, "I don't suppose you know why Eddie left before he graduated?"

Bev shook her head. "No. I rarely ran into Jervis or Molly. I'm not sure I even knew he had. But whaddya suppose possessed him to come back?"

A question that had nagged at Mala for the past week. "I have no idea. Galen says he could probably find work anywhere, at a top restaurant if he wanted."

"Well, he's sure not back because of Molly and Jervis, since they both passed on years ago...."

The doorbell ringing made them both jump. Before Mala could answer it, both kids came roaring out from the kitchen, each one claiming whoever it was on the other side. Mala opened it to find Eddie standing there, a huge sack of salt slung on one hip. He glanced at the kids, sort of the way one might regard last night's still unwashed dinner dishes, then up at her.

"Hey," he said without preamble, his voice just *slightly* laced with contrition, she thought. "I used up most of what you had out there in the shed, figured I may as well pick up some more while I was out. Heard there's another storm predicted for the weekend." The kids, clearly bummed it was only Eddie, retreated down the hall, halfheartedly calling each other names. Her mother, however, had eagerly taken their place. In fact, Mala noted with a slight twinge of dread, the woman was one step removed from panting.

"Mom, Eddie King. My new tenant. Eddie, Bev Koleski. And yes, she bites."

"For godssake, Mala, where you get that mouth, I have no idea." Bev reached out to meet Eddie's already extended hand as Mala grabbed her purse off a hook on the rack. "We met, when you were here before,'' Bev said, ''but I doubt you'd remember me.''

''No, ma'am, I can't say that I do.''

Her wallet clamped in her hand, Mala wedged between them before her mother bonded for life. ''Okay, how much—''

''Forget it,'' Eddie said. ''I'll take it out in trade.''

Mala blushed. Her mother chuckled, low in her throat. Mala sent her a brief but lethal glance, then forced her focus back to the deadpan expression in those ice-blue eyes. ''Excuse me?''

The eyes thawed, just a little. Just enough to poke at the snoring hormones. Then he grinned, all bad and little boyish, and she nearly lost it. ''For the occasional use of your washer and dryer, is all I meant.''

''Oh. Um, yeah, that sounds fair to me.''

''I thought it might.''

The phone rang. ''You want me to get that?'' Bev asked.

''Please,'' Mala said, sending up a prayer of thanks. Bev shuffled away; Mala looked back at Eddie, who shifted the salt to his other hip, which of course caused Mala's gaze to likewise shift before she snapped it back up to his face. ''Well, I guess I'll just go on and put this in the shed,'' he said.

Mala sucked in a breath, let it out sharply. ''Yeah. Thanks.''

Eddie angled away, only to turn back, a combination of regret and defiance shining in his eyes. He glanced into the house over her shoulder, as if to make sure nobody else was in earshot, then said, his voice low, ''I apologize if my directness earlier upset you. I didn't mean to criticize your mothering, even if that's the way it came out. It's just that…'' He looked away for a moment, then back at her, his mouth pulled taut. ''When you live alone as long as I have, you tend to forget about things like being tactful. Or how to put across what you're thinking without—''

''—pissing people off. Yeah, I got it.''

There went that half smile again. Mala's heart stalled in her throat. ''It's okay,'' she said softly, leaning against the door frame. Leaning into that I-can-see-straight-through-you gaze, wanting to reach out to him so badly, her teeth hurt. "As it happens, you gave me some things to think about."

One brow lifted. Skeptical. Amused. "Really?"

A smile tugged at her mouth, even as a little voice said, *"Watch it, sister."*

"Yeah. Really."

One Mississippi...two Mississippi...

"Well. Okay. That's...good, then. Well...uh, tell your mama it was nice to meet her, okay?" He turned around and trudged away, his strides long and purposeful.

"Nice butt," Bev observed behind her. Mala jumped.

"Oh, geez, Ma. Besides, what can you see under that shirt he's wearing?"

"A wealth of possibilities, missy. And what was that all about?"

"You heard?"

"Enough."

"Well, it was nothing. Just a little misunderstanding." Mala managed a nonchalant shrug. "All cleared up now."

"Oh?"

The woman could pack more meaning into a two-letter word than *Webster's* in the whole flipping dictionary.

"Don't even go there, Ma," Mala said, shutting the door a bit more forcefully than necessary and heading back toward the kitchen.

"What? What did I say?"

"You don't have to *say* anything." She went into the kitchen, pulled a mug out of the dish drainer, a box of tea bags from the cupboard. "What you're thinking's written all over your face."

"Like you know what's going on in my head, little girl. Well, for your information, Miss Know-It-All, what I was thinking is that Eddie King turned out okay. Not many men can find it in themselves to apologize for anything. Give me that," she said, snatching the box from Mala's hand. "I can make my own tea. Anyway, he's a nice boy."

"Ma, he's a year older than me. He's hardly a *boy*."

"So he's a nice *man*. Even better. You know if the restaurant's open for Thanksgiving?"

Mala frowned. "It isn't. Why?"

"I just wondered if he's doing anything, that's all."

"Oh, dear God," Mala said, raising her eyes to the heavens. Well, okay, the ceiling, but it was close enough. "What have I done to deserve this?"

"So you should ask him if he'd like to have dinner with us."

Us. Meaning her parents and Mala and Steve and Sophie—whose first Thanksgiving this would be, since they didn't do Thanksgiving in Carpathia—and their five kids and her two.

"No."

"Why?"

"Because I'm not that mean. Besides, he has other plans."

"You know this, or you're only trying to get me off your case?"

"Yes."

Footsteps creaked overhead. "You know somethin'?" Bev said, "I've got half a mind to go up there and ask him myself."

Mala opened her mouth to protest, when suddenly, she didn't care anymore. What the hell did it matter to her if Eddie King accepted her mother's invitation? He certainly didn't need her protection. And with all those people around, it wasn't as if they'd even see each other. Probably. Besides, her parents had been inviting strays to holiday dinners for as long as she could remember. So big fat hairy deal.

"Fine," she said. "Go ask."

Which Bev did. Mala listened, heard faint voices upstairs, then her mother's slow, steady descent on the outside stairs.

"You're right," Bev said when she came in. "He can't make it. Says he's got plans."

So how come she felt disappointed rather than relieved?

And what kind of holiday plans could a man have who didn't know anybody in town? And how was this any of her business?

Mala shook herself, yanked open the dishwasher to stack another half dozen dishes inside. "So who was on the phone?" she asked her mother.

''The phone?'' her mother said from the kitchen table. ''Oh, right. Nobody. A hang up. Which is so rude. Geez. I mean, if you get a wrong number, the least you can do is say 'sorry' or something, y'know? And when the hell you gonna get Caller ID, anyway?''

Mala just sighed.

Chapter 4

"So," Mala said to her sister-in-law as she scraped leftover mashed potatoes into a plastic store 'n' save bowl, swearing softly when a blob landed smack on the front of her new fur-blend sweater, "how'd you enjoy your first Thanksgiving?"

Amazingly, it was just the two of them in her brother's kitchen. Sophie and Mala had combined forces to convince Bev, who'd done most of the cooking, to go play grandma and let them clean up; the living room reeked of football-crazed testosterone; and the kids were…elsewhere. The old country house was cozy and filled with laughter and leftover feast smells, and for the moment, Mala could almost believe she was as content as she would have everyone believe.

Raking one hand through her short, ash brown hair, Sophie chuckled. "I think I'm bloody glad it only comes once a year," she said in her almost-English accent, ripping off a length of aluminum foil to cover what was left of the auxiliary ham. Her square jaw and angular features prevented her from being pretty in any traditional sense of the word, but her quick smile and the love that constantly radiated from her gentle gray eyes made her as appealing as anyone Mala had ever met. "Otherwise, I'd be big as a house from overeating. Not that I won't be that in a few months, in any case.''

She patted her slightly bulging belly underneath the floppy red sweater, then wrinkled her nose, obviously tickled with her condition. Sophie and Steve had only been married since July, but having just turned thirty, the princess was thrilled about her pregnancy.

"And with those hips you *don't* have," Mala said pointedly to her skinny sister-in-law, "you'll look like you swallowed a torpedo." She opened the refrigerator, frowning at the already jam-packed interior. The ceiling shook as many small feet stormed down the upstairs hallway, accompanied by shrieks of varying degrees of intensity. Neither woman so much as glanced up. "I hate to break this to you, honey, but you can either get the rest of the turkey in here, or everything else. Not both. And no, that wasn't a call for help, bozo-hound," she said to the grinning oversize mutt wagging his entire rear end at her feet. She gently shoved at the dog with her knee. "Go away, George."

"Oh, come here, you big goof," Sophie said, collapsing into a kitchen chair. Wearing an expression that could only be translated as, *"Yes!"*, the dog pranced across the linoleum floor to gobble down whatever it was his mistress was offering. "You should really get the kids a dog," Sophie said, making kissy noises at the beast.

"Uh, no, I really shouldn't." Mala stacked the homeless containers back on the counter, then leaned against it. "So how're you feeling these days?"

"Oh, fine. The morning sickness only lasted a week or so, thank God. So I'll be really up for when Alek and Luanne bring the children after Christmas."

"Really? I can't wait to meet them."

"They feel the same way, I gather." Sophie smiled down at the dog, who'd plopped his muzzle in her lap. "I know it seems a bit precipitous, but Alek's quite keen to introduce Luanne to Steven and your parents. I think he hopes it will relieve her mind somewhat about marrying into a royal family."

"If it doesn't frighten her off completely," Mala said wryly.

But then, the circumstances surrounding the reunion of Sophie's older brother, Prince Aleksander Vlastos, and the Texan born-and-bred Luanne Evans Henderson was the stuff of soap operas, involving a secret baby and a marriage-of-convenience gone wrong, a tragic race-car crash that had taken Luanne's husband's life, a love denied for more than a decade. Due to the delicacy of the situation, Mala knew the couple weren't planning on a wedding for some time. But just a few weeks ago they'd agreed, for both their son's sake and the simple fact that they couldn't stand the thought of being separated a minute longer, to live under the same palace roof with Sophie's and Alek's octogenerian grandmother and Carpathia's reigning monarch, Princess Ivana.

Next to all that, Mala's family seemed excrutiatingly dull.

Then Mala caught Sophie's concerned frown. "But what about you?"

Mala started. "What about me?"

"You look ready to drop."

A shrug hiked up her armor another inch or two. "Just been busy, that's all. Got a new client this week. Owns a ballroom dance studio in Ann Arbor. Man's been keeping his books by hand, which means transcribing everything to the computer. Which wouldn't be so bad except the turkey couldn't see the sense in dealing with 'those pesky pennies' as he put it, so he's been rounding off all his figures."

The princess's brows dipped, even though a smile twitched around her wide mouth. "Oh, dear."

"Oh, *hell,* is more like it," Mala said, and Sophie laughed. A tiny, dark-haired girl wandered into the kitchen, a much-loved baby quilt in tow, and crawled up on Sophie's lap. "Fortunately—or unfortunately, depending on how you look at it," Mala continued, "he's also a pack rat, which means he's kept every single piece of paper the studio's generated for the past ten years. So I now have to reconstruct everything from scratch. Plus handle all my other accounts—"

"There you are, you little stinker." Mala looked up as her brother Steve popped through the door, his short, pale blond hair gleaming in the overhead light. He bent down and scooped the little girl into his enormous arms, but not before planting a kiss on his new wife's forehead.

Sophie rewarded Steve with a new-love look that only further rocked Mala's tenuous composure. ''I was just working up to putting her to bed—''

''Forget it. You've been on your feet all day. By the way, Mal, your two are begging to stay over. We thought we'd take the little ones into Detroit to go see Santa tomorrow. You okay with that?''

She snatched at a breath, then smiled. ''Please. Twist my arm.''

Her brother laughed, and it warmed Mala's heart to see how genuinely happy he was. So much had happened to him within the past year—becoming guardian to the five children after their parents' deaths, a princess hiding out from her royal duties by becoming his temporary housekeeper…their marriage. They were perfect for each other, despite the differences in their backgrounds. Still, none of the Koleskis—who'd probably been peasants back in the old country, once upon a time—had quite reconciled themselves to being part of a royal family, even though they all adored Sophie.

She watched her brother and sister-in-law as they exchanged a laugh, a look, the ordinary, effortless communication that was the foundation of a good marriage. From the living room, she heard her mother good-naturedly giving her father grief about something, her resultant whoop when he probably swatted her gently on the fanny on her way out.

Without warning, envy streaked through Mala, hot and brutal. Why did dreams seem to come true for everyone but her? When she'd married Scott at twenty-nine, she'd thought they had. She'd fully expected to have that house full of laughter and hugs and kisses, the kind of marriage her parents and most of the couples she knew had. And the worst part of it was, that nothing had prepared her for the crushing sense of failure when her marriage fell apart. Not as a mother, or in her work—she knew her worth in those areas—but as a woman incapable of finding, and keeping, a life partner.

Self-pity was for wimps, a mantra she'd repeated probably

a thousand times since Scott's departure. But the burning sensation behind her eyes warned her that hanging around would only be an exercise in masochism.

"Well," she said once Steve had departed, Rosie hitched high on his broad shoulders, "since the kids are staying, I think I'll head on home, see if I can get some work done while it's quiet."

"On a holiday?" Sophie rose from the chair, stretching out her back as though she were a lot more pregnant than she was.

"As if you don't do the same thing." The princess was the general director of a major, international charity, a position which might have taken her away from her new family even more than it did, were it not for faxes and modems that allowed her to handle many of her duties right from Spruce Lake. Still, even with a full-time housekeeper, a house with five kids in residence didn't make for an ideal work environment.

Sophie sighed. "True. It just seems a shame you can't find a better way to use your quiet time." Now she frowned at all the plastic containers lining her counter. "But don't you dare leave me with all this food. Take some of it home. Please. And here—" She opened the fridge, removed two foil-wrapped packets. "Take some of the ham and turkey, too. Oh, drat, I almost forgot—what is it they say about pregnant women losing a certain amount of brain cells? Anyway, Elizabeth called the other day, asked me if I had any ideas for Galen's baby shower."

Oh, Lord. Elizabeth and Guy Sanford. Yet another adoring wife/devoted husband combo for the gods to dangle in front of her. The containers stuffed into a plastic grocery bag, Mala headed toward the hallway. "I thought we decided not to hold it until after New Year's?"

Behind her, Sophie gave a rueful laugh. "Well, you know Elizabeth. If everything's not all mapped out at least a month ahead of time, she gets an ulcer."

Oh, yeah, she knew Elizabeth—Galen Farentino's stepsister-in-law and the Realtor who'd sold Mala her house after her divorce—only too well. What was amusing was how quickly Sophie had zeroed in on the petite blond dynamo's endearingly irritating drive to control every aspect of her—and everyone else's—experience, a trait which not even marriage to a laid-back father of three could diminish. "I haven't even had a chance to think about it. But I suppose she has a point, since Galen's due, when? Mid-January, right?"

"Something like that." Sophie stroked her tummy and sighed. "May seems light years away by comparison."

She had her two children, Mala told herself over another prick of envy. On that score, at least, she had no right to feel left out. Annoyed with herself, she leaned over and gave her royal sister-in-law a one-armed hug. "It'll happen sooner than you think, believe me. Kids!" she yelled up the stairs. "I'm leaving!" She turned back to Sophie, then shrugged into her car coat. "Tell Elizabeth we can do the shower at my place. That'll hold her for the moment."

Carrie and Lucas barrelled down the stairs, throwing themselves into their mother's arms. Her eyes burning, Mala gave each of her children a fierce hug and kiss, thinking, at least she had this. That she had a lot, actually. And it wasn't that she didn't believe in true love, she thought as she crunched through the crusted remains of Monday's snowstorm to her car. She just no longer believed it would ever happen to her.

Eddie was just putting away the pair of stockpots Galen had let him borrow, when he heard the key in the restaurant's front door. More curious than concerned, he ambled out into the dark dining room, hands in pockets, wondering who on earth would be crazy enough to come here on Thanksgiving night. Well, besides him of course.

Her head bent so that her hair partially covered her face, Mala shouldered her way through the door, a car-coated blob clutching a briefcase in one hand. She turned and saw him in the shadows, let out a yelp of alarm.

"For the love of Mike, Eddie!" she said, bumping the door shut with her rear end. "Thanks for taking five years off my life!"

"Sorry. I just didn't expect anyone."

She cleared her throat, the laugh that followed sounding

more forced than nervous. "No, it's okay. I just…" Shaking her head, she scooted past him, her sneakers silent against the tile floor, her scent whispering in her wake. "What on earth are you doing here?" she asked as she pushed open the door to the kitchen.

Eddie followed, just fast enough to keep the door from swinging back in his face. "Just putting away a few things I borrowed. You?"

Still not looking at him, Mala skittered across the kitchen and on into the office. "Galen gave me a key some time ago," she said, her voice…tight. "Since my schedule doesn't always coincide with hers." She started in poking around on the desk in the half-light spilling from the kitchen.

Eddie frowned. Something was weird, but he couldn't put his finger on it. "Y'all have a nice Thanksgiving?"

"Yes, thank you," she said stiffly. "Dammit, I can't find a thing—"

"Which was why Edison invented the lightbulb, I suppose." Eddie leaned over to flip on the light switch.

"It's okay, I've got it!"

Too late. Stark light flooded the tiny office.

Illuminating Mala's puffy eyes and blotchy skin.

Eddie took a step closer. "You been *cryin'?*"

She folded her arms as tightly across her chest as the heavy coat would allow, not looking at him. After a second, she nodded.

"Wow. The Lions must've lost, huh?"

A small laugh sputtered from her lips. "No, they won, actually." One hand darted out, started messing with something on the desk.

"Then why the tears?"

Finally, she lifted her gaze to his, her shimmering spring green eyes luminous against her flushed skin. Another strangled laugh, a shoulder hitch, then she shook her head.

"Don't know or don't want to talk about it?"

"Both," she said on a long, shuddering sigh. "I'm sorry. I…oh, God. Do you know how long it's been since anyone's seen me cry?"

Eddie thought about his options for a second or two, *getting the hell out,* being the front-runner, for at least three-quarters of that time. Then he closed the three-foot gap between the door and the front of the desk, eased a hip up onto it. Held out his hand.

Mala just stared at it.

"You know what you said about not needing a buddy?" Eddie said. "I think you were wrong."

Her gaze, more watery than ever, shifted from his out-stretched hand to his face. She sniffed, swiped at her cheek. "And you know what you said about not getting involved? I think you've forgotten *that.*"

He dropped his hand to his lap. "I know this may not make a lick of sense, but I'm not a loner because I don't like people, Mala. And I don't turn away from someone when it looks like they could use an ear to bend."

She raised an eyebrow, sniffed again, but said nothing as she picked up a folder from a standing file on the desk where Eddie knew Galen kept invoices and such.

"This mean you're not gonna tell me why you're so upset?"

"You got it." Her gaze flicked to his, then away. "I'm not a whiner, Eddie."

"You think being unhappy about something makes you a whiner?"

"No." The papers in the folder rattled softly as she skimmed through them. "I think bitching about things makes me a whiner." She popped open the briefcase, stashed the folder inside. "Either I can change whatever's bugging me, or I can't. In either case, I see little point in burdening others with my problems."

"Not even your family?"

That got a snort. "*Especially* my family. All I get out of that little exercise is yet one more thing to worry about, which is that now I've made someone else worry about *me.* So what's the point?"

Something nagged at him about that remark, like a hair in your eye you can feel but not see, but it was too late and he was too tired to figure it out right then. So instead, he linked his arms over his chest and said, "Okay, change of subject. How come you're here on Thanksgiving night? Or is that off-limits, too?"

The briefcase snapped shut, but some of the tension seemed to drain from her shoulders. "My brother and his wife are keeping the kids for the night. I figured I'd use the time to catch up on some of the work I couldn't get to because of the snow day on Monday." One hand lifted, rammed a stray piece of hair behind her ear.

"This the brother who just got married?"

"In July, yes." She took a tissue out of her coat pocket, blew her nose.

She obviously wished he'd shut up and leave her be. Had she been anyone else, he would have. Hell, had she been anyone else, he wouldn't't've even started this conversation. But Mala Koleski was the first woman he'd ever met who wasn't looking for someone to lean on, to fight her battles for her, and that intrigued the very devil out of him. In fact, it was her very self-sufficiency he found so magnetic, in large part, he supposed, because he didn't feel like he had to constantly watch his step to make sure she hadn't laid a trap for him. Shoot, at this point, he wasn't all that sure she even *liked* him.

"What was that your daughter was going on about, something about your sister-in-law being a princess?"

That actually got a little smile, which made him feel downright cocky. "It's true. Princess Sophie Ekaterina Vlastos of Carpathia, in fact."

"Carpathia? I never heard of it."

"In central Europe. Tiny. Very pretty. Well…" She hoisted the briefcase and hustled around the desk to shut the light. "G'night."

He stood at the same time, which meant she couldn't get past him without brushing against him. Her coated sleeve against his sweatered chest. Big deal. Except he could smell her hair and her skin and the tang of cold still clinging to her coat and her hair and her soft, smooth skin and his nerve endings went *What? Hey! Get back over here!* when she moved away.

Even as his brain said *Let her go, fool.*

And while his brain and his nerve endings were going at it like a football player arguing a call with a referee, she left before he even had a chance to say "Good night" back.

Mala shut her front door behind her and leaned against it, her heart thumping in her chest as if she'd just run home from the restaurant instead of driven. What she'd said back there, about not burdening other people with her problems, hadn't just been a line to get Eddie King off her case. She truly hated dumping on other people. Yet before the man sat down on the desk and stretched out his hand to her, before she dared to look up into those remarkably ingenuous blue eyes of his, she'd never even been tempted.

But boy, she'd been tempted tonight. Seriously tempted. I've-been-on-a-diet-for-three-weeks-and-someone-just-left-a-box-of-chocolates-on-the-counter tempted. And for a split second there, she'd thought, well, hey—what danger could there be in laying bare her soul to someone who'd be gone in a few months, anyway? Someone who had no vested interest in her welfare.

Her brain zipped back to the "laying bare" part of the last sentence and hovered there, cackling.

She pushed herself away from the door, down the hall and into the office, where she dropped the briefcase and sloughed off her coat, throwing it across an extra chair in the room…only to sigh and pick it up again, carting it back down the hall to the closet.

Sheesh. If she wasn't careful, she was going to give Elizabeth Sanford a run for her money for control freak of the new millennium.

And if she wasn't careful, she was going to spend the rest of her life being afraid to even be *friends* with a man. Would she ever let herself fall in love again? Uh, no, not in this lifetime. But criminy—all the guy'd said was he thought she needed a buddy. Everybody knew the ground rules, nobody was going to let anything get out of hand.…

God, he had nice hands.

She laughed out loud, thinking it—she—sounded just a bit manic in the empty house. And then she thought, Whoa—get the kids out of the house for two minutes and look what happens. I start to crack up.

Mala heard a car drive up. Her heart began to tap dance as she realized Eddie hadn't driven around to the back to park the car in the garage. Silence swallowed the engine's purr; a car door slammed, then she heard footsteps, slow and heavy, coming up onto the porch.

She could remind him that she had work to do.

Or maybe she'd get over herself and invite him in for coffee and a few minutes of adult company.

Or maybe she'd skip the coffee and conversation and just jump the man's bones—

The doorbell rang.

Mala tugged her sweater down over her hips, sucked in her stomach. She counted to twenty—slowly, long enough for the bell to ring again—then opened the front door.

Eddie stood there, alrighty, all crooked grin and big, blue eyes and wind-blown hair. Except…he wasn't alone.

"I heard something out in the alley, just as I was locking up," he said, hitching the tiny, fuzzy…thing with the please-don't-hurt-me brown eyes up higher in his arms. From what Mala could tell, he'd wrapped up the…thing in his sweater. Which got her to wondering what he had on underneath his denim jacket. "Somebody'd tied him up in a black garbage bag, tossed him in the dumpster. D'you believe that?"

The weather had been working up to something all day. Now she noticed it had started to precipitate, a nasty cocktail of snow, sleet and rain. Eddie's shoulders and wavy hair were dotted with moisture, although the…thing certainly looked snug and dry in its little cocoon.

Mala had had a dog once. A golden retriever named, originally enough, Pumpkin. Gorgeous animal. And sweet as could be. Used to lick her scabby knees while she'd sit in her window seat, reading. Growl at the kids who made fun of her for being too heavy. Then, three days before Mala's twelfth birthday, Pumpkin got run over. Mala had cried all summer over that dog, swore she'd never have another animal again. Of course, the kids had been begging for a pet for two years already, but she'd kept putting them off.

The…thing—okay, okay, the *puppy*—lifted its scrawny, prickly little muzzle and licked Eddie underneath his chin, then turned those soulful, manipulative eyes on her.

Oh, God—it was *shivering*. And obviously frightened out of its little doggy wits. Mala's stomach clenched at the idea that someone could be so cruel.

With a heavy, heavy sigh, she reached out. "C'mere, cutie," she cooed, cudding the stinky, trembling fur ball against her chest.

And she had to admit, the sight of Eddie King's full-blown grin was almost worth the prospect of being kept awake all night by a whimpering mongrel.

Chapter 5

Eddie hadn't really expected her to take the dog from him. In fact, all he'd wanted to do was to make sure it was okay to keep it in his apartment overnight until he could take it to the local animal shelter.

"No sense in my taking on a pet," he said as he followed her back into the kitchen. "Seeings as I don't stay in any one place for longer than a few months, usually. But it never even occurred to me that you might want him."

"I don't." The pup still cradled to her breasts, she flicked on the kitchen light. Over her jeans, she wore this pretty sweater, a deep red fluffy thing with a great big floppy collar that framed her jawline. That it now probably smelled like wet dog didn't seem to bother her any. "I have no intention of keeping him, either. So we'll have to figure out something before the kids get home tomorrow, or I'm doomed."

"How come?" He glanced around the spanking clean room, took in the artwork-and-magnet littered refrigerator, the cutesy country decorations. "You allergic or something?"

"No. I just don't need another body to be responsible for. And the kids are still too young to take care of an animal."

"That's nuts. The girl's, what? Six, seven? That's plenty old enough to feed him, take him for walks..."

Her eyes flashed. "I don't want a pet, Eddie. But I agree with you—you certainly couldn't leave the poor thing where you found him." She visibly shuddered. "How anyone could do that to an animal..."

With a shake of her head, Mala clumsily lowered her rump to the braided rug centered on the beige linoleum floor, cooing to the pup still cradled in her arms. She kept up her one-sided conversation in a real soothing voice, low and soft, but the poor little guy just kept shaking up a storm, alternately giving Eddie these furtive little bug-eyed glances from the safety of Mala's embrace and jabbing his snout into the crook of her arm.

"Let's see...why don't you bring me a towel from the linen cupboard outside the bathroom? One of the old ones, from the bottom shelf."

A minute later, he handed her the rattiest towel he could find—which wasn't saying a whole lot—then squatted beside her, his knees creaking. "I probably wouldn't've brought him back here, but it being Thanksgiving night and all, I didn't know what else to do with him."

She'd carefully unwrapped the critter from his sweater, immediately replacing it with the towel. "S'okay," she said, briskly rubbing the tiny thing, who rewarded her efforts with a series of faint, ineffectual growls. Mala laughed, then removed the towel, only to laugh harder at the sight of what now looked like an eight-inch tall porcupine. Clearly mortified, the black-and-brown pup tucked its pointy little tail between its legs, then scampered underneath a worn, white-washed cupboard on the other side of the kitchen table, where it peered out at the two of them with huge, cautious eyes.

Mala rearranged herself to sit back on her heels, gently slapping her thighs with her hands. "C'mon, sweetie, it's okay..."

The snout vanished.

"Okay, fine, be that way. But I bet I know what *you* want." She got up, went over to the counter and began hauling covered bowls and things out of a plastic grocery bag. Thanksgiving leftovers, Eddie assumed. Sure enough, he heard the crackle of foil being unwrapped, then watched as she began shredding pieces of turkey into a margarine tub she'd grabbed from a whole mess of them underneath the sink. Seconds later, she knelt down again, maybe five feet from the cupboard.

"Hey, muttsky…come see what I've got."

The snout reappeared, whiskers twitching around a shiny black nose.

"Now, you know and I know you're hungry," she said softly, "so just get your fuzzy little butt out here…come on…that's a boy…just a few steps farther…"

His belly hugging the floor, the dog slunk over to Mala, snatched a piece of turkey from her hand, then streaked back to his hiding place to scarf it down.

Eddie picked his sweater up off the floor, shook it out, slipped it back on over his T-shirt. "You've gotta admit, he's a cute little bugger."

"I'm not keeping the dog," she said, again settling cross-legged onto the rug and holding out another piece of turkey. The dog repeated the slink-snatch-retreat routine twice more, but by the fourth time, he apparently decided nobody was gonna stick him in another garbage bag so he might as well just stay put and let the nice lady pet him while he ate.

"Okay, that's all," she said a few seconds later, holding her hands up in front of the pup to show him they were empty. The beast planted his bony butt on the floor, wagging his tail, and yipped. Mala laughed, then sighed. "I can't keep you," she said, only to sigh again when the pup crawled into her lap, curled up, let out a huge, contented sigh and promptly passed out. "I can't," she whispered, stroking his head.

Eddie frowned. Any fool could see she wanted the dog, that it had already wormed past her defenses and into her heart. Yet there she sat, obviously tearing herself up over this, like she was being pressured to take in an ex-con or something rather than a five-pound puppy. A little on the aggravated side, although he wasn't really sure why, Eddie got to his feet and said, "I guess I should go," except she said, almost at the same time, "Would you like a sandwich or something?"

She won't let you go without feeding you first, either.

The thought slammed into him, ricocheting around his brain for a couple real scary seconds before she looked up. And he saw an ache in her expression that just plumb twisted his gut all to hell.

"You know, there's nothing says you can't keep the dog," he said, wondering where the hell he got off trying to convince this woman to take a chance on anything. All he knew was, he hated seeing that pain in her eyes, hated even more knowing there wasn't a damn thing he could do to take it away.

She looked away. "I know."

Against his better judgment, he squatted beside them, playing with one of the dog's floppy little ears for a moment and inhaling that soft, sweet scent that he knew he'd already be able to identify blindfolded as Mala's. He'd been around plenty of sweet-smelling women in his day, but none of them had ever stirred up feelings inside him the way this one did. Dumb feelings, most of them, of belonging and trust and hope. Little boy dreams, he realized.

And he hadn't been a little boy in a very long time.

Yet he didn't move away, either from her or the feelings, so that when he said, "So you'll at least think about it?" his breath stirred the fine, silky hairs at her temple. She shuddered, just slightly, in response, rousing deeper, stronger feelings that were anything but those of a little boy.

"I'll think about it," she said.

"Then I guess I'll stay and have that sandwich," he said, even though he had no idea what one thing had to do with the other.

For an hour, maybe a bit longer, they sat across from each other at her kitchen table and listened to golden oldies on the radio and the sleet *tick-tick* against the window, while they drank coffee and ate turkey and ham sandwiches and pumpkin pie and talked about safe things, like how the restaurant was doing and her plans for fixing up the house one day. Then the pup, who'd been snoozing nearby in a little box Mala had lined with an old blanket, woke up and actually asked to go outside to do his business.

"Sure wish it was that easy to housebreak kids," Mala said, drying him off again with the towel when he scampered back in, his fur glistening with melting sleet. Still seated at the table, Eddie laughed, which made her feel really, really good. Sophomoric, but good.

Why he'd accepted her invitation, she had no idea. And her issuing the invitation to begin with wasn't exactly the smartest thing she'd ever done. She was playing with fire, and she knew it. But Eddie King made her laugh, too, more than she had in a long time. He could tell a wicked story, in that quiet drawl of his. And, boy, did he have a ton of them stored up from his exploits as a gypsy chef, as he called himself. Yes, she wondered about his sudden loquaciousness, for maybe, oh, two seconds. But it was nice, how he made her forget, just for a little while, that she was the mother of two high-maintenance children and the sole proprietor of a struggling new business and a woman with a shattered marriage on her résumé.

That she was, at times, almost unbearably lonely, unable to reconcile her basic female need for the company and attention of a man with her resolve to stop making herself crazy trying to find something that obviously didn't exist. Not for her, anyway. It was a good thing, then, she told herself as she poured them both their second cups of coffee, that the long-legged, soft-speaking man currently sitting in her kitchen was a nomad, a loner, the kind of man who wouldn't let another human being past that veneer of nonchalance for love nor money.

And that she had no business trying. Everything else aside, it wasn't fair, trying to get a peek at his pysche when she'd been so adamant about not revealing hers.

But where was the harm in a question or two?

"So, what did you do for dinner today?"

His mouth hitched up as he stirred his coffee. "Cooked it."

"But the restaurant—"

"Not there. At a homeless shelter in Detroit."

Why his answer should derail her, she didn't know. But it did. "Oh. Wow. That's really…nice."

His mouth quirked up on one side, Eddie arched back, linking his hands behind his head. "Does that make you uncomfortable?"

Her brows lifted. "No. Why should it? I was just thinking that maybe if you didn't keep it such a secret, other people might be goaded into being more generous with their time, too."

His hands still laced behind his head, his gaze never wavered. "I wasn't tryin' to keep it a secret. Just don't see the point in going around, callin' attention to myself. Besides, guilt's a lousy motivator, Mala."

"Whatever works."

"But it doesn't. Trust me on this, folks who are down on their luck can spot someone who's in it to appease their own conscience faster than this little guy can wolf down a piece of turkey." He picked up a scrap from his plate and waved it at the dog, who tripped all over himself in his split to get to the loot.

She watched as the pup demonstrated Eddie's simile, telling herself it wasn't prying if he'd given her the opening. "Sounds as though you're speaking from experience."

He glanced at her, then wiped his fingers on a napkin, which he balled up and tossed onto the plate before getting up from the chair and striding over to the back door. His hands rammed in his back pockets, he stared out the paned glass at the driving sleet. "I never had to live on the streets, if that's what you mean."

"But…?"

Silence yawned between them as he obviously wrestled with how much more to say. "But I can't say as I'd ever had what you'd call a real home, either."

Mala studied her cup of coffee for several seconds, debating how far to push. Out of the corner of her eye, she noticed the dog prance over to him and plop its tiny behind on his booted foot. She now watched as Eddie leaned down and scooped the puppy up to nestle against his chest, a smile teasing his lips as the wriggling mutt's tongue darted out to lick his chin.

"And what's to prevent you from having one now?" she said at last.

He turned, his expression bemused. "You know, I've never yet met a woman who didn't think, given enough time, she could domesticate me."

At that, Mala let out a laugh. "Hey, I got all I can handle just trying to civilize my kids. Trust me—you're in no danger from me."

"Maybe it's you who's in danger from me."

Her heart jolted. "Meaning?"

His eyes never left hers, even as his fingers methodically scratched behind the pup's ears. "You know how long it's been since I've been in a woman's company as long as I've been in yours tonight?"

Irritation knifed through her. "Yeah, well, nobody's tied you down. You got intimacy issues, the door's right over there."

"This has nothing to do with intimacy issues, Miz Oprah." His obvious frustration stopped her short. "And God knows, I'm not into dredging up memories, but…" He let the pup down, then raked a hand through his hair, his features contorted with obvious conflict. His hand slapped back to his side, his eyes searing into hers.

"My father took off before I was born," he said. "My mother's parents kicked her out, I gather, and it wasn't until I was nearly born that my great-grandmother, who was living in Austin at the time, apparently took pity on her and took her in. Except they fought all the time, and it seemed like every week, Mama'd be draggin' me off to some motel or somethin' in the middle of the night, only to drag me back to her grandmother's the next day. But then Mama died when I was six, her folks were already gone, too, and I guess my great-grandmother decided she had better things to do with her life than worry over six-year-old boys. So she sent me off to Longview to live with some cousin or other who eventually got tired of me, too, and sent me on to someone else. To make a long story short, for most of my childhood, I got passed from relative to relative like a Christmas fruitcake."

The bluntness, the brevity of his accounting didn't fool Mala for a minute. Nor was its significance lost on her. "What about your father? Did you ever hear from him? Do you even know who he—"

"No."

Up to that point, Eddie might have evaded an issue, but Mala would bet her Sara Lee cheesecake he'd never outright lied about it. Now, however, alarms went off, big-time.

"Were you…mistreated?"

He gave a rueful laugh. "Hell, Mala—you gotta notice somebody before you can mistreat them."

"Oh, Eddie…"

His eyes blazed. "Don't. I didn't tell you because I wanted your sympathy."

"I didn't think you had," she shot back. "That doesn't mean I'm not going to be angry. Why on earth didn't one of your relatives turn you over to Social Services if taking care of you was such a hardship?"

Eddie shrugged. "Who knows? Dumb southern pride, maybe. Or else it took less effort to ignore me than it did to see if maybe there was some other solution. Besides, there were a *lot* of relatives."

"Then how did you end up here? Michigan's a long way from Texas."

For the first time in several minutes, his expression softened. "Molly Middleton was my mother's third cousin. She and Mama had been pretty close, though, even though Molly was a couple years older. But she fell in love young, too, with a soldier stationed at Fort Bliss who hailed from these parts. They got married when she wasn't but eighteen, and they ended up back here after his tour was up. After my mother left El Paso, though, they lost touch, so she knew nothing about me, or even that Mama had died. So it wasn't until I was nearly out of school before somebody happened to mention it to her in a Christmas card. She wrote to me right away, asked if I'd like to come up here to finish school. And since that was the first time any of my kin had shown the slightest enthusiasm for having me come live with them, I figured I may as well go."

Mala frowned. Something wasn't jibing. "Then why didn't you stay long enough to graduate?"

He reached for his coffee, taking a long sip before answering. Then he shrugged, looking down at the dog. "Oh, I don't know. Chalk it up to turning eighteen and realizin' I was no longer anybody's burden."

"But you weren't a burden to Molly and Jervis."

"In my mind, I was."

"So why didn't you leave before?"

A slight smile touched his lips, even as she saw him tense, just a little, as if the conversation had taken a turn he hadn't planned on. "You've got a real thing for making sure all the pieces fit, don't you?"

"I'm an accountant, Eddie. I can't even stand a messy sock drawer."

He chuckled a little at that, then shrugged, looking elsewhere. "I don't really have an answer for that. Why I didn't go off on my own before. God knows, nobody would've cared if I had. I suppose…" He squinted, as if trying to find just the right words. "I suppose it was just time, you know? I mean, it's not like I was much good in school, anyway, or figured on going on to college, so I decided there really wasn't much reason to hang around. Molly and Jervis did their best to talk me out of it, of course, but they were wasting their breath. And after so many years of living with folks who didn't want me around, living on my own was heaven."

"And is it still heaven, living by yourself?"

His gaze was steady. "It's…safe."

"Because you've convinced yourself that you're unloveable?"

Mala nearly slapped her hand over her mouth. Geez Louise, she was becoming more like her mother every minute, just spewing out whatever happened to be passing through her brain. Eddie, however, didn't seem nearly as taken aback as she was. Although one eyebrow did work its way north. "No. Because I'm no good at living with anyone else."

"You don't know that."

"I've been married, Mala. In my early twenties, right out of the service. A gal I'd met while I was stationed at Camp Pendleton. It lasted three months.''

The very flatness of his words twisted her heart. "And that makes you a failure?"

"No, it makes me a realist. Years of conditioning to stay out of the way, to not do anything that would get me booted someplace else, is damn poor preparation for sharing a home, let alone a life."

"And you're telling me this because?"

His smile was sad. "Why do you think?"

Their gazes wrestled with each other for several seconds until Mala bolted from her chair and over to the sink where she rammed on the water to wash the few plates from their meal. A dozen unfinished thoughts buzzed in her head like a crossed party line: If he felt he had to warn her off, why the hell was he here to begin with? And as much as she ached for what had happened to him, she found it hard to believe that somebody like Eddie would buy into his own hard-luck story.

And why, *why* did she care so much?

She heard the chair scrape across the floor, Eddie's booted footsteps approach.

"I didn't mean to upset you," he said quietly.

"I'm not upset."

"Like hell. You scrub those plates any harder, you're gonna take the flowers right off."

She could practically feel his heat, he was standing so close. Close enough to touch her, if he'd wanted to. Obviously he didn't. For which Mala was both profoundly grateful and sharply disappointed, which is about when she got clobbered with the realization that if she'd been suckered into taking in a dog she didn't even want, what chance did she have against a man she *did?*

"Mala. I'm just trying to be honest here."

About what? she wanted to scream. Clearly, not about why he'd left Spruce Lake twenty years ago. And why was he warning her off, which she assumed was his definition of being "honest," when they'd already established that nothing was going to happen? Except, unless she was mistaken, something sure as hell *was* happening.

Wasn't it?

Frustrated and more confused than ever, Mala slammed down the faucet handle, staring at the water swirling down the drain while she tried to come up with some reason for her acting, well, nuts. Some reason other than the real one, which was that Eddie King was seriously getting to her, heart, soul and libido.

And what was she supposed to do with *that?*

Swiping a piece of hair off her face with the back of her wrist, she looked out into the blackness through her window and managed to separate a single thread of the truth from the tangled mass in her brain. "I'm just frustrated," she finally said.

"About what?"

"About how awful it must have been for you, being treated the way you were after your mother died. And I think—my God, what if that happened to one of my babies? I mean, I know I'm being totally irrational, because my family would be there for my kids. But just the thought that, if something happened to me, nobody would love my children...." She grabbed a dish towel, violently dried her hands. "The thought that *any* child would be unwanted makes me ill."

It wasn't the truth. Not all of it, anyway. But for the moment, it would have to do.

It wasn't that Eddie didn't believe her. In fact, for a split second, he thought about what it might be like, having someone care about him half as much as this woman cared about her family. Not that that would change anything, or who he was, but all those old, mothballed yearnings from so many years ago suddenly clawed to the front of his brain, where there was no ignoring them.

He still wasn't real sure what had possessed him to tell her all that stuff. Hell, for somebody not given to talking much, he'd sure made up for it tonight. But he was just as glad he had, because now he knew exactly how dangerous it would be to follow through on his body's inclinations. The word "dispassionate" was not in the lady's vocabulary. Granted, it was her energy and enthusiasm for life that had attracted him all those years ago, still attracted him now. However, being attracted to something doesn't mean it's any good for you.

But if she thought he couldn't see how she'd sidestepped the truth just as neatly as he had earlier, when her question about why he'd left town before graduation had blindsided him, she had another one coming.

He knew better than to touch her. He really did. But that little hissy fit had sent that strand of hair right back into her eyes, and before he even knew what he was doing, he'd smoothed it off her face, making his heart nearly pound out of his chest for his trouble.

Her gaze snapped to his, sending a bittersweet yearning glimmering through him. Her lips parted—in surprise, he supposed—and he decided there was no harm in looking at her mouth, just for a minute. Except then he found himself wanting to say something dumb. Like, *"Do you have any idea how incredible you are?"*

"Eddie?"

"Yeah?"

"Two words—*mixed signals.*"

He blew out a breath. "I was afraid of that." Then he said, "Did you know I used to work in the diner, when we were in school?"

"I…" Her brows dipped. "You did?"

"Yeah. In fact, it was old Al Jackson who first taught me to cook. In any case, I used to watch you from the back, when you'd come in with your girlfriends. You always sat in the corner booth, always ordered a large fries and a Cherry Coke."

Her eyes seemed glued to his. "Why are you telling me this?"

"Damned if I know. No, no…that's not true. See, Al did more than just teach me how to cook. Took him a while, but he eventually got it through my thick head that I was more than just somebody's castoff. And maybe I'm way outta line, here, but something tells me you feel the same way."

Her eyes widened and her mouth fell open on a soft gasp, but she remained silent, which Eddie figured was a noteworthy occasion.

"But you're right," Eddie went on while he had the chance. "I shouldn't've stayed tonight. I shouldn't be wanting to touch you the way I want to touch you, because I know nothing good can come of it, especially for you. So when I walk out of here tonight, that'll be the last time the two of us'll be alone if I can help it. But I just thought you should know, Miss Mala, that you fascinated the very devil out of me back then."

Her pupils had gone dark as pitch; her breathing, shallow. "And now?"

He smiled. "I'm not seventeen anymore."

"I see," she said quietly, and he heard, in those few words, the bitterness of failure.

He knuckled her chin, lifting her face so their gazes tangled. "No, you don't. And now who's sending mixed signals?" he said, only to feel his heart cramp when her eyes filled with tears. "Darlin', listen to me—my guess is you're hurting because of what your husband did to you and the kids, so you're real gun-shy right now—"

"It goes deeper than that—"

"—but eventually that hurt's gonna heal up," he said, plowing through her objections before she convinced him of something he didn't want to be convinced about, "and then some smart man's gonna come along who sees what I see—a helluva gal with more love to give than she knows what to do with." He dropped his hand, sliding it into his pocket. "And you don't need me around, confusing the issue with sex. Which is all it could be between us, honey."

After a long moment, she lifted one hand to his face, skimming her fingertips down his cheek. He steeled himself against the crackle of desire her touch set off, but he didn't have near as much luck against the look in her eyes.

"I don't mean to be sending out mixed signals, either," she said quietly. "I know our getting involved is a complication neither of us needs. Or wants. But all I have to say is, twenty years ago, I used to drive myself nuts fantasizing about how you kissed. And if you walk out that door tonight without giving me a chance to find out, I may have to hurt you.''

And before Eddie had half a chance to protest—not that he would have, but he might not have minded at least a second or two to think about things—she grabbed his sweater and lifted her chin and, well, it would've been downright rude not to give the lady what she wanted.

Chapter 6

Damn, she was good at this, he thought as her luscious mouth molded to his just right and her body melted into his even better. And she was just as soft as he'd expected, softer, and so giving and honest and fired up, it was everything he could do not to ease her down onto the floor right there and then. That first kiss led to two, then three, each one deeper and hotter and more persuasive. He got so hard, it almost hurt. But oh, it was a sweet ache, wanting her this bad.

Somehow, though for the life of him he didn't know how, just enough blood stayed in his brain to keep him from making a total ass of himself, as well as to keep his hands from straying where he damn well knew they shouldn't. Not tonight. Not with her. Except then she said, "Touch me," and he froze, just for a second, until he could force the words, "I thought you just wanted a kiss," out of his mouth and into hers. And she said "I lied," and he had to pull back, because he knew the moment he made contact with any of the several places on her body that were calling so loudly to him, he was a goner.

"No," he said, breathing hard and shaking his head, realizing he was the closest he'd come to crying in probably twenty-five years. Everything throbbed. His head, his heart, his…everything. But just as he clamped his hands on her shoulders, trying to think of some way to convince her that he wasn't rejecting her, she startled him by bursting into laughter.

"Some bad boy you are," she said over her giggles.

He frowned, there being too little blood in his head to make sense of her words. Then he noticed how her lips were swollen and how her breasts—those breasts that could have been his, had it not been for…something; oh, yeah, his conscience—were rising and falling *so* temptingly such a short distance away.

"What?" he said, stupidly.

She seemed to ponder things for a moment, then looped her arms around his neck and snuggled up to him, which wasn't doing a damned thing for his blood distribution problem. "When we were in school," she said, and Eddie forced himself to concentrate on her words, "that's what all the girls said, you know. That you'd be the type to take whatever you could get from a girl, then never even look at her the next day."

He frowned. "Why would y'all think that?"

She shrugged. "Because we led dull, boring little lives? And you were the closest any of us were going to get to something even remotely dangerous. Except…"

"Except…?"

"Except something told me, even then, you weren't really dangerous. At least, not in the way they thought."

He frowned harder. "Then you obviously have no idea how difficult it was for me to stop tonight."

"Uh, yeah, I do, actually. Which only proves my point."

"So, what are you saying? That you just gave me some kind of test?"

Out popped the dimples. "What do you think? And since the kissing seemed to be going so well…" She ended the sentence with a shrug, then patted his face with one hand. "But you're right. It wouldn't have been a good idea. At least, that's what I intend to keep telling myself until I actually believe it."

A minute later, he was standing outside, in the cold, dreary night, thinking that chivalry was highly overrated.

* * *

To be honest, Eddie had thought real hard about moving out,
after that night and that kiss and Mala's softness and her com-
ments afterward and his body's reaction to all of the above.

The lady was lonely and vulnerable and obviously…needy.
And while Eddie wasn't lonely—he didn't think, anyway—or
vulnerable—ever—he was finding himself a bit on the…needy
side himself these days. To ease those needs in all that fragrant,
giving softness was a temptation he wasn't all that sure he
could withstand for long. Because it was one thing, keeping
things on an even keel when he knew Mala wasn't interested,
quite another thing entirely when it hit him just how easy it
would be to fall in…into bed with her.

However, what with one thing and another and having to
spend even more time at the restaurant since Galen was nearing
the end of her pregnancy, he didn't get around to looking for
another place. And besides, he didn't think it was exactly right,
leaving Mala without a tenant so close to Christmas and all.
So he stayed put. And occasionally, a thought sauntered
through about maybe going to a bar or someplace and finding
someone to help relieve all these pesky needs. Except after
twenty or thirty seconds' deliberation, he always came to the
same conclusion, which was that such things didn't hold the
allure they once did. Not that they ever really had, if you wanna
know the truth.

So he found other activities to occupy the little free time he
had. He drove around some, to Battle Creek and places like
that, when the weather wasn't piss-awful, or went into Detroit,
or went to the movies at the mall. Since he didn't have a TV,
he read a lot. While that didn't exactly do much for those
needs—which by the third week in December had become a
near constant ache—at least his brain was getting a decent
workout, and that had to count for something.

A lot of folks would probably say he didn't have much of a
life, but the life he did have suited him fine. Or at least, it had
up until about a month ago. Now, however, Eddie found himself feeling restless and agitated, like he had an itch so deep
inside he couldn't even tell where it was, let alone get at it. He

thought maybe spending so much time in this hick town was getting to him, so he made up his mind that his next job would be in another big city. Maybe Chicago or Phoenix or Vegas, someplace he hadn't been before.

In any case, between his avoiding Mala, and her and the kids avoiding him, they didn't see much of each other to speak of. Yet he was acutely aware of their comings and goings, their routine and when that routine got shaken up. He knew when they went to school, and because he was off on Mondays, he knew when they got home and that Mala always met them at the bus. There were days when Lucas's near constant whining nearly drove him up the wall, but there were times when he could hear both kids' laughter, too, and he had to admit, he liked that.

A lot.

And he could see them from his window—you know, when he just happened to be passing by and they just happened to be outside—cavorting in the snow with the pup. Who Mala never did quite get around to finding another home for. And who was turning into one of the oddest looking dogs he'd ever seen. Like an electrified hot dog. Grateful, they'd named him, because he'd come to them on Thanksgiving. The kids were crazy about him, though, so Eddie felt good about bringing the mutt to Mala that night. He thought maybe he heard her laugh more these days, too, but that might've just been his imagination.

No, no…there was that time in the grocery store, maybe a couple weeks back. He'd just run in to pick up a loaf of bread and some cold cuts, and over "Jingle Bell Rock" on the loudspeaker system, he heard giggling over in the next aisle. So he'd poked his head around to see Mala and her two, all by themselves way down at the other end in the cereal section. There she was in her car coat and one of those long skirts she wore, dancing and singing right along with the music, holding Lucas's hands and making him dance right along with her, even though he kept collapsing in laughter. Carrie was in the buggy, trying to yell, "Mama! Stop! Somebody'll see us!" except she kept laughing so hard herself, she could barely get the words out. Suddenly, some old prune-faced lady wheeled her buggy into the aisle, her eyes popping wide open like she'd just happened onto a freak show. Naturally, Mala squelched her performance, but the kids only laughed all the harder at their mother's attempt to keep a straight face.

Eddie had left before they caught sight of him, but the memory had stuck with him for the rest of the evening, making him smile whenever he thought about that gal doing the two-step with her little boy, right smack in the middle of the supermarket. And if the scene had provoked an ache of a different sort, well, there was no point in ruminating about that too hard.

So. Several weeks had passed in this way, with Eddie keeping his distance and all, until one Monday about two weeks before Christmas, when for some reason he glanced up from the political thriller he'd been reading and realized it was nearly time for the kids to come home from school. But Mala's car wasn't in the driveway—and wasn't it just like her to name the damn thing Whitey Ford?—which meant she wasn't home to meet the bus. And something nagged at him that maybe he should go check that everything was okay.

Then he told himself it was none of his business, that Mala would've made whatever arrangements were necessary with her mother or whoever. So he went back to reading, for about all of thirty seconds, only to throw the book down in disgust, yank on his boots and jacket, and head out the door.

The cold air bit at Eddie's ears and cheeks as he hiked his jacket collar up around his neck, chewing himself out for not bothering to grab a scarf or gloves. It hadn't snowed in about a week, but the temperatures hadn't made it above freezing once since then, and the weak late afternoon sun didn't do diddly to warm things up any. His boots slipped now and again as he trudged down the street—he only happened to know where the stop was because he'd driven by a couple times when the bus was there. If somebody else was there to pick them up, he'd see whoever it was long before he actually got to the stop, so he could just turn right around and go back home, no harm done.

He was maybe a block away when the big yellow bus

groaned up to the corner; he didn't recognize anybody in the cluster of heavily-clothed adults who cared enough about their kids to pick them up. Shoot, Eddie couldn't recall anybody ever giving a damn whether he even got *on* the school bus, let alone whether he got off it. Out of the blue, he remembered how once, when he couldn't've been more than seven, he'd gotten off at the wrong stop and wandered around for what seemed like hours until he finally found his way back to his cousin's house, only to find out that nobody'd even missed him.

He used to wonder why other kids would *wish* to be invisible.

The doors screeched open, disgorged maybe a half-dozen occupants, including Carrie and Lucas. Everybody else got paired up with their respective grown-ups, but sure enough, when all the bodies were sorted out, Mala's two were alone. One of the parents bent down, apparently asking them if they needed any help.

"It's okay—I've got 'em," Eddie called out.

And thus the die was cast.

Carrie jerked around first, suspicion narrowing those blue eyes. Eddie thought about Mala's fears that the kids might get too attached and almost laughed. At the moment, Carrie was regarding him with about the same enthusiasm she might a plateful of boogers. She looked like a grape—purple pants, purple sneakers, purple fuzzy coat with the hood up, a froth of orange curls competing with the white fake fur trim. A backpack hung limply from one hand; some papers or something from the other.

"Where's Mama?"

I ate her, Eddie was tempted to say, but somehow, he didn't figure the kid was into dark humor. "I don't know," he answered honestly, noticing that Lucas's miniature Lions jacket was unzipped underneath a quivering lower lip. "But when I saw she wasn't home, I thought maybe I should meet the bus. Hey, buddy," he said to Lucas. "It's colder'n all get-out out here. How come your jacket's open?"

Carrie frowned, hitching her backpack up on her shoulder. "She always calls Grandma if she can't be here—"

"Carrie wouldn't zip it for me."

"I *can't* zip your jacket, stupid," she said, although Eddie could hear just a twinge of guilt in there somewhere. "The zipper's stuck."

"It is, huh?" Eddie said. Lucas nodded, wide-eyed behind the glasses. "Well, c'mere—let's have a look…" He squatted down in front of the little boy, fought with the zipper for a second or two, then did up the jacket, his insides going all funny at the breathy little "Thanks" he got in reply.

"Anyways, you didn't have to come," he heard behind him as he stood up again. "I mean, it's not like we don't know how to get home by ourselves. It's only three blocks, geez. My friend Rachel's house is farther than that. And I know where the key's hidden an' everything."

Eddie was about to say something to Miss Know-It-All when Lucas startled the bejeezus out of him by slipping his mittened hand into his.

"So you didn't have to come," Carrie repeated as they all started walking back toward the house, but her bravado was kinda limp around the edges, Eddie thought. Hugging her papers to her chest as she carefully negotiated an ice-crusted sidewalk where nobody had bothered to shovel, she asked, "What d'you think might've happened to her?"

"Now, I'm sure your mama's just fine," he said, even though he really shouldn't have been offering reassurances about things when he didn't have the facts. He realized Lucas had tilted his head to peer up at Eddie from underneath the cuff of his heavy knit cap, worry and trust commingling in the kid's big blue eyes. "I'm sure of it," he said, and Lucas nodded.

"I'll call Grandma and ask her to come stay with us," Carrie announced, and Eddie wasn't sure whether to feel relieved or disappointed.

They walked the three blocks in what Eddie had a definite feeling was uncharacteristic silence, broken only by Lucas's softly telling him that he wrote his numbers all the way to twenty-seven that day, and that the teacher had given him a sticker that said Way to Go! on it. He seemed very proud of both of those things, so Eddie figured he should acknowledge the accomplishment in some way.

"That's really cool, buddy. Bet nobody else in your class can do that."

With his free hand, the child dragged a padded mitten across his reddened, slightly runny nose. "Actually, Tara Jacobson can write up to a hunnerd," he rasped. "But this was the first time *I* got past twelve."

Something tugged at Eddie's heart, a feeling that only intensified when he gently squeezed the little hand in his and got a shy grin in return.

They'd reached the house by then; sure enough, Carrie battled her way behind a privet hedge under the windows, returning a few seconds later with a key. She clomped up the stairs and opened the front door with a flourish. Grateful exploded out onto the porch, yapping and spinning in circles. Lucas plopped his butt on the top step, dissolving into giggles when the excited pup knocked him onto his back.

"We're fine now," he heard Carrie say. His grin from watching Lucas and the pup fading, Eddie looked over at her. "You don't have to stay. Like I said, I'll call Nana—"

"Uh-uh." Lucas shoved the dog off of him and struggled to sit up, wiping dog slobber off his face. "Mama says we're not supposed to be alone."

"*You're* not supposed to be alone, 'cuz you're a baby—"

"I am not!"

"You just turned six. I'm seven—"

"Which is still too young to stay by yourself," Eddie said, walking up the steps and purposely planting himself so that he towered over the little girl.

She was clearly unimpressed. "We're not stupid," she said, unabashedly meeting his gaze three feet over her head. "We know not to touch the stove or plug anything in or turn on the hot water or answer the door or say Mama's not home if someone calls. Even Lucas knows how to dial 9-1-1."

Oh, boy, did she have her mother's chin thrust down pat. Eddie crossed his arms. "Oh? And exactly how many times has your mama ever actually left you by yourselves?"

The chin went up another notch. "Lots—"

"Nuh-uh!" Lucas said.

Carrie shot her brother a venomous look, after which she developed a profound interest in the toe of one sneaker.

"Yeah, well," Eddie said, walking over to the door and pushing it open, "whether she has or not, I'm not about to. So you're stuck with me until your mama gets home, Carrie. Deal with it."

With a toss of her curls, Carrie spun on her heel and flounced inside. Eddie followed, wondering just what he'd gotten himself into.

Mala threw the jack into the car's trunk, slammed it shut, then scooted around to the driver's side. Dammit to hell and back again—of all the times for her cell phone to go *pfft* on her! She'd been down to the wire as it was, leaving the nursery so late. But who knew the tire would blow? Well, okay, it wasn't as if it was a complete surprise, considering the condition the damn things were in. Hell, she'd seen heavier treads on a condom.

In any case, she'd be lucky to get to Big-O on the spare, let alone home. She simultaneously calculated how much breathing room she had on her credit card while reminding herself that she could call home from the tire place—she knew Carrie knew how to get in and what not to do, but still—and maybe phone her mother, too, see if Bev could scoot over there until she was done.

Fifteen minutes and a near heart attack later—she hadn't paid as much for the whole car as what these tires were going to cost—she called her mother, figuring Bev could be on her way while she talked to the kids. Hopefully, Lucas wouldn't be totally freaked out—

"No!" she said, loudly, as her mother's answering machine picked up. The guy at the counter gave her a funny look; she turned away. The place smelled like ripe rubber and stale cigarettes and men who apparently thought deodorant was for sissies. On an empty stomach, this was not good. Geez, Louise, her mother left the *longest* message—

"Ma! Ma! Pick up, it's me… Ma?" She waited a good ten seconds, but it was clear that her mother had actually had the audacity to leave the house without informing her daughter of her whereabouts.

Mala stabbed at the release button, then dialed her house, fully expecting to hear her daughter's voice. Instead, she got a "Y'ello?" in a deep, male, very familiar Texan drawl. The dog yipped in the background.

"Eddie?"

"Hey, Mala—where are you? Hey, kids," she heard him call out, "it's your mama. She's okay." Then to her. "You are, aren't you? Okay?"

"What? Yes, yes, I'm fine. Well, not *fine,* but the only thing in imminent danger of destructing is my charge card. My tire blew, followed immediately by my cell phone, so I couldn't call and I couldn't get anywhere where there was a phone until I'd changed the tire—"

"Whoa—you changed the tire by yourself?"

"Yes, Eddie," she said patiently. "My *mother* showed me how when I was sixteen." In the resulting silence, she asked, "But how'd you—? I mean, why'd you—?"

"Noticed your car wasn't there, figured something was up, went to get the kids. They're right here, by the way, eating peanut butter crackers. That okay?"

She realized she was picturing all those loose limbs leaning against her kitchen counter and that her brain had grabbed her by the libido and yanked her back to the night of The Kiss. She'd only seen him in passing, and not even that, really, unless you counted watching the guy come and go from the garage as "passing."

Damn, they kept the heat up in here.

"Peanut butter?" she asked in the midst of shucking off her car coat. "You sure you got the right kids? I mean, it's sometimes hard to tell one prissy little girl wearing purple from another."

Eddie's chuckle sent this little trickle of…something la-di-da-ing through her veins. "Pair of redheads, right? Boy has glasses, girl has attitude?"

"Yeah, you got the right kids." Suddenly, her heart twisted in her chest. "Oh, God, Eddie, thanks so much for picking them up. I've never missed the bus before, unless I'd arranged with my mother to pick them up instead…" To her annoyance, her voice cracked.

"Hey…lighten up. It's okay, they're okay. No harm done. So…when you think you'll be home?"

"Oh, Lord, I have no idea. Depends on how fast they can change out these tires. I tried getting my mother, but she's not home either—"

"For cryin' out loud, Mala. Stop worrying, okay? I'll stay as long as I have to."

"But you said you weren't a kid person."

The silence this time fairly crackled. "I think we'll all survive for the next couple of hours," he said quietly. "Long as you tell me what they usually do now, so they don't try and pull one over on me, we'll do just fine—"

"Hey, miss?"

"Hang on a sec," she said to Eddie, then looked over. The balding, paunchy guy behind the counter was glowering at her. "Thought you said this was gonna be a short call?"

"That was before I knew how much the tires were going to cost me." She waved him off, then again held her phone to her ear. Eddie was chuckling.

"Now I know where Carrie gets it."

A small, tired laugh wriggled from her throat. "Start 'em out early is my motto. Anyway, you don't have to—"

"You want me to sit 'em down in front of a slasher movie?"

"No!"

"Then just tell me what you want me to do."

She let out a long, long sigh. "You really want to get down and dirty with first grade math and Dr. Seuss?"

"I think I can handle it."

"Then go for it. I'm sure Carrie will tell you what she's got for homework, and Lucas has books in his room. He's just learning to read—"

"Miss! Please!"

"See you later," she said into the phone as she chased it into the cradle. "And thanks again."

She hung up, surprised to discover she actually felt better now than she had five minutes ago. It was that making-her-laugh thing, she realized.

Eddie also made her hot, but let's not go there.

With a whooshed sigh, she tramped across the waiting room and flopped into a vinyl chair to wait. The tire place was a few minutes outside of town, opposite a medium-size strip mall she rarely went to, next to a fairly popular steak-house type joint she *never* went to. The parking lots adjoined; from her seat, she could watch the restaurant patrons coming and going. Not that this was particularly entertaining, but it beat all to heck the beat-up three-year-old *Newsweek* lying forlornly on the table next to her. At four o'clock, the place wasn't exactly hopping, and between the stifling heat in the room and the adrenaline crash after finding out the kids were being taken care of, she nearly dozed off, until a car door slamming jerked her awake.

It had begun to get dark, the bright lights inside preventing her from clearly seeing outside. On a yawn, she tried to focus out the plate glass window. Then her heart knocked, just once and very painfully, at the sight of the tall, broad-shouldered man in a black wool topcoat with his back to her as he double-checked to make sure his door was locked. She couldn't quite tell, but his hair sure looked red from here…

Alarm streaked through her as she waited, breath held, for the man to turn around so she could see his face. After what seemed like forever, he finally did…and she sagged with relief. It wasn't Scott.

But, as if startled out of a nightmare, her pulse still pounded, her breath came in short, ragged gasps. And her throat clogged with the effort not to dissolve into tears.

Mala shut her eyes, riding out the unexpected panicked reaction. For God's sake—it wasn't as if she hadn't seen a man in a black topcoat since Scott's departure. And after three years, she'd thought that was all behind her.

She'd thought she was free.

Still shaking, she grabbed the mangled magazine and slapped through the limp pages, even though she had no idea what she was seeing. Anger seeped through the remnants of her agitation, revving her heart rate even more. After all the pains she'd taken…

Well. One thing was for certain—she'd have to be more on guard than ever. If the simple sight of someone who looked vaguely like her ex-husband could derail her like that…

It's okay, she told herself. *No regrets.*

No recriminations.

"Ma'am?"

She jerked her head up, her brow knotted. Another man stood behind the counter, younger, his overalls baggy. A scraggly goatee quivered when he smiled. "You're all set to go."

"Oh. Oh, great."

Her knees were still shaking as she stood and slipped her coat back on, an affliction which had suffused her entire body by the time she got in the car. "For God's sake, girl—get a grip!" she muttered as she started the car. Okay, so maybe she was overworked and stressed and hungry and had been spending far too much time obsessing about a man she knew she didn't want, couldn't have and should be ashamed of herself for even *thinking* about…having. But still, that was no reason to be hallucinating ex-husbands.

She popped a Fleetwood Mac tape into the player, forced the heebie-jeebies from her brain. The past was just that—the past. Now, all she had to worry about was picking up something for dinner, then going home to face her dirty house, several hours of work, her children…

And that man she'd been spending far too much time obsessing about.

Okay. Like Mala had said, Carrie had pretty much taken care of her homework on her own—actually, when Eddie had offered his help, he'd gotten the primmest, prissiest "No, thank you" ever bestowed in history. And he'd managed maybe twenty minutes of listening to Lucas stumble over "the" and "in" and "not" about fifty thousand times before he decided

Mala was right, he didn't have to do this. So, in time-honored male tradition, Eddie wandered out into the toy-and-clothes strewn living room, crouching in front of the glass-fronted case housing the video collection. A couple of old black-and-white jobbers, about a million Disney movies, and some unopened, very dusty, workout tapes. No cable that he could tell, no satellite, no *TV Guide,* even.

"We're not allowed to watch TV before dinner," Carrie said behind him.

So much for that.

Eddie twisted around to find her standing a few feet away, hugging herself. "Oh? How come?"

"I heard her tell Uncle Steve she doesn't want us brain-dead before we hit…" A neat little crease wedged between her amber brows. "Pu-something."

Eddie choked back a grin. "Puberty?"

"Yeah."

"Oh. Well." He stood. "Guess I can't fault her there."

The pup prancing along beside him, Lucas wandered in, his hands rammed in the pockets of his baggy little jeans. "So…" Eddie matched Lucas's stance. "Whaddya think we should do now?"

"We could play a game," Lucas said. "I've got Candyland."

Eddie dimly remembered that his mama had gotten Candyland for him one Christmas. He hadn't much cared for it then, as he recalled.

"Candyland is for babies," Carrie pronounced.

"Is not!"

"Is, too—"

"Okay, guys, knock it off." He and Carrie glared at each other as he wondered what sort of game Carrie would consider sophisticated enough to suit her. With Eddie's luck, probably poker. "You know what, y'all…I'm really not much good at games."

Silence jittered between them for another several seconds, until Lucas said, "Hey, Carrie! Maybe Eddie could put up the Christmas decanations!"

"Decor-*a*-tions," Carrie corrected, rolling her eyes. "Honestly."

But when the eyes stopped rolling, Eddie caught the hopeful look in them. Which immediately got to arguing with the you-really-shouldn't twitching in his stomach.

His hand snaked up to rub the back of his neck. Ah, hell…rescuing the kids from the bus stop was one thing. That was simply being neighborly. And feeding them, making sure they got their homework done…well, shoot, anybody would've done that. Putting up Christmas stuff, though…well, that was getting just a little too personal. Too close. And, hey, Mala said she didn't want the kids to get too close, right? So Eddie frowned and shook his head and said, "Gee, guys, I dunno. Seems to me most women have real definite ideas about stuff like that. I mean, I wouldn't want to step on your mama's toes."

In what Eddie figured was a rare moment of shared commiseration, the two kids looked at each other. Then Carrie said, "You mean you don't want to."

"Did I say that? What I said was, it's dangerous for a man to—"

"Never mind. It's okay," she said softly, and Eddie thought, *Oh, hell.* Except then she said, "Mama bought a whole bunch of stuff the day after Thanksgiving, 'cuz she promised we were going to have outside lights this year. But I counted on my calendar an' Christmas is only nine days away, an' everybody I know has had their lights up 'n' stuff for ages already. We're the only house that doesn't have lights for three *blocks*. Well, 'cept for Mr. Liebowicz, where we take piano, but Mama said that's 'cuz he's Jewish and celebrates Chanukah instead. 'Cept my teacher said that Chanukah is called The Festival of Lights, so I don't see why Mr. Liebowicz couldn't have lights if he wanted, do you? Mom's friend Nancy is Jewish, too, but her husband isn't, so their kids get Christmas *and* Chanukah, which *really* isn't fair. And we don't even have a *tree* yet."

And Eddie thought, *oh, hell,* again.

"Guess your mama's been kinda busy, huh?"

One shoulder hitched. "I guess."

Lucas gave him a big blue stare from behind his glasses. Eddie sighed.

It'd been years since he'd put up lights, since that Christmas he spent here with Molly and Jervis, in fact. And it was colder'n a witch's booty out there. And Mala probably would get mad at him. Or them. Or both.

And they were both looking at him with those dad-blasted big blue eyes.

Oh, *hell.*

"So," Eddie said on a rush of air, "you know where your mama put the decorations?"

The grins that streaked across both faces knocked him for a loop, is what. And the way they and the pup all stumbled all over each other to get to the hall, chattering and pointing to the closet, where apparently the elves has stashed the loot…well, he wasn't going to lie and say it didn't do something to his insides.

Then there were the giggles and cries of delight as he handed down each Wal-Mart bag, loaded with all kinds of lights and garlands and bows and gutter hooks and—oh, Lord, only Mala would think of this—heavy-duty extention cords, and he thought, this was what childhood was supposed to sound like.

But Mala was right. He didn't dare come across like Santa Claus. So he put on as stern a face as he could dredge up, then pointed to the living room.

"Before a single light goes up, that room gets cleaned."

Carrie and Lucas looked at each other, then stomped off, both sets of arms crossed over their chests.

"I *knew* there'd be a catch," Carrie said, tossing him her best ticked-off glare.

"Yeah," replied an equally indignant Lucas. "Whatever that means."

Chapter 7

In the rapidly fading light, Mala could just make out, as she approached her house, a man hanging precariously over the edge of her roof. Since tangling with a million other after-work shoppers in the grocery store had done little to calm her jangled nerves, her heart now rocketed into her throat. In general terms, she was a firm believer that the only life forms that properly belonged on roofs were birds and the occasional squirrel.

Once in the driveway, she could barely get her car door open for the crush of small, chattering bodies. Words pelted her as she at last emerged, including "lights," "cool," "finally" and something about "stupid old Becky O'Brien."

She crunched her way across the frozen snow, grocery bags and purse clutched in one hand, Lucas hanging on to the other. From her porch roof to the second story stretched her aluminum extension ladder; like a crippled centipede, icicle lights already dangled across the lower half of the house, while garlands wound around the porch posts and swagged across the lintel. Eddie looked down. Grinned. "Hey."

At that precise moment, between her nerves and her wrong-time-of-month hormones, she realized just how much of a mess she was. That a woman can only go so long without male…companionship, let's say, before she explodes. And seeing all that litheness up on her roof—never mind why he was up there, it meant *she* wasn't, and that was cause for immense gratitude—and that grin, and realizing that this guy had put himself out more for her kids than the sperm donor had in the whole three years he'd actually been in residence was doing absolutely terrible things to her self-control. Like shredding it into itsy, bitsy, not-worth-spit pieces. Not that she was about to let anyone in on that fact. "Hey, yourself. How the heck did you get suckered into this?"

He leaned back on his haunches, which meant, for the next few moments, at least, Mala could breathe again. "It was either this or Candyland."

That choice might have driven Mala to the roof herself. "Ah…ohmigod, Eddie—be careful!"

He'd tugged a length of icicle lights out of their box and had now cantilevered his entire torso out over the roof to drape them along the edge.

"It's okay, Mama," Carrie said, looking up with adoration gleaming in her eyes. "He's been doing this for like an hour already and he only slipped once."

Mala's eyes shot to his. Eddie chuckled. "I know where the icy spots are now, no problem. Hey, kids—why don't y'all go back inside and see if you can find me the bags with the colored lights in them?"

Kids vanished. Eddie glanced down, still stringing, still grinning. "This doesn't make you nervous or anything, does it?"

Mala shifted the grocery bags. Warm, rotisserie chicken-scent wafted up, tormenting her. "Oh, no. I didn't need that extra five years of my life, anyway."

"Don't tell me you're scared of heights?"

"Okay. I won't."

"Then how the Sam Hill did you plan on getting lights up here, anyway?"

"I didn't. My plan ended at the porch roof."

He chuckled again. "Wuss."

"But a *living* wuss."

Another soft laugh, warm and gentle, floated down. There was no put-down in his teasing, she realized. No attempt at humiliation. Instead, it actually made her feel good. Alive. And almost normal in a situation that was anything but. "Anyway, so how *did* they talk you into doing this?"

"Three words. Big blue eyes."

Mala melted, right then and there, felt tears sting which she quickly sent packing. Criminy, her hormones were really doing a number tonight. Just because he was a nice guy didn't mean… She glanced at the front door, which the kids had left open, then back up at Eddie, crouched like a cat.

"You must be freezing your butt off."

"Hard to tell. It went numb a half hour ago."

She laughed, then frowned. "You know, you don't have to—"

"You say that far too much, lady, you know that?" he said gently, then shimmied down the ladder to the porch roof, called out to the kids. "Y'all find those lights yet?"

They came scampering back outside, bags banging against legs. Eddie knelt by the gutter, held out his hand. "Give 'em to your mama, so she can pass 'em to me."

Realizing she'd been shocked into silence—not an everyday occurrence—Mala traded the grocery bags for the lights, told Carrie and Lucas to take the bags to the kitchen, then handed Eddie the lights, during which process she found her voice.

"It's just that I don't like putting people out," she said as Eddie opened the next box. His eyes darted to hers just as the streetlight flickered into life, illuminating his benign expression.

"I see. Well, you wanna hop on up here and take over?"

Her mouth twisted. "I'd rather shovel."

"Yeah, I kinda figured you'd see it my way. But just for the record, you're not puttin' me out, Mala. Actually, I'm kinda enjoying myself. Numb ass and all. And besides, outdoing *that*—" his voice lowered, he nodded across the street at the O'Brien's tribute to Coney Island "—has just become a matter of honor."

A laugh sputtered from her throat. "God. You are such a man."

Silence stretched between them, during which he gave her a look which she couldn't see but her knees caught, anyway. "Rumor has it. Although I don't get much chance to prove it these days."

Oh, God: "And, um, trying to blind the other half of the neighborhood does it for you, huh?"

Another grin spread across that long, lean face, this one slow and lazy and everything a grin could be. "For starters."

Oh…*God.*

Then he said, "Been a long time since I've watched any football, too," and Mala burst out laughing, partly from panic, partly from relief. She suddenly felt a lot better. She also suddenly felt a lot worse, which didn't make sense, but then, nothing did. And hadn't, she realized, for some time. She sucked in a breath, extremely grateful that it was too dark for him to see her sizzling cheeks.

"Got the new tires okay?" he said.

Nothing like being dragged back to reality. "Oh, yeah. And I have to admit, there's a lot to be said for feeling the suckers actually grip the road. In fact, I hit a patch of ice over on Main, the car didn't even flinch."

"Well, that's real good. And you *really* changed out the flat by yourself?"

"Yes, Eddie, I really did."

"I'll be damned. You are one helluva lady, you know that? What was in those bags?"

Her brows lifted. "Dinner."

"Great. I'm starved. If there's enough, that is."

She wasn't sure whether to laugh or…what. "There's plenty, but…excuse me? Did I miss something?"

"Like you inviting me?"

"Yeah, that's it."

He shrugged. "Just figured dinner was as good a way as any to even up the score. For freezing my butt off."

She flushed. "Oh. Well, uh, sure. But…"

"But what?"

"It's just…" Way in the very pit of her stomach, the trembling started. "Criminy, Eddie—you're the fabulous cook. Not me. I mean, I can manage the basics okay—my mother taught me how to cook when I was twelve—but we're talking meat loaf and tuna casserole and sticking something in the broiler kind of cooking. Nothing like what you do. And then tonight, things got so screwed up, I just picked up a rotisserie chicken and some potato salad from the grocery store deli. Don't get me wrong, I certainly cook for my kids, almost every night, but I was running late and I still have all this work to do—"

"Whoa…*whoa.*" Eddie stopped what he was doing, his hand propped on one knee, his brow tightly drawn as he looked down at her. "You think there's something wrong with taking the convenient route, every once in a while?"

"No, of course not. It's just—"

The words caught in her throat, as the shakes assaulted her all over again. She couldn't talk, couldn't breathe. But this was ridiculous, after all this time…

A gasp popped from her mouth as she felt Eddie's arm go around her shoulders, especially since she hadn't even heard him jump off the porch roof. "Criminy, Mala—are you okay?"

"What?" His solidity, his nearness, were nearly more than she could deal with. No man other than her brother or father had touched her since Scott, and the sudden, vicious need to be held was nearly overwhelming. She couldn't…

She lifted a hand to her head, swallowing down the sickness and the need, both, then nodded. "Yes. Yes, I'm fine. I just got a little dizzy there, for a moment." She dared to lift her eyes. He clearly wasn't buying it. "It's okay, Eddie. Really. I just haven't eaten in a while, that's all."

"Then I suggest we remedy that as soon as possible," he said, dropping his arm and walking back toward the porch. Then he twisted around, one finger pointed. "And don't you dare let me hear you apologizin' like that again, you hear me?" The hand dropped. "If I've got the gall to invite myself to dinner, then I can damn well deal with whatever you give me.

And rotisserie chicken and potato salad beats the hell out of another sandwich.''

Then he turned his back to her, tweaking with the strands of lights looped around the garlands framing the porch. His scent lingered in her nostrils, his touch in her nerve endings. He'd just fussed at her, she realized. But his words had felt like a caress. Not like a series of blows.

She scrambled for her control as if it were a fumbled football.

"A s-sandwich?" she said. "You're kidding?"

"Nope. After all the cooking I do for other people the rest of the week, I don't cook much for myself when I'm on my own. Okay, let's plug these suckers in and see what we've got." He took the porch steps two at a time, crossed to the outlet next to the front door, then picked up the plug and yelled inside. "Hey, kids! Showtime!"

Ten seconds later, after they'd all been dispatched to the sidewalk to get the maximum effect, he plugged in the cord...and the house flashed into brilliance, the colored lights sparkling like candy over the dangling, glittering icicle lights. The kids both whooped in delight, clapping their hands, as a shard of bitter disappointment sliced through Mala. This was what she'd envisioned when she'd married Scott, what she'd envisioned from the time she was a little girl dreaming of her own white knight, magic moments like this that bind a family together. A husband who adored her, who'd freeze his backside off to bring smiles like that to his children's faces. Only the man now loping down the steps toward them wasn't her husband, wasn't even part of her family, but just a nice guy who'd be gone in a few months.

She supposed after all this time she should at least be grateful for this much, since this was obviously as good as it was going to get.

"Well, how's it look?" Eddie said beside her, beaming nearly as much as the kids. Mala glanced over at him, her heart's stuttering shoving aside her own maudlin thoughts long enough to realize that's exactly what was going on here: the child who never got anyone's approval.

"It's absolutely gorgeous, Eddie," she said with a sharp nod, and knew, without looking at him, that, this time, he wanted to kiss *her*.

He didn't get it. He'd managed to get through the last fifteen years without worrying about another human being. At least, not on a personal level. So what sort of power or pull, or whatever the hell this was, did this woman and her kids have over him, that he found himself in immiment danger of doing so now?

"Carrie?" Mala called down the hall from the kitchen doorway, drying her hands on a dishtowel—she'd out and out refused to let him help with the dishes—her hair hanging all loose and soft to her shoulders, sleek as mink. "Time for your bath, honey."

"Aw, Mama—"

"Now, Carrie. Chop-chop."

Oh, man, he'd wanted to kiss her so bad out there, he thought he'd pop.

Not that he wasn't still in control, even if Miss Mala and her softness and sense of humor and whatever had just set her off like that were all combining to give that control a run for its money. He just had to be careful, was all, maybe remind himself a little more firmly that nobody ruled Eddie King but Eddie King.

"Coffee?" she asked.

He hesitated, figuring he really should go. Not wanting to. "I don't want to keep you from your work or anything."

All those curves of hers, even underneath layers of sweaters, swayed gracefully as she walked across the kitchen. "I can't get anything done until they're in bed, anyway."

"Then coffee sounds great."

So she went about putting on the coffee while he watched her, the pup curled up at his feet, thinking about how much energy he'd wasted growing up on being angry at all those people who periodically discarded him like last week's Sunday paper. How he'd been so sure the only way to protect himself was to turn off his emotions, not letting anyone or anything get to him. Maybe he hadn't much liked himself like that, but he hadn't known what else to do. Wasn't until after his divorce that it finally dawned on him he'd been going at things all wrong, that there was more to survival than just sandbagging your feelings. No, the key, he finally realized, was making sure you always held the upper hand, see. Controlling your own destiny, or fate, or whatever. He didn't have to be a bastard. He just had to be the one in charge.

And wanting to help had nothing to do with getting emotionally involved.

That'd been the only reason he'd wrangled that dinner invitation, because he hated to see people miserable. He had a ton of food upstairs, although the part about his cooking for himself hadn't been a lie. But from the moment he saw Mala get out of her car this evening, he could tell, just from the way she held herself, all cautious and careful like she'd break if she moved too fast, that something was wrong or something had happened, one or the other. And it was like…like something had shattered inside him, seeing her like that. Oh, he'd told himself it was none of his business, that she had plenty of people around to lean on, to confide in, that they'd done this dance before and she would only push away any offer of help or solace or whatever it was he thought he was offering, he wasn't really sure. And that she was right, there was no point in his going and getting himself all tangled up with her and the kids when he wasn't going to be around.

Except he was here, at the moment, and all those other people weren't.

And none of *that* explained this god-all drive to kiss the woman senseless.

And none of that explained why he was still sitting at her kitchen table, talking about going to get a fool Christmas tree and wanting to basically do whatever it took to relieve some of that tension she hauled around with her like the junk in her car.

He wondered when the last time was anybody had made slow, sweet love to this lady.

He wondered where he'd last seen his brain.

"Oh, God, yes, the Christmas tree," she said on a long sigh.

From down the hall, he heard the bath water get turned on. "I know, I've got to figure out how to work it in, somehow…but when is a good question. And then there's the rest of the shopping to do and the presents to wrap…and I've got ten year-end statements to finish up and gross receipts taxes to file and…"

She stopped, pressing her lips together, like she'd already let more out than she was supposed to.

"When's the last time you did something just for yourself, Miss Mala?"

Her laugh was tired. "When I was twelve?"

Eddie frowned. "You've got family all around you. Why don't you let them take some of the burden?"

Before she could tell him to take a flying leap, Lucas came in, already in his pajamas, and crawled up onto her lap, managing to bump his foot on the table leg, which prompted great buckets of tears. Eddie's stomach knotted when he caught Mala's weary sigh. But then she threaded her arms around Lucas's waist from behind, holding him tight and shushing him until he stopped crying. When the storm had more or less passed, she nestled her cheek on top of his bristly hair, even though it was obvious that every bit of the tension had come right back to roost in her shoulders, the set to her mouth.

"What's in the cup?" the kid asked.

"Coffee."

"C'n I have some?"

"Not tonight. You've already brushed your teeth. Hey, while Carrie's taking her bath, why don't you go watch one of your Pooh tapes, huh?"

The little boy snuggled closer to his mama. "It's all dark in there."

"So turn on the hall light first. Which you can do from the kitchen door."

Lucas shook his head.

"Hey, big guy," Mala said softly, but firmly. "You can do this. Besides, Grateful'll go with you." The pup scrambled up on his stubby legs at the sound of his name, only too eager to accept his new mission.

Lucas seemed to consider this for a minute, then finally slid off Mala's lap. He and the dog padded toward the door that led to the hallway, only to hesitate when he got there.

"I'm right here, honey," Mala said. And finally, the kid flipped on the hall light switch, then cautiously crossed the threshhold into the Great Unknown. A few seconds later, the TV blared on. Mala glanced over at Eddie and swiped her hair behind her ear, then toyed with the handle of her mug. "My family does help out, to answer your earlier question. A lot," she added, and he could hear the guilt in her voice. "They take the kids off my hands now and then, stuff like that."

"So you can do what? Shackle yourself to your computer?"

Her gaze shot to his. "How would you know—"

"The light's always on in your office when I get off work. And nowhere else," he added when she opened her mouth.

Her mouth clamped shut; color flooded her cheeks as she reached out to fiddle with the salt shaker. "I don't have much choice about that, Eddie. If I don't work, we don't eat."

"And if you use yourself up, there won't be a mama around *to* feed them, will there?"

"Says the man who has no one to answer to but himself."

Ignoring the sting of the justified barb, Eddie leaned foward and said softly, "I watched my mother literally work herself to death, dragging herself home every night, too exhausted to even eat." Then, before she could go all sappy and sympathetic on him, he said, "Your folks don't even know about your panic attacks, do they?"

She froze. "What?"

"You nearly lost it tonight, Mala. I've worked around enough stressed-out folks to know the signs. And somehow, I doubt that was the first time."

"That's ridiculous. I told you, I hadn't eaten—"

"You didn't faint, lady. You freaked out."

Another one of those fake laughs fell from her lips. "Please, Eddie. I hardly *freaked out*." She got up from the table, snatched up the mugs. "I'm telling you, it's nothing. And it's really none of your business."

"How can something be 'nothing' and 'none of my business' at the same time?"

She didn't answer. So, Eddie, whose good sense had clearly left the building, went on as she trooped over to the sink, "Something's sure as hell got you good and shook up. Now if you don't want to confide in me, fine. You're right—it's none of my business. But you better damn sight confide in somebody, and soon, before you really fall apart."

She turned, the mugs still clutched in her white-knuckled hands. "I'm not—"

"Mala—I've been there. I know what it's like, letting life smack you around instead of taking charge of it. And I'm thinking that's what's changed about you—you used to be on top of things. I could tell that much, even from a distance. It's part of what fascinated me about you. Made me respect you. Especially seeing as how, at that point in my life, I was anything but on top of things. Now you look like all these obligations of yours are about to take you down for the last time."

Something like fear flashed in her eyes, like she'd caught a glimpse of a monster she hadn't realized had gotten loose from its cage. But he saw her rein it in, stuff it back wherever she kept it from causing any trouble. She even tried a smile.

"Now you sound like my mother."

"Then maybe you should listen to her."

Her eyes blazed. "Excuse me, but where the *hell* do you get off giving out advice about how other people should run their lives?"

"I don't know. I've never done it before and I sure as hell don't know why I'm doing it now. But I also know what it's like to deny there's anything wrong. To convince yourself you're okay, everything's okay, because the alternative's too damned scary to contemplate."

Her mouth compressed into a thin, flat line before she whipped back around, clunking the mugs onto the counter.

"Dammit to hell, Mala…what is wrong with you—?"

"Nothing! There is nothing…wrong…with…*me,*" she said in a savage whisper.

''Mama!'' came from down the hall. ''C'n I get out of the tub?''

He saw her spine get all board-straight as she marshalled that inner strength that kept mothers going no matter what. ''Sure, honey. I'll be right there.'' But when she turned around, tears glittered in her eyes. ''Thanks for putting up the lights. But you need to go now.''

He covered the space between her and the table in three strides, yanked on his jacket. It made no sense, him getting mad when he'd been the one butting in. It made even less sense, that he should give a damn to begin with.

But God help him, he did.

''*I'm* not your problem, darlin','' he said, making good and sure he had her undivided attention. ''And whatever your problem *is,* it's not going to leave when I do.''

Lucas had crashed practically the instant his head hit the pillow. Carrie, however, was still wired at nine o'clock, much to Mala's chagrin. Her brains felt as if they were boiling; all she wanted was to sit in the dark, to be quiet, to think. Not listen to a child prattling on at forty miles an hour. But Mama-duty came first. Mama-duty always came first. And then there was work, and her family, and the car and the house and…

When *was* the last time she'd done something, just for herself?

Guilt tore at her for even daring to think such a thing. She loved being a mother. She loved being *these* kids' mother, even if she sometimes wondered if she'd live to see their teen years, she thought with a wry smile. But sometimes, she just got so tired.…

''Mama?''

She jerked herself out of her reverie and looked down at Carrie, frowning up at her from her Little Mermaid figured pillow. For a child who was otherwise as practical as an old lady, Carrie was heavily into fantasy characters—mermaids and fairies and unicorns and the like, splashed all over her pink-walled room.

"What's wrong?" the child said, her brow crumpled. "You look all sad."

Mala pushed back the Raggedy Ann curls off her daughter's forehead. "Just pooped, sweetie, that's all."

"You and Eddie had a fight, didn't you?"

Mala's hand stilled. "What are you talking about?"

"When I was in the bathtub. I heard you."

Oh, Lord. "No, Carrie. We didn't have a fight. Exactly. Just a...disagreement." She got up from the bed, picked the day's clothes off the floor and tossed them in the laundry basket in the closet, then put the books they'd been reading back on the bookshelf over Carrie's little white desk. In other words, stalling. "Grown-ups do that, sometimes."

"Yeah, I guess. I mean, Nana Bev and Pop sure do. Lots."

Mala didn't think she'd equate her parents' fine-honed fussing at each other with what had just transpired between Eddie and her, but no way was she going there. "Yes, they do," she said, sitting heavily on the edge of Carrie's bed again. "And it doesn't really mean anything, does it?"

Then Carrie gave her one of those wise-woman looks Mala had come to dread. "Eddie's nice, Mama. But he's *so* not right for you."

Mala did well to get out, "Oh?"

"Yeah. I mean, first off, you get all nervous around him. And secondly, he told us he's not going to be around after Galen has her baby." She shrugged, all nonchalance. "So what would be the point of liking him?"

The "nervous" part of that comment would have to wait a minute, but she could at least deal with the other. So Eddie had warned off her kids, too, huh? Smart man. Still, she heard the wistfulness in her daughter's voice, knew the one thing she'd most dreaded had apparently come to pass: Carrie, at least—and she suspected Lucas as well—had already become attached to the gentle, crazy buttinski who lived upstairs.

Not that she blamed them.

"You can like someone who's only in your life temporarily, you know." Mala thought—hard—for a moment, then said, "Remember last summer, when you took care of the kindergarten guinea pig? You loved him, didn't you?'' Carrie nodded. "But you also knew you'd have to give him up when school started again, right?''

Carrie crossed her arms over her chest and said, "Mama... Eddie's not a guinea pig.''

Mala managed a laugh. "True. But the principle's the same.'' She messed with Carrie's covers for a second, then said carefully, "Lots of people come and go in our lives, honey. That's just the way life is. That doesn't mean we can't just...enjoy his company while he's here.''

After a moment, Carrie sighed. "Yeah. I guess. But I know I'm gonna miss him when he's gone.''

"Well, that's not for at least three months yet, so if I were you, I wouldn't worry my pretty little head about it. Okay?''

Instead of answering, Carrie flung out her arms, silently asking for a hug which Mala gladly gave. And in answer to the child's unasked question, Mala leaned back and whispered, "You've got a lot of people who love you who aren't going anywhere, like me and Nana Bev and Pop-Pop, and Uncle Steve and Aunt Sophie...you hear me?''

After a moment, a little smile tilted the child's lips. "Yeah, Mama. I hear you.''

"Good. Now go to sleep before I keel over on top of you.''

Carrie giggled and gave her one last kiss, then flopped over on her side. Like her brother, she was out before Mala clicked off the bedside lamp.

Then she peeked into Lucas's night-light illuminated room— there was absolutely no convincing him that monsters didn't lurk in every shadow—her thoughts tumbling all over each other as she watched the tiny boy snooze, one arm strangling Mr. Boffin, a disreputable teddy bear he'd had since he was two, and his wadded up beebee. And any other night, she would have continued down the hall toward her office to cram in another couple hours work, maybe, before she called it a night.

Except tonight, all she could hear were Eddie's words pinging around in her decrepit brain.

As well as his footsteps overhead.

Oh, yeah, Carrie…he makes me nervous. Only that's not exactly the word she'd use. And while she stood there, staring at one of her many responsibilities, the tumbling thoughts began to untangle themselves and settle down, all neatly laid out so she could actually she what she had. Let's see…there was Eddie's advice that she should take charge of her life, do something just for her…and then there was hers to Carrie, that enjoyment-while-he-was-here business…

And when you added those together, what did you get?

Trouble, my friends, right here in Spruce Lake.

Not to mention the fact that she was furious with him for sticking in his nose where it didn't belong.

Again.

The pup click-clicked over the bare floor to her, then sat down and pricked up his ears, as if to say, "Well? You gonna follow through on this or what?"

Great. Now she was having telepathic conversations with a dog.

Then, gathering in her brain like storm clouds, a million previously ungelled thoughts about her and Scott and their marriage suddenly coalesced. For three years, her accountant brain had been trying to analyze what had gone wrong with her marriage, but she could never make the figures add up.

Until tonight.

She looked at her son again. Then down the hall, where a mountain of invoices and tax forms awaited her attention. Then up at the ceiling, where, in the apartment just on the other side of that ceiling, the bad boy of her dreams awaited her attention, too.

Maybe.

Oh, God.

It was nearly ten. Eddie had turned out all his lights, except for one living room lamp, and was just getting ready to close up for the night when he felt the house's faint shudder from the front door being opened. He twisted open the miniblinds just enough to see Mala, all wrapped up in one of her long sweaters, make her way down to the gate, the pup bouncing along beside her. She opened the gate and went out onto the sidewalk, twisting around to look up at the still lit Christmas lights while the dog did his thing. A few seconds later, she called to the dog, retraced her steps. Then he heard the door shut, saw the yard plunge into darkness.

A minute later, he heard her footsteps on the outside staircase.

His heart stopped, only to start booming like a kettledrum while he waited. Finally, after about ten years, he heard her tentative knock on the door.

Since he'd moved in, Mala had never, not once, come up to his apartment.

He opened the door. "Hey—"

"This will just take a minute. I can't leave the kids," she said, her voice rattling with cold. Now, Mala Koleski was not a small woman, by any means. Yet, standing there on the landing outside his door, she looked about as frail and fragile as a body could look.

So Eddie leaned against the door frame, his arms crossed, figuring if she wasn't going to freeze, neither would he. She took a deep breath, swept her hair away from her face. "Okay, I'm here for two reasons. The first one is, to tell you yeah, something kind of did happen today, and I do need to talk to someone, but I can't lay this on my family because…well, I just can't."

"So I win."

"Aren't you thrilled?"

Eddie reached inside, grabbed his jacket from off the back of a chair, handed it to her. "I won't be if you turn into an ice sculpture. Put this on."

She stared at the jacket for a second or two, apparently decided it wouldn't change the course of her life to just do what he asked, then said, "I thought I saw my husband today."

Eddie felt his brow pucker. "Oh?"

"Yeah. Only it turned out, it wasn't him. But…" Her hand drifted to her throat as she glanced away for a second, then looked back at him. "But seeing him—or thinking I saw him— apparently rattled loose some things I thought I'd handled."

"About his cheating on you?"

She rubbed her arms, hitched one shoulder. "That was the least of it."

"And what does that mean?"

But she'd gone someplace inside herself for a moment. "The funny thing was, he never raised his voice. Never seemed to get angry." She looked up, her brow knotted. "I...I wasn't even aware of what was happening, why I was questioning everything I was doing, even stupid little things like whether I was buying the right toilet paper. The cheating might have been the last straw, but it was his reaction when I told him to get out that finally opened my eyes, made me realize what kind of man I'd married."

"Let me guess. He told you it was your fault."

A sardonic smile pulled at her mouth. "Bingo. And unfortunately, he'd done his job so well over the four years of our marriage, I believed him."

Eddie felt something cold and malevolent snake through his veins. "And your next sentence better have something to do with your knowing that's not true."

Mala nodded, then let out her breath in a frosted cloud. "I know that. Now. But that's not what still bugs me." She backed up to lean against the railing, her arms crossed. "What still bothers me is how I could date a man for almost two years, and be so naive, and so blind, I never saw the signs."

"You ever stop to think maybe there weren't any?"

She glanced up at him, then away, shaking her head. "There had to be," she said softly, sadly. "But I was so...I don't know. Relieved, I guess, that I'd finally found somebody, somebody who didn't mind that I was smart, that I wasn't a cute little thing...I don't know," she said again. "Oh, *God,* Eddie—I wanted to make my marriage work. Like my parents have. Like my grandparents did. But I failed."

Eddie swore. Mala looked at him, amused. "Nice language."

"And there's a lot more where that came from. Dammit, Mala—the guy puts you down for four years, cheats on you, has never contacted you or the kids since your divorce, and *you* failed?''

''I picked him, didn't I?''

Eddie forked a hand through his hair, jammed his hands on his hips. ''How do you figure it's your fault your ex was a horse's ass?''

''I don't. But the judgment call was mine. And it hit me tonight that Scott was only one in a long line of bozos, which would seem to indicate that I have a true knack for being attracted to men who couldn't be worse for me.'' She looked him dead in the eye. ''And that includes you.''

Well, shoot—what was he supposed to say to that? He *was* bad for her. But he'd never be bad *to* her. A difference he felt obligated to point out.

''I know that,'' she said, looking up at him, her expression all sweet and earnest and explosively dangerous. ''I really do. And I'm by no means comparing you with Scott. He was rat poison. You're…you're more like chocolate praline cheesecake. Both of you are deadly, but at least I'd die happy with the cheesecake. Which leads me to…'' She paused, sucked in a breath. ''…the second reason I'm here. I, uh…oh, God.''

He thought maybe she blushed, but he couldn't quite tell in the low light. ''Okay, I can do this.'' Another deep breath, a nervous laugh. ''You know what you said earlier, about my never doing anything just for me? Well…much as I hate to admit it, you were right about that, too. Which is why I'm about to ask a favor of you. It's kind of a 'book club' favor— you know, where you buy four books at the special introductory price with no obligation to buy anything else, ever?''

''Mala…you just lost me—''

''Eddie, don't stop me now or I'll never get this out.''

He held up his hands in surrender. She crossed her arms, took one last breath, then said, ''How does the idea of an affair grab you?''

Chapter 8

He froze. Mala wasn't sure if that was a good sign or not.

Oh, Lord, she was shaking so hard, she was going to lose ten pounds before he got around to answering.

"You don't mean that," he finally said.

"Oh, b-believe me, I do. If you're still as interested as you were a few weeks ag-go."

He rammed that hand through his hair again, squinted at her. Let out a sharp sigh. "Interest has nothing to do with this."

"So you are?"

"I'd be lying if I said no."

"So what's the problem?"

"Look at you. You're trembling worse than that pup did when I first brought him here."

"It's c-cold."

She might feel better about this if she didn't have to look at him because everybody always said she couldn't lie worth diddly because it always showed on her face.

Eddie sighed. "Mala, honey, it's not that I'm not real flattered—not to mention tempted—but where the devil is this coming from? I thought we agreed—"

''—not to get involved. Yes, we did. But that's the beauty of this.''

He looked at her for a long second, then said, ''I think I need to sit down,'' so he came outside and sat, then reached up and grabbed her hand, yanking her down beside him. ''Okay,'' he said on a stream of frosted air, ''you wanna explain what this is all about?''

Any other time, she might have found his confusion endearing. As it was, she was just getting irritated that she had to justify herself when she knew damn well what she was offering was a dream come true. For most men, anyway.

''What this is all about, is that I hadn't given a moment's thought to having sex until you waltzed back into my life.'' She stared at her hands, knotted on her knees. ''Now I can't think of anything else. I thought, when you walked out of the apartment three weeks ago, that I'd cool down, get over it.'' She looked at him. ''I didn't. And then, with everything that's been going on…'' The thought drifted off, unfinished. ''You want to know what Mala wants? You. In my bed. Or yours, I'm not picky.''

There. That wasn't so hard, was it?

After a minute, he looked away, his brow creased. ''I don't want to hurt you, Mala. And I can't see any way around it, if we do what you're suggestin'.''

''But don't you see? If I *know* you're going to walk out of my life, how can I get hurt? I mean, this is a first for me, to peek ahead at the end of the book so I already know how it turns out. Sooo, no nasty surprises waiting to clunk me on the head.''

He gave her a strange, but understandable, look. Then averted his gaze again. ''Don't take this the wrong way, but you're off your rocker.''

''Hey, buster, you have nobody to blame but yourself for this one.''

''Me?''

''Yeah, you,'' she said patiently, as if to a small child. ''It's very simple. I'm never getting married again. *You're* never getting married again. You're not going to stay, I don't want to even have to think about the future. I don't want to think, period. Or worry or wonder about what might come of the affair. I just want sex. Sex with someone I like and I think I can trust. But nothing more. I want you to do for me what those lights do for this tired old house—bring a little sparkle to my existence and make me forget, from time to time, about everything except the sex. And if that sounds selfish and unladylike, well, tough beans. And how come you haven't interrupted me yet?''

''Because I'm gonna be really ticked off if I wake up and discover this is all a dream.''

''So you think it's a good idea?''

''Hell, no. I think it's the dumbest idea I've ever heard.'' He scrubbed one palm over his jaw, then folded his hands together between his knees.

She waited, heart thudding away, while he sighed and rubbed his face and sighed some more and shook his head and finally said, ''I walked out once before, when you wanted more from me than seemed right. Don't think I've got it in me to be so gallant a second time.''

''Was that a yes?''

He leaned over, frustration flashing in those ice-chip eyes before he cupped her jaw in his palms, lowered his mouth to his. And she thought, as his tongue and hers got better acquainted, as he closed her within the shelter of those arms, *This is nice.*

Maybe too nice.

But it was too late to turn back now.

He broke the kiss; Mala tilted her head, touched his mouth. ''I'm not going to change the rules on you, Eddie. I swear. And if I thought there was even a chance that *you* would try to change the rules, I wouldn't even be asking this.''

There went that serious face again. ''You ever have an affair before, Miss Mala?''

''Not like this, no.''

''Then why now?''

''Because it didn't make sense before?''

He closed the two inches between them, again taking her

mouth. Fire leapt to life, deep within her, quickly turning into a vicious, gnawing hunger that might have scared her, if she hadn't been so sure she was doing the right thing. Well, maybe not cosmically right, but right for now. Which had been the revelation that had led her here to begin with, that maybe it wasn't a horrible thing to live for the moment, every decade or so.

''So when you figure we should, um, get started?'' he whispered into her mouth, and she felt something like excitement start humming inside her. Especially when he started trailing a whole bunch of hot little kisses down her neck.

Now would be good, she thought, then sighed, only partly because it was such a relief to find out his mouth was so much more than just decoration. ''There's a good q-question. Not when the kids are around.''

He pulled back, frowning. ''So I assume that lets out to-night.''

''Unfortunately, yes.''

''I can be real quiet.''

''That makes one of us, then.''

Oh, dear God—his eyes were going to burn a hole straight through her. ''You're a screamer?''

''When the occasion demands it.''

Eddie groaned, then tilted back his head. *''Thank you,''* he said, and she laughed and started to say, ''Sounds as if you're definitely warming up to the idea,'' except then she noticed his hand had braved sweater and jacket to reach her breast, causing her to seriously reconsider her previous stance. Especially when he deftly popped open the front hook of her bra and claimed what was only too willing to be claimed.

Speaking of warming up. How the man's hand could be warm after twenty minutes outside, she didn't know, and frankly didn't care. His touch was so tender she thought she'd pass out. Her breast was just sort of floating in his palm, grinning.

''You're not playing fair,'' she said, leaning closer. Nipping his earlobe.

''Damn straight,'' he said, thumbing her nipple, which naturally provoked a little whimpering hiss on her part and a croaking *"When?"* on his.

"To-tomorrow night," she got out, thinking if they didn't resolve this soon, she was going to explode right there on the steps, thereby giving half the town the thrill of their lives. "I'll get my parents to keep the kids."

"I won't be through at the restaurant until after ten," he purred in her ear, whereupon she mused that, after three years, it wasn't going to take a helluva long time to reach flashpoint.

"They can sp—spend the night over there."

He shifted to the other breast, and she bit her lip to keep from saying something stupid, like *Take me. Now.* "On a school night?" he said.

What? Oh, right. She frowned, desperate for a coherent thought, brightening when she thought of one. "Presents!" she said, wondering if he could feel her nails digging into his shoulders. "To wrap. Kids…oh, *crud!* Someone's coming! Eddie! Eddie, cut it out!"

She popped up, leaving Eddie's lovely, warm, talented hand down there on the landing with him and her breasts up here wondering where the nice man had gone. But before she got down two steps, the nice man grabbed her by the wrist, pulled her back to him. Even in the dark, she could see the laughter in those bad boy eyes. "And I thought you were hot, darlin'."

"Criminy, Eddie, keep your voice down!" she whispered, then waited, listening to Eddie's low chuckle until whoever it was, crazy enough to be out walking this time of night, passed. When she was sure the man was out of earshot, she said, still in a low voice, "Hot, yes. Kinky, no. Audiences do *not* turn me on."

Still laughing, Eddie let her go, then propped his chin in his hand. "'Night, darlin'," he said. "Sweet dreams."

She muttered something totally inane, then got the hell away from the man while she still remembered she even *had* children.

"But you never let the kids stay overnight on a school night," her mother said the next morning when Mala called from her cell phone, on her way to the first of three appointments.

"And I wouldn't now, except I suddenly realized how close it is to Christmas and I've got a million presents to wrap and this is the only night I have to do it. I mean, unless you and Pop have plans…"

"No, no, it's okay. You know we love to have the kids, anytime. It's you who never wants to bend a rule. You sure you're okay?"

Mala turned onto the highway. If all went well, she'd be done in Ann Arbor by ten, back in Spruce Lake for her eleven-thirty with Hinkle Hardware with time to spare. "Of course I'm okay. Why wouldn't I be okay?"

"You tell me."

"I'm fine, Ma."

"You sound strange."

"Strange?"

"Well, not strange, exactly. Different. Like…excited or something?"

That would be the sound of my blood boiling. "Must be the cell phone connection. Sounds a little weird on my end, too. Anyway, so I'll bring the kids over after school, if that's okay?"

"Whatever. You *sure* you're okay?"

"Good-*bye,* Ma."

Of course she was okay, if you discounted the fact that her stomach was tied in about a million knots and she hadn't been exactly able to sleep last night.

She really had made plans to get naked with Eddie King, hadn't she?

Yes, dear, you certainly did. And how do we feel about that this morning?

Don't ask.

She wondered if he fully realized what he was about to get into. As it were. That underneath her floppy sweaters and long skirts was an equally floppy body. Well, okay, not floppy, exactly. Just…relaxed. A little lumpy, a little saggy.

Terrific. Now she sounded like an old mattress.

Actually, if it weren't for this nagging sense of sheer terror about the prospect of shedding her clothes in front of a man who didn't have a spare ounce of fat on him anywhere, she generally didn't have a problem with how she looked. In fact, Mala and her body had reached an understanding some time ago: she would feed it whatever it wanted in exchange for good health and great boobs. The hips, she could do without, but boobs without butt just looked funny, anyway.

She frowned, pulled into the passing lane to ditch some slob in a pickup out for a Sunday stroll, even though it was Tuesday. Man, these new tires sure made a difference… Anyway, where was she? Oh, right. Thinking about her naked body. Except she quickly decided thinking about *Eddie's* naked body was a much more worthwhile activity.

Her hormones murmured their collective agreement.

How in heaven's name was she gonna make it to ten-thirty tonight?

"Eddie!" Hannah Braden swept into the kitchen, her short blond hair radiating from her scalp like a million golden pins. An early season flu had taken out two waitresses and three of Eddie's kitchen staff, but not, apparently, the rest of Spruce Lake, all of whom apparently decided to give themselves a break from Christmas shopping and dine out this evening. At *Galen's.* And he couldn't touch the staff for the pizzeria next door, which was just as busy, if not even more so. "Two more grilled chicken marsalas, three tortellini with pesto sauce and the swordfish special," she read off her order pad, grabbing a serving platter to load up the orders Eddie had just set under the warming lights.

"Got it," Eddie said, tossing another set of chicken breasts on the grill, grabbing a swordfish steak from the fridge. "That's it for the swordfish, Hannah," he called out. "You mind erasing it from the chalkboard when you get a chance?"

"Sure thing," the college student said, swooping out the swinging door, tray held high.

Thank God Galen's crew was as good as it was. They'd been going like gangbusters since a little after five; it was just about eight, another hour to go, and nobody'd bitched even once about the nonstop pace. Nobody'd gotten a break, either, but he could tell one or two of them were beginning to wilt a bit around the edges.

The swordfish running out was a surprise, though. He'd figured he'd have more than enough, especially for a Tuesday night. He didn't have to come up with another special—he imagined most of the customers would understand—but Galen had driven home that the specials were what brought the customers in, and brought them back. He had no time to do anything fancy, but there was always a ton of linguine on hand, and vegetables, and…

He got Marlene started on chopping up peppers and tomatoes, told Dilman to set the pasta maker for linguine, then went back to the chicken and swordfish, sternly telling himself he could not be tired tonight. That he *would* not be tired tonight. That if he had to cook another hundred dinners in the next hour, he was not going to disappoint Miss Mala.

At last, the final orders went out, the last dishes went into the industrial dishwasher, the last pot got cleaned and hung up. The staff practically staggered out the door, one of them coughing ominously. Eddie wandered out into the blissfully quiet dining room where Hannah and Jolie, the other waitress, were doing the final cleanup, too pooped to joke around like they usually did. Ellen, the cashier, was just finishing up the final talley and readying the bank bag to slip into the night depository.

"We did great tonight," the sprayed-to-stay blonde said in her gravelled voice. "Things keep up like this, maybe Galen should think about expanding."

Eddie slid bonelessly into the nearest booth, thinking long and hard about the merits of intravenous Vitamin E. "Maybe."

"She couldn't do it herself, though. Even after she has the baby. *Especially* after she has the baby. She'd need someone else, full-time."

Eddie yawned, scrubbing one hand over his face. "Uh-huh." Maybe a ten-minute nap, right here…

"You got a lot of compliments tonight, especially on the vegetarian linguine."

"Uh-huh."

He heard Ellen's cackly laugh. "Hey. You alive down there?"

"'Pends on your definition of alive," he mumbled, cheek in palm, eyes closed, realizing he had just about enough energy to feel real sorry for himself. He was going to do well to get himself up out of this booth, let alone get anything else up. All that lush softness, just waiting for him, and not a damn thing he could do about it.

He heard the door swing open. Ellen going back to the office, presumably. A few seconds later, it opened again.

"Now who do you suppose that is at the door?" she muttered, then slalomed around the mismatched tables and chairs to the front door. "We're closed," she yelled through the glass. "Come back tomorrow." Eddie heard a man's voice, asking something, but he couldn't stir up enough interest to listen carefully. "Tomorrow," Ellen repeated. "He's gone home. Which is where I'm going," she now said to Eddie, who hauled open one eyelid to peer at her as she shrugged into her coat. "You planning on spending the night in that booth?"

With a supreme effort, Eddie shook his head, pushing himself into something vaguely resembling an upright position. "Uh-uh," he said on another enormous yawn as he stretched hard enough to make his spine pop. "Got me a date, as a matter of fact," he said, and Ellen hooted with laughter.

"What you got," she said, "is a problem. Or your date does, is any case. Well, hon, I'm off. Here's hoping tomorrow night's not quite so crazy, huh?"

A minute later, she was gone, as was everybody else. Eddie locked up, grateful to realize there was still some feeling left in his limbs after all, shut the lights, then slipped out into the frosty night. The sharp air slapped him in the face, waking him up some; by the time he walked the four blocks home, maybe he'd actually be more than one notch above comatose.

He saw the man immediately, standing under the streetlight on the corner. Middle-aged, stubby, wearing a dark parka and knit cap, the end of a cigarette clutched between a gloved thumb and forefinger. Not that Eddie knew everyone in Spruce Lake by any means, but he sensed this guy wasn't a regular, especially as the regulars had no reason to hang out on Main Street in twenty-degree weather this late at night.

"Hey," the man said, pitching the stub into the gutter.

Awake now, and on alert, Eddie stopped, nodded. "Can I help you with something?"

"You Eddie King?"

His stomach jumped. But, since he knew he wasn't in trouble with the law, and he seriously doubted he'd done anything to warrant the attention of a hit man, he answered. "Yes, sir. What can I do for you?"

Craggy features shifted into a grin. "Heh, heh…one of the waitresses, she told me what you looked like, and I knew I hadn't seen anybody come out who'd fit that description, no matter what that lady said." The man extended his hand. "I've been looking for you for a long time, Mr. King. Name's Tony Scalia. I'm a private investigator. And your father's gonna be one happy sonuvabitch when I tell him I finally hooked up with you."

"He owns a construction company in Albuquerque," Eddie said, clearly too tired and too distracted to notice Mala wasn't wearing a bra underneath her velour lounging pajamas. "Did I tell you that?"

"Mmm-hmm." *At least three times,* Mala thought but did not say, as she moved to a plate the last batch of cookies which, she'd remembered right before Eddie's arrival, she'd promised to send to Lucas's class tomorrow. For the past half-hour, she'd measured and stirred and baked and listened to the stunned ramblings of a man who would have been her lover by now, had it not been for one P.I.'s lousy sense of timing. Although, to tell the truth, she wasn't all that surprised that things hadn't worked out. The whole time she was wrapping presents, taking a bubble bath, shaving her legs, she couldn't shake the feeling that it would all be for naught. And that was before she remembered the cookies.

But it was okay, she told herself, far less disappointed than she'd thought she'd be. All thoughts—well, most of them, anyway—of hanky-panky flew out the window the instant she'd opened her door to Eddie's nearly incoherent apology/explanation. She'd taken him by the hand to tug him inside, only he'd given her this bemused little smile and shaken his head.

"Not tonight," he'd said, and she said, "I know. Come in anyway," and after a brief inner struggle, he had. She'd quietly fussed over him, given him hot chocolate, like she might have one of the kids, made him sit, made him talk. The drink had gone pretty much untouched, but he'd sat, occasionally scratching the pup's tummy with the toe of his boot, and he'd talked.

Well, as much as Eddie King was going to talk. There were a lot of "and then he saids" and virtually no "and you know what I feels?" to balance out the narrative with a little man-on-the-street reaction. Not that she was surprised. Irked, yes, but not surprised. Of course, it wasn't as if she could say a whole lot, considering she was the same way. But she hoped it was at least doing him some good, having a sounding board, having someone to tell what he'd just learned about his father. That Rudy Ortiz had been looking for his son off and on for years, but limited funds and Eddie's constant moving had made the search difficult, until an unexpected windfall apparently gave Eddie's father the freedom to tell the P.I. not to stop looking until he found his son.

"What are you going to do now?" she asked gently, figuring it was time for him to move past shock phase into action.

Something stirred in those clear blue eyes, almost as if he were seeing her for the first time. Then he shrugged. "Dunno. Nothing, probably." Then he frowned. "And how come you're baking at this time of night?"

"Because I didn't remember until about a half hour before you walked in the door that I'd promised to bring cookies for Lucas's class tomorrow."

The frown deepened. "Y'all never heard of Oreos up here?"

"Bite your tongue. My mother *never* did store-bought."

He settled his jaw in one palm, doing that puzzled look men

were so good at. "You're not your mother, Mala. And I guarantee you the kids'd be just as happy with Oreos."

She skimmed the last cookie off the sheet with her spatula, set it on a plate with about a thousand of its friends, and frowned pretty hard herself.

Oreos, huh?

"It's a woman thing," she said, and he snorted.

"No, it's a *you* thing."

She decided to ignore that, pushing the plate in Eddie's direction. "They're best when they're still warm." She waited until Eddie's face had assumed a sufficiently rapturous expression—*yeah, right: Oreos, my fanny*—then said, "You're not even remotely curious? About your father?"

He swallowed, then shot her a mildly ticked look. "Why should I be?" Okay, so maybe not quite that mild. "The man walked out on the woman he got pregnant. He never tried to find us when it might have done some good. So why now, after nearly forty years?"

She plopped herself in the chair at right angles to his, snitched one of her own cookies. "Maybe that's what you need to find out."

"I don't need to know anything I don't already."

"But you don't *know* anything, except the bits and pieces the P.I. told you tonight. You don't know why he left, for one thing."

"And what earthly difference would it make to me now? Just because he maybe wants to appease his own conscience doesn't mean I should make it easy for him."

"I didn't say you should. I'm only saying—"

"Mala, honey—didn't I tell you once there's no use arguing with a man who's not going to give in?"

"Yeah. So?"

"Oh, Lord," he muttered, then swiped another cookie from the plate. But he didn't eat it. "He didn't say he wanted to see me," he said softly, and her heart bled at the fresh, raw pain in his voice he was trying so hard to hide. "Just said he wanted to know where I was, that I was okay."

"So the ball's in your court."

After a beat, he said, "If he'd wanted to make contact, wouldn't he have said so?"

"Maybe. Maybe not. Maybe, after all this time, he's just as afraid as you are of being rejected."

Bitterness flared in his eyes. "I'm not *afraid* to see him. I don't want to. There's a difference."

Liar, she wanted to say. "Not as much as you might think."

He almost laughed. "You are one insufferable woman, you know that?"

"Yes, I do. But so did you before you walked in here to-night."

One eyebrow hitched. "As I recall, I didn't. You dragged me in here."

"And you stayed." His brows dipped a tad at that. "So now you have to pay the price, which is listening to my advice."

"Which is, I suppose, that you think I should haul my butt to Albuquerque to see a man who didn't even care enough to go after the woman who was carrying his child?"

She opened her mouth to say something like, *Well, duh, and how else do you think you're ever going to work through all this crap if you don't confront your father and find out what the hell happened?* Except an angel of the Lord, or somebody, smacked those words right out of her mouth, replacing them with, "I'm just saying you should keep an open mind. That's all."

Then she stood and held out a hand to help him up, since he looked perilously close to becoming fused to her kitchen chair. "And that you should go upstairs before you pass out and go to bed. Alone," she added before he had a chance to object.

On a groan, he stood, trying to stifle a yawn. Then he hooked his hands on his hips in that way he had that drove her crazy, giving her one of those half smiles of his that drove her crazier, which was definitely not fair. Especially as he swayed a little when he said, "You're not gonna have sex with me because I said I won't go see my father?"

"No. I'm not gonna have sex with you because I'm not into necrophilia." She turned him around, aimed him toward the hallway. "Go to bed, Eddie. My libido's waited three years. It can wait a little longer."

She prodded him the rest of the way toward the door, Grateful trotting happily beside them. But when they got there, he somehow twisted around to bracket her between his arms against the wall. Well, her heart rate kicked up quite nicely at that, boy. Especially when he grinned down at her, all tousled and grizzled and sleepy-sexy.

"Um…what are you doing?"

"At the moment?" He shrugged. "Thinkin' about how pretty you are. And how you're one of the nicest gals I've ever known. And that, come to think of it, maybe I'm not all that tired." His gaze drifted south, then he got this cute little puzzled look on his face. "When did you take off your bra?"

"About an hour before you got here. And it's taken you this long to notice, bud, I think this has lost cause written all over—"

It got lost in the kiss that swooped down out of nowhere and opened up a world of possibilities she wouldn't have considered even two minutes before. Even half asleep, the man kissed better than most other men fully awake, and just like that— bam!—anticipation blossomed into a hot, sweet, *mm-mm-good* knot between her legs. So she wriggled and shimmied and looped her arms around his neck, letting him have at it, at *her,* whereupon he began a leisurely and thorough investigation of her neck.

"I sure do like the way you smell, Miss Mala," Eddie murmured from somewhere around her clavicle, and she smiled and murmured, "Same here," except then he said, "Hell. I probably smell like sauteed garlic."

She laughed, thinking, *Gee, whiz, I'm having fun,* then said, "Hey. Some of us get off on sauteed garlic."

"Speaking of getting off…" Somebody's finger—and hey, it wasn't hers—casually sauntered into her cleavage, joining with a thumb—which wasn't hers either—to toy with her top button. Except then the person attached to the fingers yawned.

Now she sighed. "Eddie, old boy—I hate to dent your male ego, but you are *too* tired to do this."

He stopped nuzzling and sauntering and otherwise wreaking havoc with her…everything to give her a look that was at once dead serious and seriously thrilling. "To be an active participant, maybe. But I seem to recall promising you something tonight. And damned if I don't intend to deliver, one way or the other. Right here. Right now."

Her breath left her lungs in a sort of choked wheeze.

"Here?"

"I think asking me to move might be pushing it."

He was, however, doing a very efficient, one-handed job of undoing the little satin buttons on her jammies with those long, slender fingers of his. The only light came from a lamp in the living room, so it wasn't as if he'd be able to see much, but despite her best intentions, one or two panicked thoughts shot through. Except then he got the last button undone and slowly, reverently, brushed back the opening to reveal her 40 D's in all their glory.

She could have sworn tears pooled in his eyes. Then he let out a long, rapturous, and—she thought—blissful sigh.

"I'm almost afraid to touch you."

"They're not bubbles. They won't burst. Promise."

He let out a startled laugh, then kissed her again. And apparently her reassurance had done the trick, because he touched, too. And, oh, how he touched, with a tenderness that scared her half to death. Then his mouth strayed down to join the party and she heard whimpers and moans come out of her throat because he was so incredibly good at what he was doing and she was so incredibly glad he'd decided to stay. A draft skittered across her heated skin as he tugged down the pajama bottoms, and he palmed her soft belly and sighed again and said something about her being a helluva woman, which earned him a good twenty, thirty Brownie points right there. And the knot—we all remember the knot, right?—got deliciously hotter and tighter and sweeter until she thought, on a giggle, "I'm ready for my orgasm now, Mr. King." Except she stopped giggling when his fingers dipped inside her, touching her in all the best places.

She murmured something about this not seeming fair, to

which he said, simply, "Shut up and let me do this," and she thought, *oh, okay* as she clung to him, the wall solid and cool against her back, idly thinking of all the puns she could now make using the word *entryway* and how she'd never be able to look at the one where she now stood the same way again. And wasn't it odd that she didn't feel the least bit strange, letting this man do these things to her, when she wasn't at all the kind of woman who normally let men do what Eddie was doing?

Then that thought said *"See ya,"* leaving a glorious, dizzying joy in its place as that which she had so long awaited swept through her.

And swept through her.

And…swept…through…her….

And, boy oh boy, was she glad they were alone in the house and that it was winter and the windows were closed, because—probably since it'd been three years and all—she truly outdid herself in the scream department.

Eddie held her for a long time afterward—which was a damn good thing because she would have crumpled to the floor otherwise—stroking her bottom, her back, kissing her hair as she nestled against all that gentle solidness, listening to his heartbeat thundering in his chest. Then he pulled her pajama bottoms back up, letting them snap gently against the small of her back, and cradled her jaw in his palm, his thumb whispering over her cheek. And the longing and wonder in his expression scared her all over again, because that might mean this was more than sex, and if that was the case, she was in big trouble.

Then she heard a key turn in the lock and *knew* she was in big trouble.

Chapter 9

His brain still half fogged, Eddie couldn't at first figure out why Mala had jumped away from him, frantically trying to button up her pajama top, or why the dog, who'd been conspicuously absent for the past few minutes, was suddenly yapping and scratching at the—

"Door!" Mala rasped, bug-eyed, and it finally clicked that they were about to have company and that, whoever it was, they probably were going to be shocked at discovering him there with her in her pajamas looking suspiciously like a woman who'd made a recent trip to Shangri-La.

A second later, Mala's mother burst into the house, hand-in-hand with a very unhappy Carrie wearing her nightgown underneath her purple parka, followed by a heavy-set, gray-haired man with an even unhappier Lucas in his arms.

"Ma! Pop! What—? Ohmigod—" Just that fast, the woman whose cries of pleasure had twisted him inside out crammed on her Mama hat, as Mala dropped to her knees in front of her about-to-cry daughter, palming her little face and trying to elbow the dog out of her way. "Criminy, sweetie, you're burning up!"

"I don't feel good…"

"Swear to God," her mother said, "they were both fine when we put them to bed at eight-thirty."

"Then this one wakes up cryin' and pukin' his guts out," said the man holding Lucas—Mala's father, obviously. "Must be this damn flu goin' around."

"Marty, for godsake, watch your language. Anyway, we would've kept them, you know that, but they both said they wanted to come home, so there wasn't a whole lot we could say. And why is it so dark in here?" Bev finished, reaching for the switch to the overhead.

"No, Ma…it's okay—"

Light flooded the entryway; Eddie cringed as understanding streaked across both parents' faces. Yeah, Mala'd gotten herself pulled back together, but she was wearing pajamas, she wasn't wearing a bra, and her face and neck were positively ablaze with beard burns.

"Mommy," Carrie said. "I think I'm gonna throw up."

Mala scooped her up and whisked her down the hall, while Bev, after a very pointed glance in Eddie's direction, carted off Lucas to his bedroom.

Leaving Eddie with Mala's father and consequently wishing he were dead.

A big man, Mala's father. Early sixties, maybe. Tall as Eddie, a good deal heavier. Not somebody you'd want to mess with. Especially, Eddie figured, when it came to his daughter.

The two men stood in the hallway, Marty with his arms crossed, Eddie with his fingers jammed in his back pockets, both of them staring after the women. From the bathroom came faint, frantic, barfing sounds.

"Poor little guys," Marty said, and Eddie said, "Yeah, it's tough," probably too quickly.

"So." Marty swiveled his large head, his eyes narrowed. "You the new tenant?"

"Yes, sir, I am." He stuck out his hand. "Eddie King."

The handshake was short and strong. "Marty Koleski. Bev and me, we was up to *Galen's* a few weeks ago. You're one helluva chef, boy."

"Thank you."

"Break my daughter's heart and you're dead meat."

"Yes, sir, I'll be sure to keep that in mind."

Marty nodded, just once, then said, "So. You follow football?"

They got the kids tucked into bed, although Mala imagined she'd be up most of the night with them. She didn't like to give them medicine unless it was absolutely necessary, so she'd have to keep an eye on the fevers. But Galen's stepdaughter Wendy had just had it, and she was fine within twenty-four hours, so maybe this wouldn't be too bad.

"God, I'm sorry, baby," Bev whispered.

Tucking Carrie's sheets around her shoulders, she darted a glance at her mother. "About?"

"It was so late, Marty and me thought we'd just slip in instead of ringing the bell. I was even gonna spend the night and not wake you...."

Mala threw her mother a "shut up" look, then kissed her fretfully dozing daughter on the cheek before ushering her mother from the room.

"I mean," Bev continued sotto voce the instant they were in the hall, never mind that Marty and Eddie—wherever they were—could probably hear everything she was saying, "I never even imagined you and he would be...you know."

"Ma! Please!" In the silence that followed, they could hear voices coming from the living room, so Bev grabbed Mala by the arm and hauled her into the kitchen.

"You think I don't know what was going on?" Bev said the instant the door closed behind them. "For godssake, you're not even buttoned up right. Not to mention the beard burns."

"Oh, geez, Ma..."

"Not that I'm embarrassed or nothing. Hell, I'm thrilled. It's not healthy, refusing to let a man get near you. Here's a newsflash for you, baby—there's life after Scott."

Mala sank down on one of the kitchen chairs, her face buried in her hands. Terrific. Now her mother was going to think she and Eddie had something going—as in, something *real*—since there was no way in hell she was going to tell her mother they were just…just…

Oh, hell…the woman had had a hard enough time dealing with Mala's divorce; finding out her daughter was just in it for the sex would probably send her over the edge.

"Mama!"

Mala pushed herself up from the table, half thought about rebuttoning her top, immediately dismissed the idea. "Thanks for taking care of the kids and bringing them home, but you can go away now."

"And now you're mad, right?"

"No, Ma," she said wearily. "Why would I be mad? Because you brought my sick kids home so their own mother could take care of them?"

"No. Because—"

"Ma-maaaa!"

Mala was already out the door, heading off Lucas in the hall just in time to push him into the bathroom before he upchucked all over the hall runner. "Go home," she called over her shoulder to her mother. "Please."

"How'm I gonna leave you with this—?"

"Ma!"

"Okay, Miss Stubborn. But you call me if you need me, got it?"

When Mala herded her whimpering son out the bathroom a few minutes later, the house was blissfully parent-free. She tucked Lucas back in, stroked his prickly hair for a second before he asked for something to drink. On her way to the kitchen to get some ginger ale, she heard voices from Carrie's room. She peered into the dimly lit room, saw Eddie standing at the foot of her daughter's bed, his hands tucked in his back pockets as usual. For some reason, it hadn't occurred to her he'd still be there. When she found her voice, she said to Carrie, "I'm going to get Lucas some ginger ale, sweetie. Would you like some?"

Carrie nodded. Eddie followed Mala down the hall.

"And why are *you* still here?" she said, yanking open the refrigerator door.

"You think I'm gonna leave you to take care of two sick kids all by yourself all night, you're crazy," he said quietly, taking the bottle from her hands and pouring out two cups of soda.

She stood with her arms crossed for a moment, trying to fit this into her brain. "Eddie, for crying out loud, you're half dead on your feet—"

"And you're not?"

"They're my kids. It comes with the territory. And I can tell you from experience, this isn't going to be fun."

He stood less than a foot in front of her, his hands clamped around the cups. "I kinda figured that much."

"Eddie, I wouldn't even let my *mother* stay."

"I'm not your mother. And I'm not leaving. So deal with it."

Then he walked out of the kitchen, leaving Mala wondering if this was what getting caught in quicksand felt like. Because if he kept doing stuff like this, it was going to be real hard to keep from getting attached to the man.

If...oh, dear God...she wasn't already.

Eddie woke up with a start, momentarily disoriented until he figured out where he was. He lay half-sprawled on Mala's sofa, one foot on the floor, a puny afghan covering his chest. Irritatingly cheerful sunlight knifed through a gap in the drapes, which meant it was morning.

He sat up with a groan, which got the pup to jumping all over the place in his split to go outside. Last Eddie remembered, he'd gotten Lucas settled back in bed after at least the kid's sixth trip to the john to throw up, then gone out to the living room to just sit for a spell, rest his eyes.

Grateful *yarped* at him, butt in air, wagging his stubby little tail. Eddie dragged himself off the sofa and into the kitchen to let the blasted beast out.

When he was fully awake, he was going to have to take a real serious look at what he was getting himself into here. Why was it, everytime he turned around, it seemed this woman and/ or her kids needed something, and he seemed to be the one picked to take care of whatever it was they needed? Not that he minded, but then, that was the problem, his *not* minding. In fact, other than the fact that he might never walk straight again, he thought, rubbing his lower back as he went to check up on the other human beings in the house, he wasn't minding being a part of this at all.

Which was just plain stupid, and he damn well knew it. Sex was one thing; taking care of a pair of sick kids because he wasn't the kind of man who could just go off and leave it all to their mama, well, there was nothing wrong about that, either. But there was no sense letting anybody get used to this. What had happened over the past few days wasn't anything but a set of extenuating circumstances. Didn't mean he was going to allow himself to get sucked into thinking he was anything but what he was—a man who didn't really belong anyplace.

A man who couldn't love anybody the way these people deserved to be loved.

He peered into Lucas's room; the kid was sound asleep, clutching that pitiful-looking bear of his, his breathing normal. Well, good. He'd felt sorry for the kid, sure, being sick and all, but Eddie just naturally felt bad when somebody was hurting. It didn't mean anything out-of-the-ordinary. Besides, it would take a real special person to be able to put up with the kid's whining the way his mother did. That much patience, Eddie didn't have.

Then he looked in on Carrie, who was also dead to the world, those red curls of hers sprawled all over her pillow. Like this, she almost looked like a sweet kid, Eddie thought wryly, only then noticing that Mala was on the other side of her daughter's bed, asleep sitting up, half-draped across the bed beside her little girl. And he got to thinking about how much she loved these two little pills, and his heart got all twisted up inside him, especially when he thought about her response to his touch last night. Which, considering everything that had transpired right after, he hadn't been able to do much about. Then something knotted in his gut, right below the twisted heart, and he thought, shoot—at this rate, his insides were going to look like they had been set upon by manic Boy Scouts.

The woman made him feel good, he realized. And not just physically, although he had no doubt, if they ever actually got around to doing what they were supposed to have done last night, she would be no slouch in that department. But *good,* good. Like he mattered. Like she gave a damn what he thought, what he was feeling. When he talked to her, she'd get this little frown of concentration on her face, like she was determined to absorb every word. He liked that. Hell, he could get a woman to sleep with, anytime, even if he didn't always take advantage of every opportunity that tried to crawl into his lap. But having someone to talk to—well, that was a new experience for him. He couldn't remember ever liking a woman the way he liked Mala Koleski, and that's why he knew this could be really bad news, if he didn't watch his step.

He considered leaving her be, then thought, no, she couldn't possibly be comfortable like that.

Mala jerked awake at his touch on her shoulder, confusion heavy in her eyes when she looked up at him. Her hair was a mess, and her cheek was all creased from sleeping on the rumpled sheet. But she looked even softer than she usually did, and when she frowned as she laid a hand on Carrie's cheek to feel her temperature, all those knots inside him got pulled another notch tighter.

She awkwardly pulled herself to her feet, swiping her hair out of her face when they got to the hall.

"What time is it?" she whispered on a yawn, picking up speed as she got closer to her room.

"About eight. They both look down for the count, you should go get some sleep yourself—"

"Can't. I've got two appointments I can't cancel. God, I hope my mother can come sit for a couple hours." She scooted inside her room, called out from inside, "And don't you dare volunteer."

"Not to worry." Eddie leaned against the doorway, figuring considering where he'd touched and all last night, peeking into her bedroom wasn't exactly a violation of her privacy. "Far as I'm concerned, it's definitely time for the next shift."

Shoo-eee, that bed looked good. For more reasons than one.

That nice, soft comforter and all those pillows… And it would smell all pretty and sweet, he bet. Just like Mala.

Who paused in the middle of fighting her way into a very unsexy, white terry cloth robe and shot him a funny look, like she could hear his thoughts.

Then she swept past him, her slippers shooshing against the hall runner as she ducked into the bathroom, began fussing around with towels and things.

"Did you get any rest?" she asked.

"Some, I guess, since I came to on your sofa. Which, by the way, leaves a lot to be desired as a place to sleep." He watched as she squirted some minty-smelling goop into the toilet, swished around the johnny mop. "Mala, honey, I think your mama would understand if the place wasn't spanking clean."

Her movements hitched for a second, but she said, "Has nothing to do with my mother," rinsed her hands in the sink, then zipped past him back into the hall and toward the kitchen. Eddie followed. "And trust me," she said, "the floor wasn't any better. But I was afraid if I went to bed, I wouldn't hear Carrie if she called."

Mala dragged a can of coffee out of the refrigerator just as the dog yipped at the back door. Eddie let him in, shivering in the blast of frigid air that came in with him. "Thought mothers heard every noise their kids made?"

"Not this one," she said, counting out spoonfuls of coffee into the basket. "I sleep like the dead. So when the kids are sick, I pretty much have to stay with them. Whaddya want for breakfast? Oh, Lord—" she rammed home the coffee basket, spun around and took off for the door. "I've got to call the kids in sick. I'll be right back."

Warning! Warning! Domesticity alert!

"You know," Eddie said, inching toward the back door, "if you don't need me anymore, I think I'm just going to go on, catch a few hours sleep before I have to go into work."

Mala turned, one hand on the doorjamb, other on her hip, and all he could think was, *"Uh-oh."*

"I see."

"No, I don't think you do. And both of us are too damned tired to get into this right now."

"Oh, Eddie, give me a break." Mala walked back toward him, pushing her hair behind her ear before planting her hands on hips that Eddie was sorely regretting not having been able to guide over his own last night. "Sexual encounter is over, crisis is over, so what's the point of hanging around, right? I mean, God forbid you might actually find yourself getting too comfortable around here."

"Now, just hold on a dadburned minute! Who was the one who said she didn't want me getting involved with her kids?"

"Yeah, well, that got shot to hell the minute you put up those damn Christmas lights." She took a step closer, eyes flashing. "Here's a newsflash for ya, buddy—a man who doesn't want to get involved wouldn't have volunteered to spend the night watching a six-year-old lose his cookies every twenty minutes. You *are* involved, Eddie, whether you like it or not. Maybe not forever, and maybe more than either of us had planned on, but somehow or other, it happened. I wouldn't've gotten through last night without your help, much as it pains me to admit it. So all I'm trying to do is show my appreciation with some bacon and eggs, only you…you…"

With a strangled growl, she threw her hands into the air. "*God!* Did it ever, just once, occur to you that you don't always have to have a *reason* to hang around? That maybe your company is worthwhile, all by itself?"

Silence cracked between them for several seconds. Then Eddie said, "You through?"

Her chin went up, but her eyes narrowed. "For the moment."

He grabbed his jacket off the back of one of the chairs, where he'd left it the night before, slapping it over his shoulder as he jabbed one finger at the most infuriating women he'd ever met in his life. "And maybe it's about time you got it through *your* head that you're worth a helluva lot more than some safety-net fling with a man who you know damn well isn't gonna hang around."

"That's my choice, Eddie. And you know my reasons."

"Well, not getting tied down's mine. And the same goes."

By rights, that should have been his exit line. But for some fool reason, he just stood there, staring her down, until she finally said, like a challenge, "This mean the affair's off?"

The suggestion startled him far more than it should have. "You want out?"

After an obvious struggle of several seconds' duration, she shook her head.

"Good. 'Cause after last night, you owe me one. Big time."

Then he left, wondering exactly who'd won that argument.

Mala had left the kitchen full of fury and righteous indignation. Ten minutes later, she returned in a daze, her hand over her mouth.

She'd turned the phone's ringer down sometime in the middle of the night, on the off chance a wrong number or something might wake up the kids. Granted, the phone rarely rang that late, but you never knew. And she figured the world could do without her for a few hours, in any case. When she'd gone in just now to call the school, there'd been two messages, both left before seven. One was from her mother, telling Mala to call her if she needed anything.

And then there was the other one.

On autopilot, Mala poured herself a cup of coffee, feeling as though the house's silence had sucked out her brain. She heard Eddie's footsteps overhead, thought briefly how odd it was, his hearing from his father last night.

She could still smell him, on her skin, her pajamas. Could still feel him, where he'd touched inside her. Could still see the terror in those hot blue eyes, the panic in his voice just now, that she might try to trap him.

God. Was a there a more muleheaded man on the face of the earth?

Or a more hopeless woman?

She gulped down the first few swallows of coffee, then wandered down the hall to check again on the kids. They were still asleep, at peace and mercifully oblivious that their mother was *this close* to a nervous breakdown. Oh, all right, so she was being a little overdramatic, but she was sleep deprived and in shock. She was entitled.

A minute later, she was back at the kitchen table in a catatonic trance, ignoring the dog and trying to convince herself her life hadn't just gone to hell in a handbasket. The good news was she had new tires, the kids were already better and her period of celibacy had just officially, if not technically, ended. The bad news was it was next door to Christmas and she still hadn't put up a tree or finished her shopping or done her cards, her mother was undoubtedly hearing wedding bells, her father had probably put Eddie under twenty-four hour surveillance, and everything she'd said to Eddie about just wanting sex and nothing else had basically been a lie and everything Eddie had said to her about not wanting to get involved hadn't been. And if she had an ounce of smarts she'd call things off with Eddie right this minute, except she had about as much intention of doing that as she had of telling her mother when she'd *really* lost her virginity.

And oh, yeah—after three years of total noncommunication, her ex-husband had left a message on her answering machine, saying he wanted to see her. Just what she needed to add to the joy of this holiday season, a visit from the ghost of Husbands Past.

Ho, ho, ho.

Chapter 10

It was nearly five, right after Eddie finished checking in the night's supply of meat and poultry, when Galen waddled into the restaurant. It looked like they were gonna be shorthanded again tonight, since only three of the cooking staff had shown up so far. They were all occupied on the other side of the kitchen, mercifully; Eddie frowned, something he'd been doing a lot since storming out of Mala's kitchen that morning.

"What are you doin' here?"

Galen lifted one eyebrow, amusement twinkling in her eyes. She removed the coat that didn't even begin to close over her huge middle and plopped it on the coatrack by the back door. "Last time I checked, I owned the place." Eddie grunted. "And aren't we in a grouchy mood today?"

Eddie grunted again. Wasn't like he could tell her—or anybody, for that matter—what was really bugging him. Between his father's making contact with him, and his making contact of an entirely different nature with Mala...well, right now, he didn't think his sorry brain could get any more balled up than it was. So instead, he mumbled something about not getting much sleep due to Mala's kids being sick the night before and how he'd stayed up with them.

Now the other eyebrow raised, which is when Eddie realized just how tired he was, since he sure as hell wouldn't've admitted such a thing if he'd been fully awake. Mercifully, Galen said nothing, other than to ask him to come into the office.

"Close the door," she said, wedging herself behind the desk. "And take a load off." Eddie did, although he was mildly afraid if she kept him too long, he'd conk out right there in the chair. She riffled through some papers on her desk for a moment, then looked up at him with a pleased grin. "Business has been great, hasn't it?"

"I guess. I know I've been cookin' my butt off these past couple of weeks."

"I'll say you have. In fact, if I were the jealous type, I'd be pretty upset right about now."

Eddie was startled to feel his neck warm. "Don't be. From what I can tell, there's plenty of folks wondering when you'll be back."

"And I have it on good authority from the trusty grapevine that plenty of people will be very sorry when you go." She paused. "Me being one of them."

Something prickly crawled up Eddie's back. "What're you gettin' at, Galen?"

She folded her hands together on her desk, then said, "There's a classy, well-established restaurant called *Gardner's* out on the highway in a high-traffic area, right next to a major mall. You know it?"

"I think maybe I've passed it now and again."

"Well, the owners are tired of the Michigan winters or something and want out as soon as possible. It's a good deal, an even better opportunity…and I want it for a second location. Trouble is, I obviously can't be in two places at once. And with the baby, I'm going to have to cut back as it is. So…I'd like to give you first crack at it."

He stilled. "What?"

"Manager/head chef to begin. Full partner, if you want to buy in at some point down the road." When he didn't reply,

Galen let out an exasperated breath. "Oh, come on, Eddie— you're wasted as just a cook, and you know it. You're too talented, and too smart, to keep doing this itinerant number forever. Look, Mala and I went over the books a couple nights back. Not only are gross receipts up, but so are profits. You're more than a terrific chef, Eddie. You've got a good business head on your shoulders, if these numbers are any indication. And you're good with the staff, too. Believe me, if anyone had found you to be a pain in the can, I'd've known about it long ago."

Eddie tried to breathe normally through the bands constricting his chest. "I told you, I don't like cookin' the same kind of food—"

"That's entirely up to you. *Gardner's* is already heavily continental, so you could build on that. Some French, some Italian? Maybe even some Mexican? Shoot, Eddie—you can be as creative as you like, I don't care."

"Mala and I were going over the books…"

Suspicion curled in his belly. "You've known me less than a month. Don't you think making me an offer like this is kind of a big risk?"

"You're talking to a woman who moved here from Pittsburgh on little more than a hunch. I sank everything I had into this place, without a clue whether it would even fly. Believe me, this doesn't even come close."

Eddie looked her in the eye. "I'm very flattered. But I can't accept."

"Which is what I expected you to say. But the offer's open, Eddie. Del's encouraging me to go ahead and get my bid in now, even though I can't do anything about it until after the baby's born. So if you change your mind—"

He stood then. "I won't. In fact…" Lying wasn't his strong suit, God knew. And this wasn't as much of a lie as it was a half truth: he'd gone to the library this morning, searched for jobs on the Internet. Hadn't made up his mind until just this second, though. "I've got another job lined up in Vegas, starting April first. I figured that'd give you more than enough time for your maternity leave after the baby comes.''

"I see.'' She messed with something on her desk. "Does Mala know about this?''

"If she had, don't you think she would've brought it up in your conversation about my...capabilities?''

Galen's head snapped up, making Eddie realize he'd just made his second blunder in ten minutes. "I was talking about the apartment, Eddie. Mala knows nothing about my plans, not yet. Or that I was planning on making you this offer.'' Her eyes narrowed. "Is there...something going on between you two?''

Eddie crossed his arms. "Not meanin' to be disrespectful, but I'm not sure how that's any of your concern.''

"True,'' Galen said quietly, her gaze linked with his. "But Mala's one of my best friends. I gather she's been through a lot, from what her brother has told Del and me. And she's lonely, although I sometimes think everyone else knows that but her. So just...tread carefully.''

"No problem,'' Eddie said tightly, then stomped back to the kitchen, where he determined that if he never set foot in a dadburned small town again, it would be too soon.

The chore list was up, and everyone was busy, but there were a boatload more items on the list than hands to carry them out. Eddie stalked to the refrigerator, dragged out a bag of bell peppers which he then slammed onto the wooden island in the center of the kitchen.

"Where the hell's my knife?''

His favorite appeared, seemingly out of nowhere, followed by a blur as Delman skittered away to his station on the other side of the kitchen.

"Hey, Eddie,'' Marlene yelled from the stove where she was stirring a sauce she'd gotten going two hours before, her dark face glowing from the scented steam. "You wouldn't by any chance be in a bad mood, would you?''

With one swift move, he neatly eviscerated the first pepper. "As a matter of fact, I am. Wanna make something of it?''

Marlene just laughed. "No. But I guess I'll be staying out of your way as long as you got that knife in your hand."

Wham! One pepper, guillotined. *Wham, wham, wham!* Followed in rapid succession by its comrades.

It was more than small-town protectiveness threatening to strangle him, he knew that. Hell, he felt like those people in the original *Star Wars* film, caught in that garbage compactor and in imminent danger of being turned into waffles. For the first time in years, he felt like he was losing control of his life. That events were conspiring against him like they hadn't since he was a kid. And he did not like it, not one bit. For someone who'd devoted his entire adult life to avoiding complications, he was sure up to his butt in 'em now, boy.

That P.I. swore that Eddie's father wouldn't try to get in touch with him, but for all Eddie knew, the man was on his way to Spruce Lake at this very minute, determined to have a reunion Eddie had never wanted. God, he wanted to jump in the Camaro and take off. But this time, he couldn't. He'd made a commitment to Galen, and he wouldn't, couldn't, break it.

And then she goes and makes him that offer, to boot. Wasn't like he hadn't had similar offers before, which she already knew. What was so scary about this one, though, was how much it tempted him. Truth was, the moving around was beginning to get old. And his own place…

But not here. Not where Mala was. Because if he stayed, he'd hurt her.

Even more than if he left.

The peppers done, he moved on to onions, checked the clock—two hours before opening.

Bad enough he'd gone along, was still going along, with Mala's sex-and-nothing-but-sex scheme. Take two achy people, one of whom could persuade the devil he needed to be saved if you gave her long enough, and bam! Down goes a guard Eddie knew he had no business letting down. Sure, she *said* she wasn't looking for anything permanent, that she knew he was bad for her—which sure as hell was true enough—that she knew exactly what she was doing… And maybe she did. But this was asking for trouble, and he damn well knew it. What if she didn't know herself quite as well as she thought she did? What then? The last thing Eddie needed was Mala's broken heart on his conscience. Not to mention her daddy taking out a contract on his life.

It wasn't just Eddie's being bad for Mala that made this such a dumb idea. It was that Mala was just as bad for Eddie. Because, like it or not, he got ideas when he was around her. Ideas about fittin' in. About home. About things that simply weren't gonna happen, whether he stayed or not.

Which meant, if he had a shred of decency and honor left in his sorry body, he'd tell her the deal was off.

He brought the knife down so hard on the chopping board, everybody in the kitchen jumped a foot.

"Mama! Uncle Steve's here! An' he's got a *tree!*"

Clutching her sweater closed, Mala traipsed down the hall toward the front door, wondering how it was that two kids who had been virtually lifeless less than twenty-four hours earlier could be so damn energetic now. Ever since early this afternoon, they'd done nothing but race and tear around the house, shattering her concentration to smithereens. They had slept, after all. She hadn't.

But then she caught a whiff of Noble fir and saw her brother's goofy grin and the way the kids were just about to turn inside out from excitement and somehow, things didn't seem quite so bad.

"What on earth—?"

"Ma said you didn't have one yet, and I was in the neighborhood, so here." Steve shouldered his way inside with the enormous tree, thunked it in the middle of the hall. Needles and water flew everywhere.

"You lie like a rug. And I love you to pieces," she said, fighting through the branches to give him a hug. "Geez, what'd you do? Get the biggest one they had? And where's everybody else?"

"Waiting at home, probably wondering where I am. Where you want it?"

"Oh, shoot…the stand's still out in the garage. Just prop it against the wall, I'll deal with it after dinner."

"Aw, Mama…" Carrie said, just as Mala caught her brother mouthing, "We need to talk."

She frowned at Steve, then turned to her daughter. "Another hour won't kill you, missy. Now why don't you two go back to watching your movie, and finish your soup before it gets cold."

"Awww…"

"Now, Carrie."

The kids tromped back to the living room. Mala crossed her arms. "What?"

"Heard somebody left a message on your machine today."

Oh, my. She hadn't seen a murderous expression like that on Steve's face since the *last* time she'd heard from Scott. Well, if she hadn't wanted the Koleski Mafia to close ranks around her, she should't've told her mother to begin with.

"Ma told you, I take it?"

"Actually, it was Pop." Steve crossed his massive forearms over his open down parka, his pale brows nearly meeting. "You talk to Scott yet?"

Mala swiped her hair behind her ear, thinking how strange it was that the little brother she'd protected when she was eight and he was four now not only outweighed her by a good eighty pounds, but was the one protecting her. Or trying to, at least. Would Lucas one day be Carrie's protector? Now there was a weird thought… "Nope. He didn't leave a number and he hasn't called back."

The frown grew more serious. "You think he's in town?"

"I have no idea."

"You know, you really gotta get Caller ID—"

"Steve, relax, okay? I mean, I'll admit I was thrown when I first heard, and I probably shouldn't've told Ma until I'd had a chance to get hold of myself…but I have now. I'm fine, I swear. Whatever this is about, I can handle it."

"After what he did to you—"

"*Did,* Steve. Past tense. He can't hurt me anymore. *Nobody* can hurt me anymore." Eddie's implacable expression during their argument that morning flashed through her thought, just as her heart pinged a little too loudly against her ribs. "You got over your ex, I got over Scott."

"That's different."

"Why? Because you're a big, strong man and I'm a weak, vulnerable little woman?"

"Oh, don't go getting all feminist on me, for cripes' sake. Francine's head games were kid stuff compared to what Scott pulled on you."

"Then that just means I'm the stronger one for overcoming more than you did."

Shaking his head, Steve let out an okay-you-win chuckle. Then he bent over, grabbing her by the shoulder and planting a kiss on the top of her head. "I gotta scoot. But you hear from that bum again…"

"Thanks for the tree, sweetie. Give Sophie and the kids my love."

Steve grunted, yelled out his goodbyes to the kids, and left. Just as the phone rang.

Eddie was afraid if he rang the doorbell, or even knocked, he'd wake the kids. So he fought his way through the privet hedge to rap lightly on the living room window.

He was rewarded with a short, shrill, muffled yelp. Two seconds later, the drape twitched back to reveal Mala with her hand at her throat.

She yanked open the window. "Thanks for scaring the snot out of me."

"Bet that's not what Juliet said to Romeo."

"That's because she was a clueless, horny, fourteen-year-old. So. What do you want?"

She sounded edgy. Eddie considered the wisdom of changing his mind.

"To talk," he said.

Arms crossed over a red sweatshirt. "Thought men hated that."

"You're right."

"Oh." There went the hank of hair behind the ear. "Well. As a matter of fact, I need to talk to you, too."

Eddie felt a tremor in his gut. "Yeah?"

"Yeah. So. Shall I open the front door for you or are you planning on climbing in here?"

"I'll opt for the door."

Ten seconds later, he was inside, like to gag on evergreen scent. "You overdo the PineSol or somethin'?" he said, walking into the living room behind Mala, who, he couldn't help but notice, wasn't looking at him. "You got a tree."

"My brother showed up with it earlier. Isn't it great?"

Somehow, she didn't exactly sound thrilled. And somehow, he didn't think it had anything to do with the tree. Eddie frowned. "How come there's no stuff on the top half?"

"Short kids. So…" She sidestepped the upright vacuum, then dropped to her knees, closing up empty ornament boxes. "What'd you want to talk about?"

Something in her voice snagged his attention. He looked over, saw how the multi-colored tree lights shimmered like oil rainbows in her hair.

That her hands were shaking.

Damn.

"You first," he said.

She darted a glance at him, but surprisingly didn't argue, even though she didn't exactly launch right in, either. Instead, she got up, stacked all the boxes on the coffee table, then grabbed the vacuum.

"You really gonna do that now?"

She whipped the cord behind her. "It'll just take a sec. Kids'll never hear it."

So Eddie stood there, his arms crossed over his chest, his heart thudding *in* his chest, and waited until Miss Mala was good and ready to say whatever it was she had to say. Finally, after she put the vacuum away and carted the boxes off somewhere, she stood in front of him and said, "I talked to my ex today."

Something that felt an awful lot like a brass-knuckled fist rammed into his gut. "You're kiddin'."

"Nope. Scott Sedgewick is alive and well and wants to see me. Says he needs to…how'd he put it? Oh, yeah—*clear the air*." She pulled a face.

"Forget it, Mala."

Her brows shot up, although, to tell you the truth, Eddie wasn't sure which one of them was more surprised by his macho-protective act. "He may be toilet crud, Eddie, but he's the father of my kids. I don't think I've got a lot of choice."

"Like hell. The jerk walks out on you, you don't owe him a damn thing."

After a moment, she said, "This isn't you and your father we're talking about here," and something jammed right up into his throat. Except then she went on to say, "Besides, this isn't about owing anybody anything. It's about using this as an opportunity to prove to myself that he has no power over me anymore." She hesitated again, then said, "Not even in my memories."

He chose to ignore the point she was obviously trying to make. "So what you're sayin' is, your mind's made up?"

"I can't let the past mess with my head anymore, Eddie. But I did say I'd only meet with him in a public place, in neutral territory, if that makes you feel any better."

"It doesn't."

She cocked her head at him. "And what's it to you, whether or not I see the man I was married to for four years?"

"What is this, a trick question? I don't like the idea of you getting hurt."

Mala's gaze danced with his for several seconds before she walked over to the tree, fiddled with some ugly little felt ornament with glittery stones glued to it. "Interesting you should say that. Because ever since Scott's call, I've been doing a lot of thinking, especially about some choices I've made. Am still making. And…" She shut her eyes and swore softly, then turned to him. "Until I get this mess sorted out in my head, I've got no business fooling around with anyone else."

It took a second. "You're calling it off?"

Consternation flooded her features. "I'm…well, yeah. I guess I am. It's not that I *want* to…stop…what we were doing…it's just…'' Another cussword flew out of her mouth. ''The timing's just really lousy, and this is really, really hard, and God, I feel so stupid…''

Relief should've washed over him, that she'd said it first, that this way, Eddie didn't have to feel guilty about letting her down or hurting her feelings. Instead, he felt suckerpunched. And unaccountably pissed off.

''Is it because you think you might get back together with…what's his name?''

''Oh, my God, Eddie!'' A short, sharp laugh flew from her throat. ''Not even if the survival of the human species depended on it. No, this has to do with me and my…pattern of being attracted to men who are wrong for me and all that fun stuff. I not only have to face up to Scott, on my own, without anybody else's interference, but I have to face up to myself, which is a helluva lot harder.''

She knotted her arms over her midsection. Tears glittered in her eyes as two spots of red bloomed in her cheeks. ''And the conclusion I came to is, I gotta learn to stop myself *before* I make the mistake, to love myself enough to say 'no' when 'yes' is only gonna get me in trouble. To stop pretending I can handle the consequences, in order to justify going after things I know aren't good for me. Because I have finally gotten it through my head that it's a damn sight easier to avoid the mess to begin with than it is to clean it up afterward. And I know there's a name for women who do what I just did to you, but all I can say is, I'm so, so sorry.''

Eddie stood there, trying to figure out why what she'd just said hurt so damn bad. Except, he knew. Never mind that he'd been about to head the whole thing off at the pass himself, for almost those exact reasons. And, on some level, he was actually proud of her for having the courage to not only face the thing that had caused her so much pain, but to save her own butt. But the fact remained that it'd been a long time since he'd given anyone the opportunity to get one over on him, and now he remembered why he'd made it such a point not to.

''Hey, no problem.'' He schooled his features, dismissed the whole thing with a wave of his hand. ''You've got a lot on your plate. God knows you don't need me to complicate things.''

Her brow puckered. "You're not mad?''

He pushed a puff of air through his lips. "Why would I be mad? In fact—you're gonna love this—I was about to break it off with you."

"You…were?''

"Yeah. That's what I'd wanted to talk about. So now I don't have to. Great minds think alike, huh?''

He turned and walked to the living room doorway, then twisted back, wondering why it was such an effort to breathe right. "By the way, I guess this is as good a time as any to tell you I got a job lined up for after I leave here. In Vegas. So I'll be outta your hair by April Fool's.''

No sense in telling her about Galen's offer. But what made even less sense was how much he'd wanted to.

He'd made it all the way to the door when she called out in a whisper, "Eddie, this isn't about you. You've got to believe that.''

He tried not to let the door slam behind him.

Wasn't until he got up into the apartment that he realized he hadn't even been in Mala's long enough to take off his jacket. Why that ticked him off even more, he didn't know. It was all he could do not to stomp into the kitchen, but he knew she'd be able to hear him, and the last thing he wanted was for her to think she'd gotten to him. By the time he was ten or so, he'd gotten real good at that, not letting folks see the wounds. By the time he turned twenty, he'd gotten so good at it, he didn't even see them himself.

But the thing was, this time, there weren't *supposed* to be any wounds.

Took him less than a half dozen strides to make it into the kitchen, grab a Bud from the fridge. He didn't normally drink this late at night, but just this once wasn't gonna kill him, he didn't imagine. Then, for some reason, his eyes lit on the business cards the P.I. had given him last night. One was his, the other belonged to his father. Or the man who liked to think of himself in those terms.

Eddie viciously twisted the top off the beer, guzzled down half the bottle before coming up for air. Then he snatched his father's card off the counter.

What *would* he do if Rudy Ortiz showed up?

He tossed the card back down, not even bothering to question why he didn't just throw the damn thing in the trash. Then he wandered back out into the living room, dropped onto the edge of the sofa. Took another swig of beer.

Wasn't any of his business, whether Mala saw her ex or not. After all, like she said, the jerk was the kids' father, even if the idea of somebody like that weasling his way back into Carrie and Lucas's lives made him sick to his stomach. Lucas, especially, he needed somebody better in his life than a man so weak, he got his rocks off from bullying women. Still, that didn't change the fact that Mala and this Scott person had a history together.

Unlike Eddie, who'd never had a history with another living soul.

And who damn well intended to keep it that way.

Chapter 11

"I'm sitting with the Farentinos," Eddie said to the restaurant hostess. "They might be here already."

The forty-something brunette scanned the reservation list, quirked a very red, very flirtatious smile up at Eddie. "Yes, sir. Come this way."

Trying not to finger his tie, Eddie followed the woman through the herd of linen-swathed tables, each with a flickering, amber globe in the center. The atmosphere was strictly mid-sixties Classy Traditional: dark reds, wood panelling, intimate lighting—dim, in other words—but it wasn't off-putting or anything. And the Christmas decorations were pretty nice, mostly evergreens and tiny white lights. It was early yet, only around six—and on a Monday night, no less—but the restaurant was fairly full. Mostly older couples and families, Eddie noticed, which tended to hold true most places. The younger crowd didn't generally show up before seven-thirty.

God knew, he was here under duress, but Galen had practically threatened to fire him unless he joined Del and her for dinner tonight. When he'd accused her of trying to strong-arm him, she'd gone all indignant on him.

"Don't be ridiculous. In fact, I've already got a couple interviews set up for next week. I just want your opinion, that's all. See what your reaction is to the place, what you think I should keep, what you think I should change, that sort of thing."

Yeah, right. Like Galen Farentino listened to anybody's advice about anything. What woman did?

He spotted her vibrant, auburn hair a good fifteen feet before he reached the table, saw Del look up and smile, wave him over. Saw, too, the builder's daughter Wendy, sitting between them in a froufrou little dress like she owned the place. Eddie'd met Wendy once before, so he knew the little girl was profoundly deaf, that her mama had died right after she was born and that Galen and her stepdaughter were crazy about each other. What he didn't know was how he was supposed to communicate with her, since he didn't know sign language.

So the last thing he expected was for the kid to grin and say, "Hi," when he took his seat across from her.

"Uh, hi…Wendy."

Her grin widened. "If you…talk so I…can see your…lips," she said, slowly and deliberately, "I can under…stand you."

"Well, okay, honey, I'll be sure and do that."

Looking only marginally more comfortable than Eddie in his sport jacket and tie, Del said, signing as well as talking, since Wendy wouldn't be able to see his face, Eddie figured, "Her school has this new computer program that teaches the kids to speak. You wouldn't believe how much her speech has improved in the last few months."

The gleam of pride—and love—in Del's eyes poked at something inside Eddie, reminding him of the way Mala looked at her kids, even when they exasperated the living daylights out of her. If his mama had ever looked at him that way, it had been so long now, he couldn't remember. God knew, nobody else ever had, not even Molly and Jervis, whose expressions had more often conveyed either pity or confusion than love. Not that he blamed them.

"…I already ordered for you," Galen was saying, which got his attention. As usual, she wore little makeup, but the turquoise sweater she wore made her look real good, especially considering how pregnant she was. "The Coq Au Vin, because I know you've made it before so I want to know what you think. Hope that's okay."

In spite of himself, he grinned. "I'd be in real trouble if it wasn't." He unfolded his linen napkin, spread it over his new khakis. He hadn't had the nerve to admit to Galen on Saturday, when she'd said in that imperious tone of hers, "You do have a jacket and tie, don't you?" that, up until that day, he hadn't. But Hannah had put him onto a nearby outlet mall where he picked up a few essentials. And he had to admit, he didn't look half bad all gussied up.

He buttered a roll, glancing around. The place was easily four times the size of Galen's restaurant. "You sure you want to take on something this big?"

Del's chuckle caught his attention. "You sure you want to go there?"

Eddie felt his stomach muscles loosen, just a little. He liked Del, even if the man made him feel downright puny by comparison. But the dark-haired, gentle giant had a ready smile and honest brown eyes, and his contentment was dangerously contagious.

"Which I take it means you've always been a risk taker," Eddie said to Galen.

Her deep blue-green eyes met his for a moment, before she took a sip of water…then winced, water sloshing out of the glass when she clunked it back onto the table.

"You okay?" Del and Eddie both said at once.

"Yes, yes. Just a little twinge in my lower back. It's nothing." She looked from one to the other. "I swear. Now, what was I…oh, yes. Actually, I was thirty-five before I found my…" She glanced at Wendy, winked at Eddie.

"…wings. Before that, I didn't even know how to pay an electric bill."

"You're kidding? What happened?"

"Oh, Lord, it's a long story involving grandparents and old husbands… Trust me, you really don't want to know. But the upshot was, I got tired of being afraid to go after what I wanted.'' Her eyes twinkled over her grin. ''It just takes some of us longer to grow up, I guess.'' Eddie didn't miss the meaningful look the redhead aimed at her husband. ''To learn that facing our fears isn't fatal.''

An older, very gentlemanly waiter brought their food—prime rib for Del, stuffed sole for Galen, a chicken salad sandwich for Wendy, the Coq Au Vin for Eddie. He hadn't gotten but two bites into his meal when he was struck by an extremely irritating revelation, one made all the more irritating when Galen said, ''You can do better than that, can't you?''

''What makes you think—?''

''It's written all over your face,'' she said, smiling smugly at her own dinner.

''It's a little…bland,'' he admitted. ''But this close to Christmas, they could just be having an off night.''

''Mama? May I go…look at…the…fish?''

There was one of those fake ponds up near the cash register, Eddie remembered, complete with plastic waterlilies and about a dozen carp easily large enough to serve up as an entrée.

''You barely touched your sandwich.''

The little girl shrugged. ''Not hun…gry.''

Galen let out a long, heartfelt sigh not dissimilar to ones Eddie had heard from Mala's mouth. Only Eddie didn't hear whether or not Galen gave her daughter her permission to go, since the world had just come to a screeching halt.

Fork poised in midair, his breath, along with his most recent bite of chicken, caught in his throat.

''Eddie?'' Del's deep voice barely penetrated his concentration. ''Something wrong? Holy… Hey, honey…isn't that Mala? Over there in the red dress?''

Galen sent him a look. ''Like I can turn around.''

''She won't see if you do it now…''

''No, doofus.'' She laid her hand on her belly. ''I mean, I really can't turn around.'' She looked at Eddie. ''It is, isn't it?''

He nodded. Then he somehow managed to ask, ''Either of you know what her ex looks like?''

"Drat," Galen said. "Now I *really* wish I could turn around."

"On second thought," Del said, an evil grin teasing his mouth, "maybe you shouldn't. That dress is something else."

"Oh, *you* really know how to cheer up a woman in her last month of pregnancy...."

But Eddie barely heard them, because one, the dress really *was* something else, all right. And Mala was something else in it, especially with her hair all done up like that, classy as all get out and sexy as hell. And two, because the tall, impeccably dressed man who'd stood when she got to the table had to be Scott, if the hair color was anything to go by. Even from clear across the room, the man radiated success and breeding. Eddie would've bet the farm that the navy double-breasted pinstripe hadn't come from any outlet store, or that Scott Sedgewick hadn't been any high school dropout.

And that Mala Koleski wouldn't't've married him if he had been.

Eddie just about couldn't see for the haze of jealousy that had just sprung up out of nowhere.

Never mind that the man had been a scumbag. Was probably still a scumbag. Or that Eddie had no reason not to believe Mala when she'd told him just how slim the chances were that she'd ever get back together with the scumbag. Fact was, the father of Mala's children was a purebred, not a mutt like Eddie.

And the fact was, the first inkling Eddie got that Mala wasn't happy with the way the conversation was going, he'd be hard pressed not to kill the guy with his bare hands.

Even though none of this was his business.

Mala had insisted on taking her own car. At least, this way, she could get away if she needed to. Which either made her very smart or a big chicken. Although, frankly, at the moment, she didn't really care.

And for once, she'd had the good sense to keep her mouth shut and not tell her loving, overprotective family about this meeting. She'd even arranged to let the kids stay overnight with Elizabeth and Guy Sanford and their kids, rather than ask her folks. At best, they would have only worried; at worst, Steve and Pop would have stood guard like a pair of overzealous pit bulls.

God, it had been years since she'd been to *Gardner's*. The restaurant had been Scott's favorite before they were married, a bastion of the traditional cuisine and conservative appointments favored by old money, of which Scott was the quintessential poster child. Even though both the decor and food had slipped a bit in the past four or five years, the establishment's reputation had somehow remained intact, in large part due to the staunch loyalty of the Scott Sedgewicks of the world.

"White wine," she murmured when he asked what she'd like to drink, then immediately picked up the menu to avoid looking at him. Or to give him a chance to scrutinize her, to search for clues that her heart was beating too fast and too hard, that, despite her every effort to appear in control, her hands were so clammy, her fingers stuck to the laminated menu.

She'd spotted him first, as she crossed the room. And in those few seconds before he noticed her, she saw how little he'd changed. Although why should he have? It'd only been a little more than three years, after all. He was still tall and graceful and well-dressed to the point of obsession, as a good little hotshot finance officer should be. His auburn hair was still cut short and parted on the left, although he'd changed his glasses from the thin tortoiseshells he'd always worn to a pair of chic, black wire rims.

Same sharply defined cheekbones, same finely shaped mouth, same opaque gray eyes…

"You look…amazing," he said with something approaching genuine astonishment.

…the same charming smile that had dazzled his lonely, twenty-nine-year-old assistant into thinking she'd finally found her prince.

She didn't even try to squelch the frisson of triumph that shot through her. Granted, she'd needed the come-and-get-it red jersey dress like she needed termites, considering the stack of bills sitting on her desk. But there was no way she was meeting this man looking like the cowering little—okay, cowering *big*—mouse she'd let him turn her into. Maybe it was childish, wanting to dangle things he couldn't have in front of him, things he'd walked away from, but it was empowering, too.

She'd started wearing the loose clothing after Carrie's birth, so Scott wouldn't see, couldn't ridicule. They'd made Lucas in total darkness, too, since that was the only way Scott would make love to her by that point. Odd how she hadn't even realized how humiliating that had been, that her husband couldn't bear to look at her naked, even in the privacy of their own bedroom.

Or how ridiculous, that she should have ever been ashamed of looking like a real woman, a woman who'd given birth and nursed her babies and had boobs and hips and thighs and all those things men in some parts of the world actually revered.

Like a certain Texan, for example.

A certain Texan she'd thrown out on his ear—

No. Not now.

"Thanks," she said at last, nodding to the waitress as she set the glass of Sauvignon Blanc in front of her.

"You've finally lost weight, haven't you?"

She looked him straight in the eye. "Not an ounce."

Scott leaned back in his chair, fingering his chin before letting loose with the first and only nervous laugh she'd ever heard from his mouth, which is when she realized she'd won the first round. Damned if he was taking her taciturnity for confidence, when in fact she was petrified he'd hear her voice shake if she said more than a three-word sentence. But her insides weren't trembling from nervousness as much as from pent-up anger, the anger she'd lost somewhere along the way during her marriage.

But she didn't want him to see her angry. She didn't want him to think he affected her in any way at all.

The waitress appeared to take their order.

"Have you had enough time to decide?" Scott asked.

Oh, boy, had she. In more ways than he'd ever know, that was for sure. God knew, the last thing she felt like doing was eating—especially in this damn girdle—but eating was exactly what she intended to do.

"Yes, I'll start with the stuffed artichoke appetizer. Oh, and ranch dressing on the salad. Then the petite sirloin in mushroom and wine sauce, rare, with a baked potato, the broccoli Hollandaise, and for dessert…" She ticked her tongue against the roof of her mouth as she frowned at the menu.

"Perhaps you'd like to see the dessert cart when you finish your meal?"

She smiled up at the waitress. "Yes, I think I would."

She bit back a smile at the stiffness in Scott's voice as he ordered.

Why not just have a salad, or some grilled chicken or fish? God, Mala—how can you live with yourself, eating that much food? And your mother's cooking is a coronary waiting to happen, you know that. If you're not careful, you'll be big as a house….

The waitress wafted off. Mala sucked in a surreptitious breath, calmly folded her hands in front of her on the table. "Well?"

Scott laughed softly. "Oh, come on, Mal…let's just have dinner first."

"Forget it, Scott. Obviously, you didn't just happen to look me up because you were in town. So let's just get on with it."

Movement out of the corner of her eye caught her attention: she glanced over, saw a little towheaded girl worming her way back through the tables. Wendy Farentino, she realized. Distracted, she watched the child's progress, her heart stopping when the child reached her destination and Mala caught Eddie King's hot-ice glare.

And she realized, as her heart rate sped up and her skin flashed first hot, then cold, that all the while she'd been telling herself that Scott Sedgewick no longer had even a smidgen of power over her, she'd totally missed just how much Eddie King *did*.

And how the hell had that happened?

She forced her gaze back to Scott, who was looking at her very curiously.

"Sorry. I saw someone I knew."

"Oh? Do you need to say 'hello'?"

"No, no. Just…never mind. You were saying?"

For a second or two, she endured Scott's condescending regard. Then he wordlessly reached into his breast pocket and retrieved an envelope, which he passed to Mala.

"What's this?"

"Open it and find out."

She did, blinking three times before she could trust that she'd counted the number of zeroes correctly. Stunned, her gaze flashed to Scott's.

"What is this?"

He smiled, took a sip of his martini. Very dry, no olive. "I missed a few child support payments. Figured this would cover it."

"Like hell." She shoved the check back into the envelope, pushed it back toward him.

"Mal, what are you doing?"

"Do you even remember your children's names, Scott?"

"Don't be absurd. Of course I remember my children's names—"

"Just not their birthdays."

His jaw tightened. "Considering the way…we left things, I just thought it would be easier this way—"

"On whom? Them? Or you?"

He leaned forward, his features carefully arranged into a mask of concern. "I understand your animosity, honey. That's why…why it took me so long to get up the nerve to finally leave a message on your machine. But I've changed, Mal, I swear. I'll admit, I was a bit harsh with you when we were married—"

"Harsh?" Mala lowered her voice, grateful the tables weren't cheek by jowl in here. "You were a *prick*, Scott. You treated me as if I didn't have a brain in my head. Consequently, I have more respect for the mold on the green beans I tossed out yesterday than I have for you."

She saw a muscle tick in his jaw, saw his supreme effort to

keep control, and she thought, *Hot damn! This guy wants something from me.*

Something he wanted so badly, he wouldn't even fight back.

"That's not fair, Mala," he bit out.

"Yeah, well, neither was walking out on your kids." Then the light dawned. "Who is she, Scott?"

He jerked. "Who is who?"

"The bimbo-du-jour."

Scott sucked in a breath, tried a smile that failed miserably. "Very funny. But while my...fiancée's hardly a bimbo, her identity is immaterial. You don't know her. Someone I met in Chicago."

"Humor me."

Behind the glasses, his expression turned glacial. "Her name's Beverly Sampson. She's a doctor, a heart specialist. Our parents...are old friends."

Ah.

Mala took a sip of her wine, leaning back in a very Bette Davis pose. "What I can't figure out, is why you married me to begin with."

Three years ago, his silence would have wrecked her. Now, it was a relief. Better to know he'd never loved her, than to think he'd fallen *out* of love with her.

In other words, she'd goofed, but she hadn't failed.

Hallelujah.

Mala bent forward enough to give Scott a good view of her cleavage as well as to pick up the discarded envelope, which she fingered for a minute before waving it between them. "This is guilt money, I know that much." She threw down the envelope, then sat back, her arms crossed over her rib cage. "And you have a five-course meal in which to tell me why."

Their appetizers arrived. Mala noticed the Farentinos and Eddie getting up from their table. Once again, she caught Eddie's gaze, which was now downright scary, and momentarily panicked he'd take it on himself to mosey on over and punch Scott's lights out. God, she could practically taste the testosterone from here.

As someone who'd never, ever spurred any sort of rivalry

between a pair of chest-beating, grunting males, it stunned her to discover just how arousing the caveman routine could be. Okay, yeah, infuriating, sure—would men ever evolve past the point of thinking a woman couldn't protect herself?—but this was about something much more…basic.

And there was a lot to be said for getting back to basics.

Her jog in the conversation was enough to make Scott turn around again, then back to her. "Who's the guy?"

She shrugged, tamping down an almost insane urge to tell Scott she'd just been more turned on by Eddie's eyes than any part of Scott had been able to accomplish the entire time they'd been married. Thank God it was dark in here. "The woman's a client, owns a restaurant in town. The dark haired man's her husband, the other one's her chef while she's on maternity leave."

She decided telling him that Eddie was also her tenant would serve no useful purpose. Especially as it was more than apparent that Scott really didn't give a flying fig who any of them were, or what any of it had to do with Mala's life. Oh, no, nothing had changed. If it didn't orbit around Scott, it wasn't worth bothering about.

She held her breath as the little party wended their way back out of the dining room. But she could feel Eddie's gaze, lingering on her, on Scott, until the very last second before he disappeared into the lobby.

This was going to be the longest dinner of her life.

His stomach churning, Eddie stood in the restaurant lobby, his hands crammed in his pants pockets as he faced the dining room. He would've left already, except Galen and Wendy had disappeared into the restroom before he had a chance to say thank-you. So here he stood, staring at Mala's table, although the room was too dimly lit for him to make out much of what was going on.

It scared the very devil out of him, how much she mattered.

Del came up beside him, nudged Eddie's arm. He looked down, saw a proffered York mint in Del's hand.

"Thanks." Eddie unwrapped the mint, poked it into his mouth.

"Between my pregnant wife and my daughter," Del said good-naturedly, "I spend a lot of time hanging outside of bathrooms." His gaze drifted out to the dining room, then back to Eddie. "I hate to break this to you, buddy, but you look like someone who gives a damn."

Eddie grunted, then ambled over to a padded bench, dropped onto it.

"And walking away won't change anything. Trust me."

"And don't go readin' more into this than there is," Eddie said, crossing his arms. "Mala's a nice lady. I just don't like the idea of the jerk bothering her, is all. It's nothin' personal."

Del popped another mint into his mouth, then lowered himself onto the bench beside Eddie, his long legs sprawled out in front of him, his head resting on the bench back. "Whatever." Then he pivoted his head, a grin teasing his mouth. "But what you'd really like to do is go back in there and beat the *fap* out of the guy."

"Believe me, it's tempting."

"Looked to me like she was holding her own, though."

In spades. Oh, Eddie could tell she wasn't exactly acting like her usual smart-ass self, but she sure hadn't been runnin' scared, either. She could've taken the easy way out, not met with the creep on her own, let a lawyer or somebody run interference. But she hadn't.

Woman had a lot of guts, that was for damn sure.

Moving with surprising grace for such a big man, Del sprang back up from the bench, swiping another handful of mints from the bowl by the cash register when the cashier wasn't looking. "D'you suppose they even have a clue how much it scares us when they go off on their 'I am woman, I can damn well take care of myself' numbers? I mean, it's not like I begrudge them their independence or anything, but what're we supposed to do with our protective streak, huh? Just ignore it?" Del stared off into the dining room for a second or two, then turned back, shaking his head. "God, I hate smarmy types like that. Heads up!'' He tossed a couple more mints to Eddie, who neatly caught them.

"Did you know Scott?" Eddie asked, mulling over that protective streak business and how he'd never really noticed he'd had one before he came back here. "When they were married, I mean?"

"Nope. Wasn't around then, so I didn't have the pleasure. But Mala's brother Steve's told me plenty. Guy sounds a lot like Galen's first husband. A total control freak when it comes to women. You know, the type who's not happy unless he calls all the shots?" He stuffed another mint into his mouth, spoke around it. "And then to walk out on his own kids... There's no forgiving that in my book."

A fresh wave of anger nearly made Eddie choke on the remnants of the mint. He swallowed both of them down, then said, "Yeah. You got that right."

Mala could see Eddie sprawled on the porch's top step, his back propped against one of the railing posts, before she even pulled Whitey into the driveway.

His presence didn't surprise her. The rush of pleasure that streaked through her, however, did.

Since she hadn't been home, the Christmas lights weren't on, but the glow from the streetlight, accentuated by a single red pinpoint in the vicinity of his knees, sufficiently illuminated his slouched figure. Apprehension trampled her earlier delight: giddiness at having survived her meeting with Scott could easily lead to recklessness, if she weren't careful.

She got out of the car, mincing over the icy patches in her high heels as she approached him. He'd changed back into his jeans, she could tell, topped by a shearling-lined denim jacket she didn't remember seeing before.

"You wouldn't by chance be waiting for me, wouldja?"

"Yep." He shifted to stretch out one leg along the next to top step. For some reason, the movement made her stomach go all jittery. "Wanna make somethin' of it?"

She tucked her arms over her stomach and shivered. "It's cold."

"I like the cold."

Even from where she stood, she could hear Grateful snuffling at the front door. "Is this some Papa Bear protective thing?"

"Don't know. Haven't figured that part out yet."

"So this means you're not mad at me?"

He tilted his head. "I take it you mean about the other night?"

She nodded.

"I told you then, I wasn't mad." Harsh shadows carved his face as he looked away for a moment, than back at her. "You had your reasons. And I don't hold grudges." He took a hit off the cigarette, languidly spewed the smoke into the air. "Not for long, anyway."

"Thought you said you didn't smoke anymore?"

Eddie held up the cigarette, studying it as if he couldn't figure out how it got there. "I don't. Well, not on anything like a regular basis. I doubt one every month or so's gonna kill me. Where're the kids?"

"Spending the night with friends." The initial euphoria was beginning to wear off. Not that she wasn't proud of herself, but… "I figured…well, I wasn't sure how I might feel. Afterward. And there are times when even perfect mothers like me don't want to deal with their kids."

His chuckle spun out into the cold air. When it died out, he said softly, "I understand what you did tonight. Why you had to go fight that dragon all by yourself."

"Oh?"

"Yeah." Another pull on the cigarette, another stream of smoke released. Then he looked at her, a half smile teasing his lips. "I'm real proud of you, Miss Mala."

His compliment stole her breath. "Thanks. And I really mean that."

"I know you do." Then his gaze narrowed. "You okay?"

She climbed the steps to sit on the other side of the top step, tucking her coat under her butt. "I think I am. Or I will be, anyway."

"You gonna see him again?"

"I somehow doubt it."

"Wanna talk about it?"

"Not yet, I don't think. Not until I sort it all out in my own head a little better, anyway."

Eddie didn't look particularly pleased, but he was smart enough not to probe.

"So," she said brightly. "How come you were there to-night? At *Gardner's?*"

He propped the hand with the cigarette on his knee, seemed to take the out-of-left-field question in stride. "Galen's fixin' to buy the place. Wanted my opinion about what she might change."

"You're kidding?"

He grinned. "About her buying the place or about her wan-tin' my opinion?"

"The first."

"Nope. She's already put a bid on it, in fact. Del said some-thing about his father backing her. That developer, what's his name?"

"Hugh Farentino."

"Yeah, that's it." He angled his head to stare at her shoul-der. "That real fur?"

"What? Oh, the coat. Uh-uh. First off, who could afford it? Secondly, I doubt my conscience would let me wear a bunch of dead animals. Score one for the animal rights folks, I guess."

He laughed. Heat crawled into her belly, curled up like a fat, sassy cat, even as her thoughts settled enough to realize he'd deliberately steered the conversation away from talking about Galen's new acquisition.

Not that she would ask.

After a final drag on the cigarette, he stubbed it out on the bottom of his boot, tossed it out into the yard.

"Hey! Don't you go leaving your cigarette butts for me to clean up!"

"It's butt, singular, and I don't intend to, and you know you're startin' to sound like me."

"Am not!"

"Yes, you are, darlin'." He shifted to reach into his coat pocket, pulled out something shiny. "And it's damned cute." Palm extended, he stretched toward her. "Mint?"

"No. I'm still stuffed from dinner." And would be for at least a week.

Mala hugged her knees, looked up at the stars, found herself wanting this moment to last forever, this sense of victory over at least some of her fears. This feeling of peace in a man's company. Because she did feel peaceful around Eddie King. Safe. And no, that didn't make sense, since that would mean she'd have to totally rethink her definition of the word. But you know, after tonight? She didn't really care anymore. "Safe"—her old definition—was for wimps. And damned if she was a wimp.

"Hard to believe it's only two days to Christmas," she said.

She heard the crinkle of the candy wrapper, caught a faint whiff of chocolate and mint. "Bet the kids are like to turn themselves inside out by now."

"Bet you're right." Her full stomach groused when she bent over, rubbing at an imaginary spot on the toe of her shoe. She'd heard it in his voice, that sense of detachment, that the holiday meant little to him personally. Yet he didn't seem to begrudge Carrie and Lucas their excitement, even if he couldn't share it.

Or wouldn't.

And maybe she could change that.

And maybe you need to have your head examined.

Her sense of peace gave way to something edgier, like the feeling she used to get before an exam, that bizarre mix of confidence and doubt that had always driven her to succeed.

"So," she said, "what are you doing for Christmas?"

"Working at the same shelter I did at Thanksgiving."

"All day?"

"If you're about to invite me to spend Christmas mornin' with y'all, forget it. That's just a little too Hallmark for me, okay?"

"Why? Because of the kids?"

"Has nothin' to do with the kids." At her raised brows, he added, "I swear."

"Then it's me."

"Oh, for the love of Pete, Mala. No, it's not you, either."
His gaze had gone opaque as stone in the dark. "Which I
would've thought you'd figured out by now."

She wasn't sure what to make of that. "Then why not? I
just hate the thought of you being alone."

"I've been alone most of my life, Mala. I'm more'n used to
it."

"Which doesn't make it a good thing."

"And I suppose that's for me to decide, isn't it?" he said,
then, after a moment, got to his feet, headed down the stairs.

"Hey! Where the blue blazes do you think you're going?"

"Back to my place."

"Where you're safe from the crazy lady who keeps trying
to invite you to breakfast."

At the bottom of the steps, he turned, his thumbs hooked in
his pockets. "No. Because the only reason I was here to begin
with was to see if you needed someone to talk to. About your
ex and all. Since you don't, there's no point my hangin'
around."

The man was going to drive her totally insane.

"Dammit, Eddie—" She threw her purse at him, which
weighed all of eight ounces and which he easily caught. "You
can't have it both ways! You can't run every time somebody
tries to get close, and then accuse them of pushing you away!"

"You're nuts, you know that?" He tossed back the purse,
which she missed and nearly put out her back when she lunged
for it. "I'm not accusin' anybody of anything."

"And I'm a size three." She stood, smacking at the back of
her coat, then shivered as she crossed to the door, looked for
her key in her purse. "Just because I didn't give you a blow-
by-blow description of my conversation with Scott doesn't
mean I don't want your company." *Where was the stupid…?
Oh, there.* "And just because I want your company doesn't
mean I expect a lifetime commitment. Now, if you're willing
to take a chance that I'm not going to chain you to the hot
water heater in my basement and force-feed you breakfast for
the rest of your days, you can come inside. I'll light a fire and

tell you about Scott, which is really boring, but hey, if it rings your chimes, who am I to say? And after that, we can sit and stare at the tree and tell awful jokes and maybe, if we're feeling really wild, we can watch the puppy grow.''

''Or maybe we could just cut to the chase and get naked.''

She dropped the key.

Then she turned, one brow arched, saw him still standing at the bottom of the steps, his hands tucked into his back pockets. ''I don't suppose you mean in separate rooms, huh?''

''Now, darlin', that would kinda defeat the purpose, doncha think?''

She stooped down, found the key, rammed it into the lock. The door popped open. She flicked on the hall light. Bent to greet the quivering dog. Realized she'd run out of things to do. That Eddie was on his way back up the stairs, his footsteps slow, deliberate. Promising.

Grateful dashed out onto the porch to greet his long-lost buddy, who knelt to scratch the beast's belly. Mala found herself staring at Eddie's hands.

''You...you remember that conversation we had the other night?'' she asked.

''Yep.''

''You're ignoring it, aren't you?''

Eddie looked up. Shrugged, like it really didn't matter to him, one way or the other. ''I'm not the one who changed my mind, honey.''

Then he stood, right in front of her, slipping his hands back into his pockets, but still close enough for her to feel his warmth, his quiet dominance of the space. The moment. Close enough for her to pick up the mingled scents of chocolate and mint and man and just the merest hint of tobacco, which she found exciting in a forbidden, dangerous kind of way.

Her mouth went dry, while the rest of her just went nuts.

''And, um, if I were to change it back...?''

She shuddered as one of those incredible hands lifted to her jaw, as his thumb began tracing her cheekbone with a lazy sensuousness that threatened to debone her. His head dipped, his mouth grazing hers. A hint. Another promise.

"I think maybe," he whispered into her mouth, "I just might find it in my heart to forgive you."

Except at that precise moment, Realization jumped to its feet at the back of Mala's buzzing, hormone-crammed brain, waving madly and shouting over the din, "Madam Chairman! Madam Chairman! Aren't you forgetting something?"

Mala backed away so suddenly she tripped over the stupid dog.

Eddie frowned. "What?"

"You know damn well *what.* Or were you just trying to save face the other night by telling me you'd been about to break it off, anyway?"

Well, at least he had the courtesy to look embarrassed. One hand lifted to the back of his neck. "I was kinda hopin' you'd forgotten that part."

"I'm a mother, Eddie. We don't forget anything."

He let out a sigh. "Okay, fine. No, I wasn't tryin' to save my butt. I mean, I was, but that's why I was going to call it off. For both our sakes. Only you beat me to the punch, and my male ego got all bent out of shape. That didn't mean I still didn't want you. Or that, after I got to thinkin' about it, that I didn't understand how much your ex's poppin' back up in your life like that must've thrown you, made you feel you had to protect yourself. Then, when I saw you with him tonight..."

His eyes burned through her. "Look, if you still feel you gotta protect yourself, that's okay. But I just want to let you know, I'm here if you need...anything. Company, comfort, mind-blowing sex, some leftover lasagna..."

Mala burst into startled laughter, wanting to touch him so badly, she thought she'd burn up. Afraid if she did, she would. "Do I have to pick?"

"Only whether I go upstairs or come inside with you."

Oh, God. Oh, Lord. Oh, blessed Mother and all the saints and anybody else who might be listening—what *was* a girl to do? And then it hit her, with a force strong enough to make her heart nearly leap out of her chest, that for all Eddie said he was there for her, he was there just as much for *him.*

That he'd changed *his* mind first. After all, who had shown up on whose doorstep?

Like a wall sliding back to reveal a secret passage she hadn't known existed, or even been looking for, she saw a chance. A slim one, God knew, and one she wouldn't have dared take even a week ago. A chance to heal, to show this lonely, proud man—a man who, heaven help her, she was growing to love with everything she had in her—what could be his.

It meant risking everything: her heart, her peace, her barely recovered self-confidence. Even her dignity. What if he never completely warmed up to the kids? What if she couldn't convince him to take the same kind of chance she was?

But the thought of letting this opportunity slip away…

Tonight had proven she was no longer the woman she'd been when Scott left her. Or even, for that matter, the still-cautious woman she'd been a few weeks ago, when Eddie King had come strolling back into her life. Somehow or other, the cocoon of fear she'd huddled inside for the past three years had fallen away, and—ta-da!—there she was, her old giving, impetuous self, ready to try again.

Ready to live again.

From the open doorway, the pup yipped, giving them a goofy, tongue-lolling grin when they looked over.

Mala looked up into Eddie's hopeful gaze, realizing he didn't even understand what it was he was hoping for. And for a split second, she wished with all her heart she didn't have to go through what she was about to, that she could somehow sidestep the risk.

Except she'd never be able to live with herself if she didn't.

She slipped her hands inside his jacket, making the contact that would, she knew, change her life forever. "Just one question."

"And what is that?"

She smiled into his eyes. "Is the lasagna vegetable or sausage?"

He grinned back, then took her by the hand and led her into the house.

The dog seemed immensely relieved.

Chapter 12

They never made it to the bedroom. And to be perfectly honest, Eddie didn't ever remember getting naked, although he did—vaguely—remember the brief—very brief—stab of regret that he'd more or less yanked that red dress off of her before he got a real good look at her in it.

The trade-off, however, was that here they were, slick and sweaty and panting on the carpet in front of the Christmas tree, ignoring the pup's whines from the other side of the kitchen door where he'd been banished. And all Eddie could think was...

Not a whole lot, actually, since anything even approaching reasonable thought had been pretty much obliterated by this thick, fire-red I-have-surely-died-and-gone-to-heaven haze of lust. At least, he figured that's what it was, although he had to admit, he'd never had a case of it quite this bad before.

Something told him Miss Mala hadn't, either.

From God knows where, she'd produced a box of condoms—"Don't ask," she'd said—and hurled them at him, her eyes begging him to hurry.

Not that he'd needed any encouragement.

There was so much of her and she was so warm and soft and sweet-smelling—and soft—and everyplace he touched or kissed or nuzzled quivered or arched or hardened or went wet....

Her moans were the downright prettiest sounds he'd ever heard.

Sex with this woman was like being caught in a hurricane, exhilarating and frightening and exciting, all at once. He buried his face in her belly, flicking his tongue around her navel, then tracing the faintly puckered lines of her stretch marks—what would it be like, to add to those marks, to plant his own seed in her and make a baby...?

The thought shot through before he could stop it, except then she spread her legs, whimpering little *comeoncomeoncomeon* noises, and her directness arrowed straight to...someplace... but he wanted to taste her first, just enough to tease, to make her tense and cry out....

Yeah. Like that.

He slid up the length of that lush, amazing body to trap her hands with his over her head, her gaze in his...

Gotcha.

Desperate to regain control, he plunged inside her...she hissed her welcome and the old male ego sang out in triumph...only to go "Huh?" a second later when she shook her head and said, "No."

Eddie froze, next door to shattered, his mother's tiny cross shivering between them on its frail gold chain. *"No?"*

She sputtered a laugh, her eyes dark with arousal. Her hands squeezed his, still braced over her head. "Not *that* 'no,' doofus. *No,* as in, it's been three years, y'know? I'd kinda like it to last more than three seconds."

"I'm not sure I can."

One brow arched. "Try."

"If your parents show up right now—"

"—you'll make me an orphan. I know." She smiled, the tenderness in her expression damn near stealing his breath.

Now, hold on, here. This wasn't supposed to be about tenderness, this...this was supposed to be about mutual need and the easing thereof. Of comfort, yeah, but the kind of quick-fix comfort of a great meal or a full-night's sleep or a good book.

This was supposed to be about *lasagna,* for the love of Pete.

Except then Mala gently cleared her throat and said, "Hello? I'm down here?" and Eddie remembered he was inside her, and how significant that was for both of them, so he decided to concentrate on being a good lover and giving the lady what she wanted instead of straining his brain about matters he couldn't think clearly about anyway considering where most of it was at the moment.

He'd never gone slow before now, he guessed because no-body'd ever asked him to, for one thing. And because going slow was not a concept most men were prone to think about if left to their own devices.

But he'd always prided himself on being a quick study.

Except, going slow meant he had lots of time to study Mala's face, for him to hear his heart stutter in the house's deep hush as he watched her skin flush with excitement, for the thought to crystallize that he really cared about this woman and wouldn't be here right now if he didn't.

And that that thought wasn't bothering him nearly as much as it should.

Time held its breath while he and Mala luxuriated in their mating dance, while he drank in the scents of her perfume and evergreen and his own heat, and the thought *This could be yours* raced through his brain, spooking him good, and he didn't know what to do with it and he didn't want to think about that right now, all he wanted was to lose himself in her just for these few minutes....

Mala yanked her hands out from his to wrap herself around him, engulf him...Eddie shifted, lifted her hips and claimed her, almost savagely, his own shout of long awaited release mingling with her cries of gratitude to whoever cared to listen.

From behind the kitchen door, the pup started to howl.

"Damn dog," Eddie muttered in her ear, and Mala erupted with laughter. A draught chilled her damp skin as he shifted off her, cuddled her to his chest.

Good sign.

"Where'd you get this?" she said, her fingers tracing the delicate cross nestled in that just-right patch of coarse hair on his chest.

"My mama. When she died."

"You never take it off, do you?"

"Nope."

"That's sweet."

He groaned softly. She smiled, then said, fighting against the insane, overachieving part of her that wanted so badly to make things right, to make this…real, "I've never done it on the floor."

"I hate to tell you this, darlin', but the way my knees are feelin' right now, you may never do it on the floor again. At least, not with me."

She let the last part of that play on through, then said, "And here I thought you'd be able to introduce me to the wonders of unconventional sex."

Beats passed. Many, many beats, each one more torturous than the one preceding it.

"And just what gives you the idea—"

There's gonna be more than just this one time?

"—that I'm so all-fired conversant in the art of lovemaking?"

Relief positively shot through her. "Eternal optimism?"

He laughed, then gathered her even closer, which meant more to her than the sex itself but no way was she going to mention that to Eddie. "Well, maybe I can show you a thing or two," he said, and his male cockiness made her smile again. "But I'm no expert on the Kama Sutra, believe me."

"S'okay. I happen to think the missionary position is woefully underrated, anyway."

"Kinda have a soft spot in my heart for it, myself, if you wanna know the truth. But it is cold down here. And these old bones aren't quite as maleable as they used to be. So come on, Miss Mala…" He got to his feet, put out a hand to help her to hers, and she figured if he wasn't the least bit self-conscious about standing there naked in somebody's living room, why should she be? "What do you say we move to the sofa or the bed or something a little more conducive to gettin' in the mood again."

Didn't have to ask her twice.

The next few seconds were a blur as they both grabbed for the box of condoms—he won—then sprinted down the hall to her bedroom, nearly choking with laughter by the time Eddie jerked back the covers and they both dived into the bed. He sprawled over her, solid and reassuring, cradling her face in his hands as he dipped for a kiss, only to pull back, frowning down into her face.

"Your teeth are chattering."

"I get cold easily."

"I can tell." But he chivalrously reached behind him, yanking the covers up over them both before resuming his lovely onslaught on her mouth and neck and breasts and...

She wriggled underneath him. "Again, please."

"Already?"

"Look who's talking."

He grinned, then reached between them, teasing her with his fingers for several horribly wonderful seconds before letting himself inside, and she closed her eyes and sighed and silently sang praises to whatever saint there was in charge of these things—and if there wasn't, somebody had definitely missed the boat with that one—and then she opened her eyes and saw so much confusion in his expression, she nearly forgot to breathe.

She whimpered then, for herself, for him, willing him to understand that this could be so much more than the mating of two bodies. But then, maybe that was just her silly, romantic female brain talking and men never felt that way, not really. Once again, she was expecting far more than she had any right to expect.

He moved inside her, just a little, just enough...she sent up another sigh that was equal parts bliss and annoyance, that next to the indescribable joy of holding her babies for the first time, there was nothing like the feeling of having a man—correction: the *right* man—deep inside her to make her feel this...complete.

She'd gone for three years without sex, never really missed it, certainly wouldn't have said she was less of a woman for not having it, but, oh, this was...*oh!* She gasped, clung to Eddie's shoulders, wondering what he was doing, not really caring, only knowing if he stopped she'd die.

"You like that?" he whispered, and she thrust her hips upward and he laughed and said, "Guess that answers that," and then he kept doing...whatever...and she moaned a little and thought he smelled so damned good, felt even better...and she drew him closer, drew him *home,* telling him the only way she dared that he *belonged.*

And when his second release came, in perfect, earth-shattering, teeth-knocking tandem with hers, Mala smiled the smile of a woman smug in her ability to please her man.

"Scott lives in Chicago now, wants to run for city council or something...." Eddie toyed with her hair, so smooth and sleek, as she lay with her head on his chest. Pillow talk, which Eddie'd always figured was a lot more intimate than sex, usually made him nervous. Most talking made him nervous, to tell the truth. But somehow, with Mala...well, it just didn't feel threatening the way it did with other women, that's all.

"...and I guess it finally dawned on him that, hey, if anybody went poking around and discovered he'd walked out on me and hadn't sent me a penny of child support all these years, he'd be up the creek without a paddle."

"You shouldn't've let him get away with that," he said into her hair.

He felt her shrug. "I didn't need the aggravation, Eddie, believe me."

"Yeah, but he does. Maybe you don't care about his money, but his kids—"

"I wanted the kids, I can take care of the kids. Anyway...I guess he got scared, so he decided to head me off at the pass. Hands me this huge check, as if that's supposed to take care of it."

"And you handed it back."

She raised up, looked at him. "You saw?"

"Yeah."

With a sigh, she cuddled back against him, her arm snaked around his waist. "He never even asked about them."

"That doesn't give him leave to pretend like they don't exist. You should've taken the money, Mala."

"And let him think that tossing a few bucks at me would somehow exonerate him? Forget it. Far as I'm concerned, let the creep squirm, wondering when or if somebody's gonna start digging around in his past, find out Mr. High-and-Mighty's nothing more than a deadbeat dad."

"But you won't force the issue."

"Why should I? It's much more fun this way."

Pride warmed Eddie's blood at the resolve in her voice. Lord, but she was fierce, this woman of...

Uh-uh. No way was he gonna finish that sentence.

"Hey—" He squeezed her shoulder. "You hungry?"

"For lasagna? No."

The laughter trembling in her words provoked a sigh. "Now, see, this is where you and me being the same age is a problem. I peaked twenty years ago. You're just getting going."

Mala twisted off of him onto her own pillow, one arm under her head, mischief dancing in those cat's eyes of hers. "Fine. So I'll give you another twenty minutes."

"Mighty generous of you."

"I thought so."

Panic viced his heart, but not because making love to her again frightened him....

"You're frowning," she said gently, skimming a knuckle down his arm. "Which means you're thinking too hard."

"I do that occasionally, you know. And with more than just my—" Her laugh cut him off. Then he flipped over, caging her between his arms, his thigh insinuating itself between her legs. "Any regrets, Miss Mala?"

"About what we just did, you mean?"

"Uh-huh."

Her smile softened into something that just plumb stole his breath. "Nary a one. Granted, the concept of living for the moment is a new one for me. But I think I like it." She laced her fingers around his neck, tugged him down to her mouth. "Kiss me, Eddie King," she whispered. "Help me celebrate my newfound freedom."

Well, now…how could he pass up an invitation like that?

Mala was awakened the next morning by a slobbery kiss on her fingers, which were hanging over the edge of the bed. Somehow, she didn't think it was Eddie. She rolled over, not bothering to pull the sheet up over her breasts, only to realize there was no one around to show them off for. Or to.

He was gone. Surprise, surprise.

Now she flopped onto her back, tugging the covers up over her since it was kind of chilly with no nice, warm man to snuggle up to.

Gee, she'd gotten used to that real fast, hadn't she?

It was still early, maybe around six-thirty. But it was Christmas Eve, which meant she had a million and one things to do, which meant lollygagging in bed was not an option. There were still presents to wrap and cookies to bake and kids to keep from climbing the walls and mothers to keep from guessing what their daughters had been doing last night….

Oh, that was worth a lazy, sated grin. Okay, so she was a little sore—if Eddie's performance last night was anything to go by, he must've been hell on wheels at seventeen—but heaven knew when they'd get that opportunity again. Or even if there would be another opportunity, since they didn't exactly discuss it.

"Hey. No whining," she muttered to herself as she swung her legs out of bed. "You knew what you were letting yourself in for." Robe and slippers donned, she made a quick pit stop before shuffling into the kitchen, letting the dog out, putting on coffee.

The phone rang, scaring her out of her wits.

"Hel—?"

"It's a boy!" Del practically shouted into her ear. "Merry Christmas! We've got a great big, gorgeous boy! Eight and a half pounds!"

With a cry of delight, Mala sagged against the counter. "Oh,

Del! How wonderful! When? What's his name? Is Galen okay?''

"She's fine! Oh, my God…it was incredible…she was in-credible…I've seen her put more effort into a sneeze, I swear…the kid just popped out—''

Mala smiled. Men were so clueless.

"—his name's Sam. After Galen's father…''

Del's voice was shaking with emotion, bringing tears to Mala's eyes as well. If Scott had even been half this excited over his childrens' births…

Envy spurted through her, so hot and fierce it scared her.

"—I gotta go make about a million more calls! Oh…what?'' Mala heard muffled conversation, then Del came back with, "Galen says she's gonna be in here until tonight, but if you could possibly stop by—''

"Like you could keep me away!'' she said brightly, grab-bing a napkin off the counter to wipe away her tears. "Con-gratulations, you guys! I'll see you later!''

Mala poured herself a cup of coffee, wandered out into the living room, discovered she'd forgotten to unplug the tree lights. Gee, that was real smart.

She squatted to yank the plug from the wall, only to crumple cross-legged on the floor by the fragrant, glittering, eccentri-cally decorated tree. The pup wriggled over and crawled into her lap; she clamped her arms around his scrawny, scratchy neck, staring at the spot in front of the tree where she and Eddie had gone at it like a pair of crazed rabbits.

And she sighed, not even realizing that tears were trickling down her cheeks.

"…so, since the baby came earlier than we'd expected, I should be ready to come back to work by March first.''

Eddie had barely heard what Galen was saying, concentrat-ing on the sleeping baby in her arms. He'd never been this close to a newborn, he realized. Wouldn't've been this close to this one, if Galen hadn't've called him this morning, asked him to come see her before she left the hospital, if it was at all possible. It wasn't like he could exactly say "no,'' not with how good she'd been to him. Besides, he genuinely liked her, and Del, and was pleased as all get-out for them. Galen had told him how much Del had worried over her with this pregnancy, what with his losing his first wife in childbirth and all. And he'd seen that worry, etched in Del's face, even when he smiled. So now that Galen had safely delivered their son, that was one thing Del didn't have to bother himself about anymore.

Of course, there were a passel more worries down the road, but Eddie didn't figure Del needed reminding about that—

"Eddie?"

He jerked his head back up, meeting Galen's beaming gaze. Sunshine streamed through the open miniblinds in the pink-walled birthing room, which with those flowered sheets and everything looked more like somebody's bedroom than any hospital room Eddie'd ever seen.

"Did you hear me? About my coming back on March first?"

"There's no hurry," he heard himself say. "I told you, my new job doesn't start until April. So you take all the time you need to be with that little boy of yours."

She gave him one of those astute looks women were so good at. "Del said there was a message on our machine at home. The Gardners accepted my offer for the restaurant."

Eddie shifted in the padded chair. "Well, hey—that's great! You sure are having one heck of a Christmas, aren't you?"

"And it would be even better if I knew I could count on you to run the new location for me." She batted her big turquoise eyes, but Eddie knew she was only half joshing. "So I wouldn't have to worry about finding someone else during these first few weeks as a new mother...?"

He stared right at her, but if he thought that was going to shake her up, or loose, he was sorely mistaken. She might've had a confidence problem at one time, but there was nothing wimpy about her now, boy. "Thought you said you had some interviews lined up?"

"I lied."

His breath left his lungs in a rush. "I'm real sorry, Galen. But the answer's still no."

Those sea-blue eyes cut straight through him for another

second or two. Then, with a sigh, Galen looked down at the snoozing infant in her arms, her long, short-nailed fingers reverently touching the baby's face, his tummy, his tiny hands. "I had five miscarriages, during my first marriage," she said. "And a tubal pregnancy that nearly killed me. I never, ever thought I'd see this day."

Something propelled Eddie to his feet and over to the side of the bed to look more closely at Galen's little miracle with his scrunched up face and thatch of nearly black hair, just like his daddy's. To Eddie's extreme surprise, he started to get all choked up.

"And to think," she said, "I almost didn't marry Del."

Eddie's gaze jerked back to Galen, even though her attention was still riveted to the baby. "Why not?"

"Because I was scared."

"Of what?"

She lifted her eyes to his. "Of feeling safe, if you can believe that."

That he understood exactly what she meant didn't make her revelation any less startling. Nor did he miss the fact that she was obviously trying to make a point, one which he heard, all right, but wasn't about to take. Women were like that, always tryin' to fix up everybody else's lives the instant they got their own worked out. If not before. But he had exactly zip time to think about all this when Mala and the kids burst into the room, everybody carrying flowers or balloons or a present of some kind. Mala stopped dead in her tracks when she saw Eddie, her cheeks red as apples, though that could've been the cold. She'd once again shrouded herself in those godawful shapeless clothes she wore, but Eddie's skin heated at the thought of what was underneath.

"Come see, come see!" Galen squealed, oblivious to the crackling going on between Mala and him, then whispered, "How the heck did you get the kids in here?"

Mala yanked her gaze away from Eddie and scooted over to the bed, pressing her hand to her heart when she saw the baby. "They're supposed to be sitting outside in the hall," she said. "Soon as no one was looking, we snuck in. Oh, my God,

Galen—he's *gorgeous!*'' Then she looked at Galen, frowning. ''I hope you don't mind. That I brought the kids?''

Galen looked sternly at the pair of redheads now ogling her child. ''You guys have your rabies shots up-to-date?''

''Huh?'' said Carrie, wrinkling her nose.

''Never mind. So whaddya think? Isn't he just the cutest thing?''

Eddie watched in amazement as Miss Priss went all tender and mushy, even though she still managed to be her usual bossy self when Lucas tried to touch the baby, except then he caught the funny look Mala was giving the baby, and suddenly he didn't know where to look that wouldn't get him in trouble. Then the baby yawned or something, which made the kids start giggling and the women just go all to pieces. And Eddie watched all this as something hot and brutal crushed against his chest, and he thought about last night, and how Mala had felt in his arms and underneath him and how he'd never known another woman like her, never would again, and how he knew he should give her up and how he knew he couldn't, at least not yet, not until he got his fill of her, and oh, sweet heavenly Father, what if he never did?

Then Del and Wendy came in from wherever they'd been, and Wendy came right up to him and gave him a big hug which he hadn't expected and didn't know what to do with, and the room swirled with all these smiles and all this laughter and none of it was for him, it never was, never would be, and who the *hell* did he think he was kidding, pretending like he was a part of this?

''I gotta go,'' he said, and bolted from the room.

Mala nearly slipped on the tile floor in her rush to get out into the hallway. ''Eddie! Wait!''

He hadn't gotten very far, a few feet, maybe. But he turned, his fists rammed into the pockets of the shearling jacket, his features strained, and she felt his fear as sharply as if it had been her own.

She understood. Sympathized, even. But damned if she was going to let him run again.

"What was that all about?"

"I don't know. I don't…" He paced away, then turned back, rammed a hand through his hair. "I suddenly felt…"

"Like you were being smothered."

"Yeah," he said on an exhaled breath.

"Hey, if it makes you feel any better, being around that much happiness makes my teeth ache, too."

After a moment, she saw him relax. Not a lot. But enough.

"So it's not just me?"

"God, no. I've just become more inured to it, that's all."

But her reassurance hadn't eased the panic in his eyes, and the hope she'd felt for a few crystal clear moments last night quickly faded. An overly cheerful orderly wheeled the lunch cart onto the floor, stopping at the room next door. Which meant Galen's was next, which was crammed with at least three people too many.

"Oh, crud—" She whirled around, one hand on the door. "I've got to get the kids out!"

Eddie grabbed her by the arm. "Wait, Mala—I just want you to know…"

"That last night was great, but—"

"Dammit, woman, you got a real problem with letting folks finish their sentences, you know that?"

She stilled, caught in that intense blue gaze, then said, "Sorry. Automatic reaction to waking up alone."

Eddie swore, then shook his head. "I'm sorry. I…needed some time to think, is all," he said, his voice no louder than a breath. "And I came down this mornin' to apologize and explain, but you'd already taken off. But I just want to say, from my standpoint, at least, last night wasn't a one-night stand. Not if you don't want it to be—"

"I don't."

"I swear, I'm gonna start clamping my hand over your mouth."

"Okay, okay…I'm sorry. You were saying?"

"As long as you understand, I can't offer you…what those people have in there. I don't know how to be the kind of man Del is. Or your brother or your father. And I still think that's not fair to you—close your mouth, Mala, until I've said my piece—but you've turned me inside out with wanting you, and I'm not just talking about sex, even though that would be the safest thing, especially since I'm still leavin', come spring, and here I am, standing here in the middle of a hospital hallway runnin' off at the mouth like a dadburned idiot...."

When she determined he'd run out of steam, she said, "Is it my turn now?"

He nodded, looking so bewildered, her heart twinged. She'd never seen a man look so...lost. And, oh, but it was so hard to stand back and give him the room he needed to find himself.

"Quit beating yourself up, okay? You don't have to apologize or explain yourself to me. All I want is to just enjoy...being with you, for as long as that lasts. But you know what? Nobody...." She swallowed, realizing she was starting to shake so hard she could barely talk. "Nobody's ever told me before that I turned him inside out. And you have no idea how much of a gift..."

Her voice caught. Eddie bent over, pressed his lips to her forehead. "Merry Christmas, Miss Mala," he whispered, then turned and strode down the hall.

Chapter 13

He'd been afraid, after the scene at the hospital the day Sam was born, that Mala'd go all mushy on him whenever they got together, which would seriously jeopardize their affair, which Eddie seriously did not want to happen. But since two weeks had passed without a single tear or shuddering sigh, Eddie had begun to breathe easier. After all, the day had been an emotional minefield, between the baby's birth and their having had sex for the first time and it being Christmas and all.

Not that her words hadn't affected him, about nobody having ever said anything like that to her before. And maybe, if he'd been smart, he shouldn't've said it to begin with. Except it was true, for one thing. And he wanted her to know she was more than just a body to him, for another. He just didn't want things to get, well, out of hand or anything.

Not that there seemed to be any danger in that, far as he could tell. She welcomed him into her bed when she could—which, with the kids being there so much, wasn't nearly as often as either of them would have liked—but didn't get all whiny and possessive when they had to be apart. Which was good. Real good. Especially as he didn't see the kids all that much, except in passing, so there was no way they were in any danger of pretending like they were a family or anything....

"Damn," he heard her say, her hand still on the kitchen phone receiver.

It was Saturday morning. She'd ambushed him when he'd come in last night, downright giddy with the news that *both* kids were spending the night elsewhere, and in fact, would be away all today as well, which was a blessing because she was hosting Galen's after-the-fact baby shower later and the last thing she needed was a pair of bickering children underfoot. So they'd taken advantage of the situation to enjoy the heck out of themselves most of the night and into this morning, but now it was nearly noon and he had to head into work in a couple hours and she had a mountain of stuff to do, she said, before the guests started arriving at two.

"What's up?" he said, sidling up to her and slipping his arms around her waist from behind, just to smell her, to feel her one last time before he left. And he knew he had to be careful, showing affection like that, but...

She sighed, leaning back against his chest, and he thought... Never mind what he thought.

"That was Tracy's mother. Where Carrie spent the night? Anyway, Tracy has a cold or something, so her mother's bringing Carrie home."

Eddie extricated himself from Mala while he still could, planted his butt on a chair to pull on his boots. "It's not that big a deal, is it? I mean, if she has to hang out during this shower thing?"

Mala gave him one of those looks women are just born knowing how to do. "In theory, no. But this *shower thing* is for women. As in, grown-ups. As in..." She waved her hand. "You wouldn't understand."

Eddie chuckled, let his foot clomp onto the floor. "I bet I can guess. Y'all talk about sex and stuff, and havin' a kid around'll cramp your style?"

"Honestly, Eddie. Why do men think that every time women get together, they talk about sex?"

"Hey. I've seen *Sex And The City*." Mala lifted her brows. "Once."

She laughed. "It's a *baby* shower, for God's sake. It's just that we can't hear ourselves think with the kids around, so we agreed we could all live without them for two hours."

Then he heard himself say, "Think she'd like to hang out with me at the restaurant? I mean, if that'd help?"

Mala gave him another look, one he couldn't translate right off, didn't figure he wanted to, but he also figured it wouldn't hurt to say, "Don't read anything into this, darlin'," and she said, "I wasn't."

Except Eddie had a very uncomfortable feeling one of them wasn't exactly being truthful, here.

In any case, that was how he came to have an oddly subdued little girl sitting up on a stool beside him as he added freshly grated Parmesean and Romano cheeses to the already ground mixture of basil, pine nuts and garlic in Galen's large marble mortar. Sure, he could make his pesto sauce in a blender—it was both quicker and easier—but there was nothing like the old-fashioned way to relieve tension. Which definitely needed relieving right about now. Carrie'd gone willingly enough with him, when her mama'd suggested it, but she wasn't exactly brimming over with enthusiasm.

"You haven't touched your pizza," he said, now adding olive oil, a few drops at a time, to the mixture, then some softened butter. He stirred, watching the kid off and on, then tasted…oh, yeah. He was *good*. Eddie picked up another spoon, dipped it into the sauce and held it out to her. "Wanna taste?" Curls danced when she shook her head. "Hey, sugar—you feelin' okay?"

Her eyes darted to his face along about the same time it hit him what he'd called her. That for some reason, he actually liked the little twerp, had ever since that afternoon when he'd put up the Christmas lights. Not that he was attached to her or anything, because he wasn't. But she was a spunky little thing, and smart, and it sickened him to think her own father had given up the chance to watch her grow up, see how she was gonna turn out.

And now, in answer to his question, she gave this sad little shrug which made Eddie's stomach flip.

"Okay, spit it out. What's the matter?"

When she looked up, he was startled to see tears hovering on her lashes. "How come you haven't been around? Don't you like me an' Lucas?"

Something like an electric jolt zinged through his veins. Eddie set the bowl of pesto aside, then started in preparing his veal cutlets. "'Course I like you. I've just been busy, is all."

"Oh." She picked up the pizza, nibbled at it, put it back down, then daintily wiped her hands on her napkin, even though they weren't dirty to begin with. "My daddy was here, did you know?"

Eddie's breathing hitched; he glanced over at the little girl, then returned to dipping the cutlets in the egg mixture Marlene had already prepared. "Oh?"

"Yeah. I heard Mama talkin' to Nana about it the other day, when she didn't know I was listening." She looked up at him, her eyes round with confusion. "He was here, but he didn't come to see me."

Oh, Lord. "Which is his loss, baby," he said carefully.

"Justin Martin, he's this kid in my class? He said I was too bossy, that nobody likes bossy girls."

"Yeah, well, some boys have trouble dealin' with strong women. So you can just tell Justin whatever-his-name-is to go…jump in a lake." Then it hit him.

He dropped a cutlet onto a platter of bread crumbs, looked her straight in the eye. "Don't tell me you think your daddy left because you're too bossy?"

She shrugged. Eddie swallowed down the choice cussword that tried real hard to get out. "That's bull, Carrie. And let me tell you something…why ever your daddy left, believe me, it's because there's somethin' wrong with *him*. Not you. You hear me?"

The little girl seemed to think that over for a minute, then said, "You think I'm strong?"

"Sure do. Just like your mama."

"Do you like Mama?"

Damn. "Everybody likes your mama, you know that."

"Daddy didn't."

"Honey, any man who'd leave your mama—" he flipped a half-dozen cutlets over in the bread crumbs "—and you and Lucas—has a serious screw loose. And you can tell anybody who asks I said so."

Carrie suddenly beamed, then picked up the pizza and took a big old chomp out of it, like the weight of the world had just been lifted from her shoulders.

Only to settle inexplicably right smack on Eddie's.

Okay, so maybe this wasn't turning out to be like any baby shower she'd ever been to. What it was, was like being trapped in an edition of *Cosmo! Live!* Which is what happened, Mala supposed, when you took a group of otherwise educated, accomplished women and detached them from their children for longer than twenty minutes. Especially *this* group of educated, accomplished women. The music was jumpin', there wasn't a thing on the food table that wasn't on the Heart Association's hit list and the hottest argument of the afternoon had been over which male movie star had the cuter butt.

God, she hadn't had this much fun since—

"It's not fair."

—this morning with Eddie.

Brows raised, Mala turned to Nancy Braden, Hannah Braden's tiny, spunky stepmother and one of Galen's best friends. "What's not fair?"

Big brown eyes sparkled underneath a froth of impossibly kinky hair. "That you're the only unmarried woman in this room *and* I'm guessing the only one who got any last night."

Mala nearly choked on one of her mother's Swedish meatballs. "Excuse me?"

"Ladies?" Nancy turned toward the clot of women in the center of Mala's living room, rapping her spoon on her plate. "Quick poll, okay? And no cheating. Who among us has had sex within the last twenty four hours?"

That got several groans, a few titters, one shriek of outright laughter—from Galen, who'd only given birth three weeks before—but not a single, solitary raised hand.

Nancy turned back to Mala with a triumphant smirk. "I rest my case."

"But I didn't say—"

A red-tipped finger snagged Mala's oversize sweater collar, tugged it down. "Ahem. Exhibit A. Fresh hickey. And a damned nice one, too."

"God, Mala." Elizabeth Sanford appeared out of nowhere, forking her fingers through her newly cut Successful Realtor blond 'do. "You're positively glowing. Is it your makeup?"

Nancy snickered. "Maybe it's Maybelline, and maybe it's—"

"Hey, Ma!" Mala caught her mother's approach out of the corner of her eyes, grabbed her by the arm and steered her toward the far end of the table. "Did you try some of Sophie's…" She glanced over. "…stuff?"

Bev gave her a squinty-eyed look, then gasped. "Ohmigod, the drought is over, isn't it?"

"And has been for some time, if those pink cheeks are any indication," Sophie said, her tummy round underneath a baggy sweater.

Talk about wanting to die. Except the worst was far from over, because then somebody—her mother, no less—said, "It's Eddie, right?" and Nancy said, "Eddie who?" which prompted somebody else to say, "Eddie King, from the restaurant, who else?" and Elizabeth clapped Mala hard enough on the back to make her choke on another meatball and said, "Way to go, *Mala!* He is so *hot!*"

At which point, Galen called out from across the room where she sat nursing Sam on Mala's sofa, "Hey, guys—have pity on the poor woman stuck over here with baby attached to her breast. What's going on?"

"Nothing!" Mala practically shrieked, her cheeks burning, and the room fell silent. Except later, when she'd escaped into the kitchen, Galen came in and put an arm around her shoulders and said in that soft way of hers, "Is he worth it?"

Mala met the redhead's trenchant gaze and sucked in a breath. "Yeah."

Galen smiled. "You know, Del didn't give up on me, even when I ran screaming in the opposite direction. He just waited until I got tired of running." She folded her arms over her middle, her smile growing wistful. Content. "And I can't tell you how glad I am he did. And you know what I think?"

"What?"

"That one day, Eddie's going to thank you for not giving up on him, either."

"...anyway, it's not a big deal or anything. Just a bunch of football fanatics yelling and screaming and stuffing their faces with junk food in front of Pop's big-screen TV."

In the midst of slipping on his Henley T-shirt, Eddie twisted around, his insides torquing at the sight of Mala lying on her side in the rumpled bed, her head propped in her hand, her dimples on full display. He'd surprised her in the middle of the day, dragging her away from her work despite her laughing shrieks of protest. Now, an hour later, her hair was an electrified mess, her skin still flushed from their lovemaking and the short nap she'd taken while he'd showered.

It had snowed again last night, just enough to brighten up the week-old slush and set her bedroom—and her—to glowing from the reflection. She'd pulled up the sheet in a half-assed nod to modesty, but her dark nipples were easily visible beneath the smooth, white cotton.

Lord above, this was The Ideal Situation for a man, wasn't it? A great lady who laughed and listened and made him feel impossibly good when he was with her, brain-scrambling sex and not a string in sight. Yet, he couldn't deny the tension that shimmered just below the surface. And the weird thing of it was, it was because she *wasn't* demanding that he felt so off-balance.

When this ended, they would have had something like three months together, which was longer than any affair he'd ever had. Longer, even, than his marriage had lasted.

Yet it would be over in a heartbeat.

"Hey," she said gently, stretching out one foot under the covers to prod him in the butt. "I know that last time was pretty good, but did you go deaf or what?"

He forced himself out of the melancholy he was too damn close to slipping into and scrambled back across the bed. *"Pretty good?"* With a growl, he loomed over her, grinning when she dissolved into giggles. Damn, but it made him feel good, making her laugh. "My ears *are* still ringing, now that you mention it, and you're tellin' me it was only *pretty good?"*

"Okay, okay," she managed breathlessly when he pretended like he was going to tickle her. "It was out of this world."

"That's more like it," Eddie said, pushing himself off the bed to stand at the edge farthest from her, only to dodge the pillow now sailing in his direction.

"God, you are such a man," she said, but she didn't seem any too upset about that fact. Nor did she seem particularly aware that the sheet had slipped.

It was everything Eddie could do not to rip off his clothes and crawl right back under those warm, sex-and-perfume scented covers and lose himself once again in all that softness and laughter and generosity. They'd even managed to get through this time without scrapping over something. Although, to tell the truth, it kind of got his blood going when they argued, made him feel like…like maybe she really gave a damn.

His heart racing, Eddie grabbed his lined flannel shirt from the chair by the bed and shrugged into it, only to find himself once again bending over Mala, his hands braced on the mattress.

"You're incredible, Miss Mala," he whispered, his insides cramping all over again at her smile, as pleased and ingenuous as a child's. Then the smile softened, the expression in those yellow-green eyes shooting straight to where he'd packed his soul away in dry ice, a thousand years ago.

"So are you, Eddie," she said. "And you haven't answered my question."

"I know I haven't," he said, straightening.

"It's just a Superbowl party, for heaven's sake.…" She threw back the sheet and got out of bed, tucking all those sweet curves into that ugly robe of hers. "And there will be so many people crammed into my parents' little house, nobody'd even know you were there." She yanked the tie closed on the robe, then giggled.

"What's so funny?"

"Me," she said with a huge grin, padding over to him and slipping her arms around his waist. "I just made love in broad daylight. Wow. I'm getting downright decadent in my old age."

Eddie waited for the familiar feeling of suffocation to claw at his lungs, more startled than not when it didn't come. But it would, if not now, then later, when he least expected it.

It always did.

He gave her a nice, slow, we-just-had-incredible-sex-in-the-middle-of-the-day kiss, then an extra one on top of her head for good measure. "So. When's this party?"

Her eyes brightened. "You'll go?"

He kissed her on the nose. "I'll think about it. Don't want your folks to go getting any wrong ideas about us, right?"

Her expression unmistakeably dimmed, even as she crossed her arms underneath her breasts and gave him one of her take-no-bull looks. "They won't. After all, you live upstairs, you're free that day and you're nuts about football. Inviting you is just the logical, not to mention polite, thing to do. There's nothing to be nervous about."

He dropped into the chair, thought about that as he yanked on his boots. Thought more about the way Mala's robe was gaping open like that. "The only thing making me nervous," he said as he got up, "is the condition I'm gonna be in if I don't get out of here within the next five seconds."

Her wicked laughter followed him as he headed out of the room and toward the front door. He'd just reached for the knob when he heard, "Oh, Eddie…?" in a gravelly, singsong voice behind him.

Against his better judgment, he turned. Mala stood in front of the stairs, pure, unadulterated trouble blooming in her great big eyes as she whipped open the front of her robe. "We'll be waiting for you," she said in what he was sure was meant to be a sultry voice, except she collapsed into helpless laughter before she finished getting the words out.

On a groan, he zipped out the door, slamming it behind him.

But he was grinning like a dadburned fool all the way to work.

* * *

She stood at the living room window like some lovesick teen-ager, watching him fold that long, lean body that had so recently been folded around hers into his car. If she had known that sex could really be this much fun, that it really was possible to find a lover who could be both tender and passionate, that this wasn't just *Redbook* hype, she'd've set her sights a damn sight higher to begin with.

Now that her mother knew about…things, she'd bugged Mala half to death about inviting Eddie to the Superbowl party, to encourage him to feel more like one of the family. When Mala finally took the bull by the horns and pointed out that Eddie was leaving in a few months, no matter what, her mother had only shrugged and smiled.

If you had to pin down why the human race had survived as long as it had, Mala mused, it would have to be because women were unshakeably optimistic.

The Koleskis' driveway looked like a used car lot, as did several of the houses Eddie had passed on the ten block walk from Mala's house. Folks took Superbowl Sunday seriously around here, looked like. It had already been dark for some time, but an overflow of kids of all shapes, sizes and hair colors had spilled out into the small, chain-link-fenced front yard, whooping and shrieking their heads off as they played a football game of their own in the deeply shadowed light spilling from the porch. Carrie spotted Eddie and made a beeline for him, chattering a mile a minute about heaven-knew-what, but Eddie noticed that Lucas was hanging back in the shadows, his hands stuffed in his jacket pockets. Eddie could see that the kid was obviously torn in two, wanting to get involved at the same time he was afraid to.

Eddie looked up at Mala's folks' front door as he sidestepped the kids to get there. Yeah, he could relate to that, boy.

And had been, before he was even as old as Lucas, Eddie realized. Maybe he'd handled his own fear of rejection, of being hurt, differently from Lucas, but when it came right down to it, whenever he looked at Lucas it was like looking at old movies of himself at that age.

He was still watching the little boy and puzzling over this when the front door swung open. Eddie whirled around to run smack into Mala's brother's steady, green-eyed gaze.

Eddie had met him on occasion, when Steve and Sophie had brought their brood into the restaurant, but it always startled him just how damn big the guy was. So when, like a big old rottweiler wagging its tail, a smile branched across Steve's face, that went a long way toward easing Eddie's mind.

"Eddie, hey! Mala told us you might stop by! Come in, come in—" Steve backed away from the door, which led directly into a small, very crowded, very blue living room with an enormous TV at one end. Right on Eddie's heels, all the kids trooped in, flopped wherever they could find a spot on the floor. "Wanna beer?"

"Yeah, sure, that'd be great."

Steve disappeared toward the sound of female cackling coming from the back of the house, leaving Eddie standing at the back of the packed room with his hands in his jeans pockets, trying not to look so much like a bump on a log.

Except at that precise moment, Mala spotted him. Her mouth dropped in surprise, then she jumped up from where she was wedged on the sofa between her father and a tall, spiky haired teenager Eddie recognized as one of Steve's soon-to-be-adopted wards. Wearing a loose white sweater and jeans, she wriggled her way through the crush of male bodies and over to Eddie, her face lit up brighter than the Christmas lights he'd finally gotten around to taking down a couple days ago. For a moment, he thought she might hug him, only to realize there was no way she'd do a thing like that. Not here, and certainly not with a dozen pairs of eyes riveted to them.

"I really didn't think you'd come."

"I didn't know I was going to, up until a little bit ago."

She reached out to briefly squeeze his arm, then said, "Well, I think you pretty much know everyone who's here. Steve and Sophie and my parents, of course. And all the kids. And—oh, wait a minute." She stuck two fingers in her mouth and whistled over the din. "Hey, Alek!"

At her call, a man with hair darker than Eddie's looked over, then stood, which is when Eddie realized he was cuddling a baby not a whole lot bigger than little Sam Farentino. Stepping over assorted children sprawled on the small patch of wall-to-wall carpet crammed between the coffee table and the TV, the man approached Eddie and Mala, a broad grin splitting handsome, angular features that looked vaguely familiar.

"Eddie King, Alek Vlastos, my brother's brother-in-law. Sophie's brother."

"Oh, right, that accounts for why you looked familiar." With a smile of his own, Eddie stuck out his hand before it occurred to him that this just wasn't any old relative-by-marriage, but a real live prince, standing here with baby spit up on his expensive sweater, surrounded by cans of domestic beer and bowls of chips, salsa and pork rinds. And looking just as happy as a clam about it, too.

The prince adjusted the sleeping baby on his shoulder, took Eddie's hand. "Ah, the chef, yes?" Laugh lines branched out from the corners of pale silver eyes, their gaze direct and honest. After a brief, strong shake, he said in his foreign-sounding accent, "Luanne and I stole an hour to ourselves and had dinner at *Galen's* the other night. It was superb."

"Thanks. That means a lot, coming from you."

The grin broadened. "Mala tells me you're from Texas?"

"Yes, sir, I am. Originally, anyway. I haven't been back there for some time."

"We just came from there. My wife was born in Sandy Springs, have you heard of it?"

"Matter of fact, I spent a summer there once. Long time ago, though—"

Then Steve shoved a can of beer into Eddie's hand, and Alek excused himself to go change the baby, and Mala told Eddie if he didn't go back to the kitchen to say hi to her mother, Bev would have both their hides.

So he did, since he was rather partial to his hide, and Bev swooped him into her arms like he'd just come back from the wars. Then she introduced him to Luanne Vlastos, a very pretty brunette who looked and sounded like she should be up for a country music award, and the whole time he was talking to her, he was trying to come to terms with her being a princess. Then Sophie came in, followed by Mala, who slyly skimmed her palm across his butt when nobody was looking, nearly making him snort beer out his nose.

By this point, he decided there were far too many female bodies crammed into the tiny kitchen—although he burned for one of those bodies so bad, he was like to self-combust—so he opted to go back to the living room and the game. Except when he stepped out into the hallway, he thought he heard crying coming from one of the rooms down the hall. Kid's crying.

He thought about going back to the kitchen to tell somebody, only to realize that, with all these kids, it probably would make more sense to find out whose kid it was first. Otherwise, there'd likely be a stampede.

The whimpering was coming from behind a partially closed door near the end of the hall. Eddie slowly pushed open the door, saw Lucas sitting with his back to the door on a twin bed with a dark blue bedspread on it. His little shoulders were shaking something fierce, making something snap inside Eddie.

"Hey, buddy," he said quietly so as not to scare the boy. He walked into the room—a half-second's glance at all the sports trophies and what-all told him this had been Steve's room, once upon a time—and around the bed, lowering himself onto the edge of the mattress. "What's up?"

Lucas skootched away from him, his arms knotted tightly over his middle. "Go 'way," he said, but not like his heart was really in it.

"You want your mama?"

"Nuh-uh."

"You hurt or something?"

He shook his head.

"Somebody say somethin' to you, hurt your feelings?"

After a second, the boy sucked in a long, shuddering breath and said, "Dylan called me a baby 'cuz I said I didn't wanna play football."

"Dylan…that's Steve's youngest boy, right?"

He nodded.

"But isn't he younger than you?"

Lucas swiped his sweatshirted sleeve across his nose. "Yeah. But he's tougher 'n' me, too."

"Says who?"

"Everybody. Carrie calls me a weenie-baby 'cuz I cry so much."

"You ever see her cry?"

"Not much."

That figured.

"Well, buddy…"

Lucas's face jerked up. "An' you think I'm a baby, too, huh?"

"Well…" *Oh, boy.* "You do kinda tend to get real upset about things that aren't really all that important."

"You mean 'cuz it's not okay for a boy to cry?"

"Didn't say that. Sure it's okay for a boy to cry, if the occasion warrants it."

"You really mean that?"

"Wouldn't say it if I didn't mean it. Shoot, it's even okay for a grown man to cry from time to time. Just not every time he gets a little scrape or bumps something, y'know?" He leaned over, whispered, "That kinda gets on people's nerves, if you wanna know the truth."

Lucas seemed to think this one over for a bit, then said, "Bet *you* don't."

"Well, I suppose it has been a while. But that doesn't mean I can't. Or won't, ever again." Then he said, before the conversation got any nearer a sore spot Eddie hadn't even know existed until about two minutes ago, "So…how come you don't wanna play football?"

Lucas just sat and stared at his knees.

"You think it's dumb or something?"

"Nuh-uh. I think it's way cool. But…I'm scared of gettin' hurt."

"That's understandable. Football can get kinda brutal."

He looked up at Eddie, his eyes all watery behind his glasses. "An' I can't always catch the ball, which makes the other kids get mad at me and yell at me an' stuff. Especially Carrie. An' my glasses get knocked off sometimes, an' then I can't see when the kids are comin' at me.''

"Yeah, I can see where that could be a problem. But you know, it doesn't make you a baby, avoiding something that could get you hurt."

The kid reached up, fiddled with his glasses. "You play football?"

"Not much anymore. But I used to some, when I was younger."

"Bet you weren't scared."

"No, but only because I was too dumb to know any better."

Lucas sorta laughed at that, which made Eddie feel pretty good. Which in turn made him feel like those damn walls were closing in on him again. "So the question is," he went on, "if you weren't so scared of gettin' hurt, and if you could catch better, would you like to play?"

That got a shrug. Which prompted Eddie to open his big mouth and say, "I suppose I could give you a few pointers," and the words exploded inside his head, because that meant sticking around, didn't it? And where'd he get off, offering to be something to this little boy he knew he couldn't be?

Then he saw the look on Lucas's face, like Eddie had just promised him the moon or something, and he felt this odd stirring inside him, something that felt an awful lot like joy, even though he felt lower than a worm at the same time.

"Hey, let's you and me go find something to eat," he said, somehow, over the tightness that had taken root smack-dab in the center of his chest. He stood up, holding out his hand to Lucas, which was another mistake because the instant that little hand landed in his, all trusting like that, Eddie's heart screamed inside his chest because, dammit, he did want to stay around and teach the kid how to play football and how not to be so scared all the time, even as he realized that was, without a doubt, the dumbest thought he'd ever had since right after his mother had died and he'd hoped with all his heart that his father would come get him and take him away to live with him.

Oh, yeah, boys cried, all right. And Eddie had done more than his fair share of it back then, and he hadn't liked it much, as he recalled. Especially the ache that came with the tears, the hollow, cramping pain that came from knowing how much it hurt when people died or went away or just plain outright let you know you weren't really wanted.

No, it didn't make you a baby, avoiding something that could hurt you. Or any less of a man. He remembered then why he lived the way he did, why he avoided entanglements. He'd been through as much pain as he ever cared to, thank you. All he wanted now was to be left alone, to live out his days in peace.

But right now, he had this little kid's hand in his, and it felt almost better than anything he'd ever known, maybe even better than how it felt to make love to the boy's mother…

…who was standing in the doorway with one of those sappy looks women get on their faces at moments like this.

Damn.

He was having some sort of crisis again. Mala could see it in his face, feel it in the waves of tension pouring off of him. Oh, he'd smiled and chatted and rooted for the Lions like everybody else, had joined in taking sides when her parents had gotten into one of their good-natured tiffs about something, but something had happened, during that talk with Lucas. Something that was making the hair stand up on the back of her neck.

It wasn't until half-time that she realized Eddie had disappeared. She didn't think he'd just leave without saying something to somebody, but…

A quick tour of the house revealed nothing. Then she happened to go into her old bedroom for a moment to get a little car out of her coat pocket to prove to Lucas that it wasn't lost, she did have it. She hadn't bothered to turn on a light, which meant she could see out into the backyard, illuminated somewhat by the lights Pop had set up around the deck. Way over by the back wall, something or somebody moved. She called Lucas and gave him the car, then sent him back to the living room before slipping on her coat and quietly letting herself outside.

Eddie was standing as far away from the house as he could get, hands in his jacket pockets, staring up at the full moon.

"The instant you howl, I'm outta here," she said from a good six feet away.

Nothing. She swallowed, stuffed her hands in her own pockets, already knowing the way a woman does that it was over. That she'd lost. But she still said, "Um, if you don't get in there soon, I can't guarantee the locusts will have left anything."

Now he twisted slightly, his expression unreadable. Bands of light from the house sliced across the yard, mingling with the deck lights, barely reaching this far back.

"I can't do this," he said.

"Do what? Eat my m-mother's cooking?"

"Your voice is shaking."

Damn. "Yeah, well, it does that when I'm scared."

He turned more fully, enough for her to see the sadness in his eyes. "And what's scaring you, Miss Mala?"

"You are. Eddie, for God's sake—it's only a Superbowl party. We didn't even arrive together."

"And I'm the only non-family member here. You think I didn't notice that?"

"Del and Galen were invited, but they opted to go to his father's instead. And the Metlocks next door didn't come because she's got a bad cold. What are you implying? That I set you up or something?"

"You tell me."

That did it. "Okay, fine. Yeah. I set you up but good, boy. Whoo-hoo, let's all get wicked Mala for daring to bring a little fun into Eddie King's life—"

"Oh, don't go getting all over-dramatic on me, Mala—"

"How is it such a crime to try to make you feel part of something?"

She watched as her words hit their target.

"How could I ever really feel a part of what y'all have? I'm just a stray, an outsider—"

"By your choice, Eddie."

"That's where you're wrong."

"No, I'm not. God—you're just like Grateful was, when you first brought him home. Remember how he'd snatch the food from my hand, then scurry back under the cupboard? How many times did he do that before he learned to trust me? How many times are you gonna stick your toe in the water before you realize you won't drown if you get all the way in?''

He snapped his head away, a muscle ticking in his jaw.

Oh, God, Eddie…you're so close. You're so…damn…close….

''And did you happen to take a good look at this family?'' she went on, desperate to at least keep him within the range of her voice, petrified if she stopped talking, he'd leave. ''My father never even finished high school. He's worked with his hands all his life. But he made good and sure both Steve and I went to college, and now my brother's married to an Oxford-graduated princess who speaks five languages. But *her* brother's married to a country girl who sounds just like you. Far as I can tell, the only requisite for fitting in around here is being human. Which is why I suppose Scott never did make the grade.''

It was brief, but she caught the smile. Then he said, ''You're asking too much of me, Mala.''

''Oh, for crying out *loud!*'' She stomped away, her arms braced across her ribs, tears burning her eyes, the back of her throat. But they were for him, she realized, far more than for her.

She turned back. ''The only thing I ask…'' *Oh, what the hell.* ''All I'm asking is for you to accept my love. Not return it,'' she added when shock streaked across his features. ''Just… accept it.''

''Dammit, Miss Mala,'' he said softly, after several excruciating seconds. ''You weren't supposed to fall in love with me.''

''So sue me.''

Anger flared in his eyes. ''This isn't fair. We both knew goin' in what the limits were, that neither of us was interested in anything permanent. So you haven't been completely honest with me, have you? You're just the same as all the rest, wantin' to clip my wings.''

''No, Eddie. You'd clipped your own wings long before I met you.''

She watched as his brows crashed together. ''And what in tarnation is that supposed to mean?''

"It means you're so damn busy blaming the past, you've totally lost sight of the present. That you work so hard at keeping yourself from getting hurt again, you refuse to grab hold of the happiness that could be yours."

"That's bull, Mala. Besides, I told you, I'm no good at this kinda thing. I don't how to be a family man."

"And you never will until you get over yourself and *try*."

He stood stiffly, not looking at her, his hands still rammed in his pockets. Then he said, "I think maybe I'd better go," and she said, "Fine."

His gaze flicked to hers. "You know I did not want to hurt you—"

"I'm not."

"—or make you mad."

"Not that, either."

"You sure?"

"Eddie, I knew what I was getting into, okay? Maybe it didn't work out the way I hoped, I'll admit that, but I knew the odds were against me."

And still he stood there, not looking at her, his jaw rigid. "I just don't want you to feel sorry for yourself," he said quietly.

"Trust me. I'm not the one I feel sorry for."

After another moment he said, "There a way out of here without goin' through the house?"

"Side gate. To your right."

She stood, listening to his heavy footsteps crunching the dry grass, then the whine of the metal gate opening, slamming shut.

Her mother was alone in the kitchen, spreading out yet more hot wings on a cookie sheet, when Mala came in. "God, Ma," she said, taking off her coat, "like dinner wasn't enough?"

Bev shoved the sheet into the oven, took one look at her daughter and frowned. "What happened?"

Well, there was little point trying to skirt the issue, wasn't there?

"Eddie went home. Said to say thanks, he had a good time."

"Oh, hell, honey…it didn't work?"

And of course, her father picked that precise moment to walk into the room. "What didn't work?"

"Mala and Eddie, whaddya think? God, men can be so dense. They just had a fight."

"We didn't have a *fight*—"

"When was this?"

"Just now," Bev said. "Out back. I saw 'em. Then he walks away, couldn't even come inside to say goodbye—"

"Ma, it's okay—"

"I'll kill 'im, swear to God—"

"*Pop!* Both of you, cut it out, because if you don't, I'm gonna cry, and that's the last thing I want to do be-cause…because…"

And on a sob, she sank into her mother's embrace, while Marty said, "What? What? Did I miss something here? I swear I'm gonna kill him!"

"Marty, put a lid on it," Bev said, then shushed Mala in her arms like she used to do when Mala was little. Except she wouldn't be shushed, so Bev moved them all out of the kitchen before anybody else came in, down the hall to Bev and Marty's bedroom, fussing at Marty to go away, this was women's stuff, only he said the hell it was, this was his daughter, so Bev gave up and told Marty to at least close the door, for godssake, and keep his mouth shut.

Then she sat with Mala on the edge of the four-poster bed that Mala used to crawl into with them when she was little and still afraid of the Bogeyman. And all these words just came pouring out of her, about how she'd given it her best shot and how she knew this was probably how it would end so she had no business feeling bad except, oh, God, the look on his face nearly killed her because he was a good man and the best thing that had ever happened to her and why couldn't he get it through his thick head that he was worthy of being loved? And Ma said, "I know, honey, I know," over and over again, while Pop just kept saying, "I don't get it. The guy dumps you, and you feel bad for *him?*"

To which her mother said, "Of course you don't get it, Marty. You're a man. And if you don't get the hell out of here, right now, you're never going to *get it* again, got it?"

And through her tears, Mala had to laugh, that after nearly forty years, her mother could still manipulate her father by threatening to withhold sex. "I just can't compete with you," she said, and her mother was obviously about to give one of her smart comebacks when her eyes suddenly went wide behind her glasses.

"Oh, my God...you really mean that, don't you?"

Mala gave a shaky sigh. And when she said, "Yes. I really do," it wasn't with anger, or even annoyance, as much as simple resignation. "No matter how hard I try to keep the house clean or the cookies baked or a man interested, you always got me beat."

Her mother stared at her for some time, as flabbergasted as Mala had ever seen her. Then she shook her head, swore, and said, "Why do women do this to themselves?"

"Do what?"

"Try to impress their own mothers. God knows, I nearly drove myself nuts, trying to meet my mother's standards. Or worse, my *grandmother's.*" She frowned at Mala. "I bet you run around cleaning the house when you know I'm coming over, don't you?"

She nodded. Sniffed.

"And because *I* baked for every class party, you feel *you* got to, right? Even when the kid tells you like five minutes before they go to bed, so you stay up half the night so you won't disappoint them?"

Mala looked at her mother. "Yeah. I do."

"And now I bet you've got come cockamamie idea that because your father and I have stuck together for all these years, we've got some kinda magic formula for marriage that you think's outta your reach, right? Well, you listen to me, little girl, and you listen good." Bev lunged over, grabbed Mala's hand. "There's nothin' magic about it. What it is, is plain bullheaded endurance, because, in case you haven't missed it, your father and me, we drive each other nuts."

"But you love each other."

"Of course we do. That don't mean we don't want to do each other in on a regular basis."

''Oh.'' Mala got up from the bed, plucked a bunch of tissues from the box on her mother's nightstand. Sat back down again. Then she went through this routine where she kept opening her mouth, but nothing came out.

''I know what you're thinkin','' her mother said.

''Good.'' Mala honked into the tissue. ''Fill me in.''

''You're thinkin', somehow it was you who screwed up, picking Scott. And it was you who screwed up, again, fallin' for Eddie. Well, let me tell you something, okay? Scott left you because, for one thing, he didn't know what to do with a good woman, and for another, he's a schmuck. But Eddie left because he's mixed up and hurting about things that have nothin' to do with you, I'll bet my life on it. And maybe you think he's the best thing that ever happened to you, and maybe he is, I don't know, but I do know that you're the best thing that ever happened to *him,* only it's gonna take him some time for him to realize that. Like I said, men are dense.''

''Then why do we love them so much?''

Bev shrugged, then dragged Mala back into her arms. ''Because who else is gonna make us feel so good about being women, huh?''

The kids had conked out by the end of the game, so Pop volunteered to help Mala get them home, which was either his way of playing the supportive father, which while annoying at the moment, was nice, or he was using this as an excuse to get close enough to Eddie to beat the snot out of him, which was both annoying and not nice at all.

Not that he said much on the short drive to her house, but then, pithy conversations weren't exactly Pop's strong suit. They carried in the kids; Mala put first Carrie, then Lucas into bed—jammies yes, teeth no—then wandered back into the kitchen, where she heard her father rummaging around in her cupboards.

''Where the hell you keep the coffee filters?''

''Right by the coffee…maker…''

She froze at the sight of the set of keys and note on the counter.

Marty looked over. ''From him, right?''

"You didn't look?"

"No, Miss Smarty-pants, I didn't look. And how'd he get in, anyway?"

"Same way you and Ma do. He knows where the key is."

"Oh." Then, "What's it say?"

She picked up the folded note, annoyed that her hand was shaking. His handwriting was terrible, which she found comforting in a perverse kind of way.

Think it's better if I just go on ahead and find someplace else for the rest of the time I'm here. Since I know you were counting on me being here through March, here's the rent to cover the two months.

This next part's real hard for me, since I'm not real good at putting things into words, but I just want you to know that I hope one day you get everything you want, Miss Mala, because nobody deserves it more than you.

Take good care of yourself,

Eddie

She handed the note to her father, and thought, well, hell— that was more than she ever got from Scott, wasn't it?

Chapter 14

February dragged by in its usual bleak way, a seemingly endless cycle of fresh snow and drab slush and muddy sneakers and squabbles when it was too icky to go outside and even more endless questions about why Eddie had moved out when Carrie had seen him at Krogers just the other day when she was in there with Nana Bev and didn't he like them anymore? Lucas, especially, seemed more inclined to moping than usual, which tore at Mala's heart. She'd find him sprawled on his bed, flipping though books he couldn't yet read, the pup stretched out beside him in silent commiseration, but if Mala asked him if he was okay, he'd just shrug.

Which was about her reaction whenever anyone asked her if she was okay, too.

She was…managing. Holding her own. Coping. She took care of her kids and met with clients and cleaned house and played with her nieces and nephews and basically acted as though nothing had changed.

Except *she* had.

Everything had.

Mala told herself it was just the never-ending gray weather

that was getting to her, combined with her surly children and the steadily escalating frenzy of tax season. But a person can only lie to herself for so long. In Mala's case, she barely made it to Valentine's day. And now it was the last day of February and she really needed to do something about finding a new tenant for the apartment, except she didn't really need to, yet, since Eddie had paid up for another month.

Seated at the computer in her home office, Mala rubbed her eyes with the heels of her hands, then she tried again to focus on the file glaring back at her and told herself, very sternly, that none of this was anybody's fault.

But God, she felt so empty inside. Worse, even, than she had with Scott. Much worse, because, after all, Scott was a scuzzbag. Eddie didn't even come close.

Did she miss the sex? Sure she did. There were nights she woke up craving Eddie's touch so much she nearly cried out with it. But she missed far, far more than that. She missed *him,* his goodness and gentleness and the way he'd poke at her fears and make her take good, long, hard looks at herself.

The tears came, as they always did. She'd never met another man like Eddie, never would again. He'd been her one last shot at a dream she'd just about given up on, the prince she'd always envisioned as sweeping her off her feet one day….

"Mama?"

She swiped at her eyes, smiled for her daughter. "What is it, honey?"

"Did you see? The crocuses came up in the backyard! Come look!" Carrie grabbed her hand and tugged her up from her chair. "Come on, Mama!"

With a sigh, Mala let her child drag her out to the backyard, where, sure enough, a whole bevy of purple and white and yellow flowers had sprung up all over the still-dead lawn. Mala smiled at the cheerful little things, willing herself to believe that, just when things look their bleakest, something good always happens….

Then the dog trotted over to the biggest, prettiest, cheeriest clump of flowers and whizzed all over them.

* * *

"No," Galen said from behind her desk. "I'm not *asking* you if you want out of your commitment."

Standing just inside the door to her office, Eddie stared at her for several seconds, then let out a short, sharp laugh. "You cannin' me?"

"I suppose you could call it that." She opened her desk drawer, pulled out an envelope which she then held out to him. "With full pay for the rest of the month, needless to say."

Eddie stared at the envelope for several seconds, then lifted his gaze to the redhead's. "Look, I don't know what Mala's told you—"

"Actually, she hasn't said a word. She's got far too much class for that. But when she asked if I minded bringing over the restaurant's paperwork to her house, rather than her coming in here, I kinda figured it out. So I just think, since you were planning to leave anyway, and I said I'd be able to come back to work the first of March, this would make things easier. For everybody."

Eddie hooked his thumbs in his pockets. "Your friendship means that much?"

She lowered the hand holding the envelope, giving him a smile that seemed almost sympathetic. "It's called loyalty, Eddie. You know—not being afraid to stick by those who mean the most to you?"

Heat raced up his neck. No way was he getting into this with her. It was none of her business, what had gone on between him and Mala. Just like it was none of her business how many sleepless nights he'd had since the Superbowl party, worrying himself half to death that he'd hurt Mala, having no earthly idea how to go about checking up on her without making everything even worse than it already was.

He turned, stomped over to the door. "I'll finish out the night—"

"That won't be necessary," Galen said softly.

His hand braced on the edge of the door, Eddie turned back, a frown biting into his forehead. "I never pegged you as bein' the vindictive sort, Galen."

Her brows lifted, but she didn't seem the least bit offended.

"Vindictive? I just gave you the one thing you clearly value over anything else in the world. Your freedom. Oh, don't give me that 'she-doesn't-understand' look. Believe me, Eddie, I understand exactly what's going on inside your head. All too well. There was a time when I thought there was nothing more precious than my independence." She stood, walked around the desk, then folded the envelope in two, stuck it in Eddie's shirt pocket. "I was wrong."

Eddie yanked the envelope from his pocket and tossed it on top of a nearby filing cabinet before striding from the office.

Only, this was the first time he could remember leaving a place when he felt so much like he'd just run straight into…nothing.

He got out onto the street, the spring sunshine barely strong enough to cut the wind's bitter chill as he strode out to his car. Okay, fine, so he'd leave. Get the hell out of this town, away from memories he'd never wanted, had been stupid enough to collect. Once he'd left Mala's, he'd found a cheesy little place on the other side of town, all the better to avoid running into her. But there'd been that day a couple weeks back when he'd gone into the Kroger's close to the restaurant to pick up some extra veggies when they'd run out and had run into Carrie and Bev. And the confusion in Carrie's eyes, not to mention the censure in Bev's, was nearly his undoing. Clear as day, those amber eyes had said, "You at least owe my daughter an apology."

So now he found himself driving the few blocks to Mala's, his heart pounding so loud it was making his head hurt. For all he knew, she might not even be home.

Except she was, on her knees out front, planting flowers of some kind along the walk. Her back was to him, but he saw her whole body stiffen when he pulled up. When she didn't turn around, he realized two things: that she knew it was him, and that she had no intention of making this easy.

Mala heard the Camaro pull up—funny how you get used to the sound of certain car engines—but she didn't turn around, not even when she heard the car door slam. Her heart pounded in her chest in tandem with Eddie's boots thunking against the concrete.

"Hey," he said softly, right behind her, and her heart jolted into her throat.

She glanced up at him, then back at the hole she was digging for the next bedding plant, trying not to react when she sensed him crouching beside her.

"You sure those won't freeze?"

"They're pansies. They can withstand just about anything. Which is kinda funny when you think about what most people mean when they say 'pansy'…"

God. She was so pathetic.

After a moment, he said, "Galen gave me my walking papers."

Her gaze shot to his. "You're kidding?"

"Nope. Good as told me to get my sorry butt out of town."

The look in his eyes would be her undoing, if she didn't hold firm now. The man didn't have a mean bone in his body; it was patently obvious that what he'd done was killing him. She also knew this was her last chance at getting him to see what he was doing to himself. "I see." She swiped at a stray piece of hair with the back of her wrist. "So…are you?"

"Figured I may as well. But…"

"What?"

He exhaled loudly beside her. "It's just I don't like leavin' things this way."

"And what way is that?"

"Like what we had was just some kind of passin'…I don't know. Like it didn't mean anything. And why are you makin' me work so hard here?"

Finally, she sat back on her heels, squinted at him in the sun. "Because maybe you're the one who's got more work to do?"

He sort of smiled at that, then shifted to lean on one knee. Her heart nearly stopped beating at that. Only then he said, "You're the first woman it's ever pained me to leave, you know that? The thought of never seeing you again…" His face contorted as he shook his head. "You and the kids mean more to me than any people I've ever known since my mother died. And I'd like to think I could come back, every now and again, and visit you all—"

"No," she said, yanking her head around before his eyes got to her again. "It's like you said, when you first told me why this wouldn't work—I deserve more than that."

Finally, she dared to look back at him, because what she was about to say wouldn't mean jack otherwise. "You asked me if I ever considered what I wanted out of life, which is what got us into this situation to begin with, since I thought having a fling with you *was* what I wanted. Well, I was wrong. And I apologize for not understanding myself better, and for not listening to you to begin with. But the fact is…" She shook her head. "I do deserve more. Certainly more than a half-assed relationship with some guy who would always have one foot out the door, ready to take off when things got too…whatever it is they get for you. So, no. Don't bother coming back just to *visit.* And if that seems too demanding, well, tough. I don't know how to love any other way."

The pain in his eyes stood out sharp and clear. "I just wish I could've left you with something other than more heartache, Miss Mala."

Against her better judgment, she reached up, felt his roughened cheek beneath her fingertips one last time. "Oh, Eddie…but you're not, don't you see? I'd gone dead inside, more than I'd even realized. It was almost as if…as if I'd let Scott take my heart with him when he left. And how dumb was that? I looked like me, sounded like me, but I sure as hell didn't *feel* like me. So thank you, Eddie King. Thank you for giving me back my heart. For giving me back *myself.*"

A second, then two, ticked by; then he leaned forward, pressed his lips into her hair.

Then he was gone.

She managed to hold on to the tears until she could no longer hear the Camaro's engine.

Eddie'd gone on ahead and moved to Vegas, figuring he might as well get settled. Except, after nearly two weeks, he was anything but. For the first time in his life, that precious freedom of his sat in his mouth like a bad taste you can't get rid of, no matter what you do. He already hated Vegas with a passion, even though, once you got out of the flashy part, the surrounding areas weren't much different than most other places. He'd even found a nice one-bedroom in a quiet complex with no kids that he could tell, nobody paid him any mind or butted in his business or stopped him to chat. Just the way he liked it.

Or had, up until one smart-mouthed, dimpled brunette had wormed her way into his life.

Fact was, not an hour went by that he didn't think about Mala, or the kids, the way Lucas would smile up at him like Eddie was the best thing since sliced bread, the way Carrie would talk his ear off.

And after these endless days in what amounted to self-exile, Eddie had to admit all the arguments he'd spent a lifetime fine-honing against making a commitment meant diddly-squat. He got along with Mala just fine, even if they did snipe at each other from time to time. He'd seen her parents in action enough to realize, well, hey, that's what people who live together *do*. An argument now and again isn't fatal, for crying out loud. And as for the kids…well, yeah, sure, they still scared him. But far as he could tell, all parents felt that way—could they keep their kids happy and healthy and safe? Would they make the right choices, or screw up, bigtime?

Eddie sank onto the edge of the bed, letting his head drop forward into his hands. What was that she'd said, about how she'd been dead inside until he'd come along? He'd tried real hard to dismiss her words as nothing more than sentimental female claptrap, until it finally got through his thick skull that he'd been feeling the same way, only he'd been doing it for so long, he thought it was normal. Hell, he hadn't been content all these years; he'd just been numb. And now that Mala had jolted him back to life, there was no going back, was there?

Fact was, he was one lonely sonuvabitch. And had been, ever since he could remember. So the question was—he lifted his head, staring at his sorry-assed reflection in the mirror over

the blond wood dresser—what in tarnation was he gonna do
about it?

What she'd said, that night at her folks, was absolutely true:
he'd based every single decision he'd made since he was seventeen on his past, not the present. And certainly not the future.
And what was worse, he'd ordered his life in part on a past
that existed only in his own head. He had some nerve, thinking
he was free when the fact was he'd been imprisoned just as
surely as if he'd been behind twenty-foot high walls.

And nobody'd built those walls but him.

If he wanted to really be free, he'd have to take some risks.
Put his butt on the line. Quit blaming the past when he didn't
even have the guts to confront it.

He wouldn't be worthy of Miss Mala otherwise.

After a second, Eddie got up, yanked the *Rand McNally
Road Atlas* out from under the phone book.

If he hauled ass, he could make it to Albuquerque in seven
hours.

He parked in front of the modest, flat-roofed house, its earthy
stucco echoing the Sandia Mountains bordering the city to the
east, stark against the blazingly blue sky. Just barely leafing
out, a pair of ash trees studded a small, still thatch-gold lawn
neatly rimmed in junipers. An older neighborhood, Eddie sur-
mised, one in which the inhabitants were, if by no means
wealthy, at least managing okay.

Sitting in his car, he took in the satellite dish perched on the
roof, the daffodils and tulips crowding a small flower bed underneath a picture window bordered in bright turquoise. In the
side yard next door, somebody's dog started yapping its fool
head off.

He'd wiggled out of the job in Vegas, never mind that he
had no idea what he'd do next. Something'd come up, he imagined. It always had before, no reason to think it wouldn't now.

Wish he could be as sure about Mala, though. It hadn't been
long enough for her to get herself involved with somebody else
or anything like that, but he doubted she was sitting around,
pining for him. She wasn't that type. Besides, maybe she'd had

enough time to think things through, realize he really wasn't any good for her, anyway.

And maybe he needed to deal with the situation staring him in the face before he got to worrying any more about that one.

He got out of the car, stuffed his sunglasses in his jacket pocket.

A pudgy, dark-haired woman, her black eyes cautious behind overlarge glasses with a lot of flashy gold trim, opened the front door, leaving the screen door as a barrier between them.

''The sign says no solicitors,'' she said, but not harshly.

''I'm not tryin' to sell anything, ma'am. I'm looking for Rudy Ortiz.''

''Why?''

''My name's Eddie King, ma'am—''

The woman's hands flew to her face as she gasped, then began rattling in Spanish. ''*Dios mio!* You're Eddie? You actually came?'' She slammed back the screen door, nearly knocking him over before she grabbed his wrist, and yanked him inside a tiled entryway that smelled of fried onions, chili powder, cumin.

''Rudy!'' she shouted down the short hallway, off to their left. ''Get out here, *pronto!*''

Then she turned back to Eddie, tears glimmering in her eyes. ''I'm Rosalita, Rudy's wife. Lita, most people call me…'' She covered her mouth for another second or two, then let her hand drop. ''Oh, my God, you have no idea what this will mean to your father. I told him, a million times, he needed to tell you, to make you understand…but no, he said. I need to leave the decision entirely in his hands. And God's.'' Then she turned, shouted down the hall a second time, her voice almost frantic.

''I'm coming, woman,'' boomed a deep male voice laced with good humor. ''You know this damn thing only goes five miles an hour on a good day!''

Eddie barely had time to puzzle over the whirring sound before his father—and his wheelchair—came into view.

Declaring the two men needed to be alone to ''hash things out,'' Lita had pushed them outside onto the backyard deck she said Rudy had built before his accident. The yard wasn't enormous by any means, but the garden, ablaze with hundreds of tulips and just-flowering fruit trees, was meticulously groomed and obviously loved.

"Pretty, isn't it? If I'm good, Lita lets me sit on the ground and dig in the dirt," Rudy said, his voice edged with laughter. "I got in two hundred bulbs last fall, nearly killed me."

Eddie turned back to this stranger who accounted for half his genes, a broad-shouldered man with granite-colored hair and deep-set eyes the color of wet wood.

"Why didn't the P.I. tell me?" he asked quietly.

"That I was…what's the term they use these days? Physically challenged?"

Eddie nodded, sipped the iced tea Lita had handed him five minutes before.

"Because I didn't want you to come see me out of pity. Or guilt. That tea okay? I've got beer—"

"No. No, this is fine." He nodded toward Rudy's useless legs, sympathy, if not much else, fisting in his gut. "When did it happen?"

"Ten, eleven years ago. Drunk driver. They didn't think I would make it." He grinned, showing off straight white teeth against his dark skin. A handsome man, still. And, Eddie had to admit even after only a few minutes, a nice one, too. "They underestimated me…good *God,* you look exactly like your mother. The eyes… Hey," he said when Eddie turned away. "I loved her. You gotta believe that."

"You *left* her," he said to the back wall. "Left us."

"Yeah, I figured that's what you thought." At his father's quietly spoken words, Eddie twisted back to see his father's face twisted in consternation. "I didn't know about you until you went to live with that cousin of your mother's up there in Michigan."

"You expect me to believe that?"

"It's true, swear to God. Terese never told me, *nobody* told me. Except Molly, she remembered your mother and I were goin' together about then. If you can call it that."

Eddie's gaze tangled with the older man's for several seconds before agitation propelled him over to the edge of the deck. "Come to think of it, maybe I will have that beer."

"Good thinkin'. Lite or regular?"

"Whatever's handy. You want me to get it?"

"I'm crippled. Not dead." On that note, Rudy wheeled himself up the ramp leading into the kitchen, retrieved a couple of cans of Bud, wheeled back. "You ready to listen now?"

Eddie set the glass of tea on a nearby table, then leaned his hips on the deck railing, popped the top of the beer. "Yeah."

Rudy took a long pull of his beer, then squinted out over the yard. "I wasn't exactly who your mama's family had in mind for their daughter to be hanging out with. The son of a Mexican migrant worker? No way. But the minute I saw her, workin' out at the Dairy Queen, I was a goner. We started seein' each other, in secret, y'know? God, she was so pretty. And sweet as they come. Anyway, one thing led to another..." He let out a sigh, then fixed Eddie with his gaze. "We thought we were bein' careful. I loved your mother, sure, would've married her if there'd been a way, but I was twenty years old. She was seventeen. Neither of us needed a kid to worry about, that was for damn sure."

His jaw tight, Eddie stared hard at his beer can.

"But that doesn't mean I would've ever walked away from her. Or you, if I'd known about you. But when I drove by to see her at the Dairy Queen that day, and they told me she'd quit, that she'd moved away...what was I to think? I may have been in love, but I wasn't completely *loco*. I figured she'd come around to their way of thinkin', that she didn't want to see me no more. So I tied one on for three days, and after I sobered up, I enlisted in the Army.

"Time goes by." He took another swallow of beer. "I get out of the Army, decide to move here, meet Lita, fall in love again. Me and Lita, we figure we'd have a batch of kids, only it didn't happen. Suddenly I get this letter from Molly, a couple months before you turned eighteen. How she found me, I have no idea. I never got a chance to ask her. But anyway, she tells me she has every reason to believe that you're my son, if I want to see you, I'd better get my butt up to Spruce Lake. Only she told you about me, and you took off before I could get there. Never even gave me a chance to explain.''

Eddie looked down, tapping the can on the railing. ''I was scared.''

''Of *what?*''

Two little words, even packed with twenty years of bitter disappointment, weren't about to wipe out a lifetime of doubt. He met Rudy's troubled gaze. ''That all you wanted to do was satisfy your curiosity, then you'd take off again.''

''Then maybe you shoulda trusted a little more—''

''In what, dammit? I'd been kicked around from place to place my whole life. Nobody'd ever wanted me, except my mother, and she was gone by the time I was six. So why should the man I had every reason to believe had *never* wanted me suddenly change his mind?''

''So it was easier to run than take the chance that maybe you were wrong? It was easier to just give up, to curse fate and God and everybody else, because you'd gotten the shaft?''

Eddie looked at his father's legs and felt a great wave of shame wash over him. ''Yes,'' he said softly.

''And that's what you've been doing your whole life, isn't it? Runnin' away?''

There was little point in pretending otherwise. ''Yeah.''

''And now you've stopped?''

A shrug. ''Thinkin' more seriously about it, that's for sure.''

Rudy chuckled. ''A woman?''

''Yeah,'' he said again.

''She why you're here?''

Eddie turned. Nodded. ''She's one of those…persuasive types.''

Another laugh rumbled up from Rudy's barrel chest. ''Yeah, I know all about those. Been married to one for nearly thirty-three years.'' He paused. ''What's her name?''

''Mala,'' Eddie said, completely unprepared for what simply uttering her name would do to him. And apparently whatever thunderstorm was going on in his head was showing on his face, because his father's expression changed, too. Not that Eddie could put it into words, but it had.

"Once I knew you existed," Rudy said quietly, "I was determined to find you. But it costs money to track somebody down, money that kept running out as fast as you kept changin' where you lived. And there were long stretches of time when I was dead broke, when I had to give up the search. And believe me, that hurt far more than this—" he swiped at his legs "—ever did. To know I had a son I'd never seen, could never seem to catch up with…"

His father scrubbed his hand over his face, then finished off his beer. "But, hey, that's all in the past, right? Good things come from bad, like the phoenix from the ashes. I used part of the settlement I got from the accident to find you, to finally get my chance to tell you my side of the story, which is all I ever wanted."

Eddie kicked back the rest of his beer as well, crushed the can against the top rail of the deck. "You expect me to believe that?"

"I don't expect anything, Eddie. Certainly not for you to feel something for somebody you don't even know. Maybe still don't wanna know. But even if you walk outta here today and never come back, never want to talk to me again, you're gonna understand that you and me, we're part of each other. If I'd known about you, I would've wanted you, no matter what. And if anybody'd bothered to look me up, tell me I had a son—a *son*," he said, wonder softening his features, "you better believe nobody would've taken better care of you. You wanna know the biggest mistake of my life?"

"What?"

"That I didn't try harder to find Terese. Or at least, find out where she was, what'd happened to her."

Scraps of bitterness swirled through him. "Why didn't you?"

"I dunno. Because maybe it was easier to let myself believe it was for the best, that it probably wouldn't've worked between us, anyway?" He batted at the air. "Who knows? But if I'd had the *cojones* to look for her, I would've at least known about you." His intense brown eyes seared into Eddie's. "I know you don't think of me as your father, maybe you never will. But if I can leave you with one piece of advice, a legacy, you could call it, it'd be this—in the long run, the safe way is usually the dumbest.''

After a moment, Eddie chuckled, then looked out over Lita's pretty backyard, thought of another woman more than a thousand miles away, planting pansies when it was still the dead of winter.

A woman who embodied the word *hope.*

"Hate my guts if you want, but don't repeat history," his father said softly behind him.

Tax season was always nuts, but this year seemed nutsier than most. No matter how much Mala nagged her clients to get her all their information as soon after January 31 as possible, every single one of them, it seemed, had called her this past week with a frantic, "I have no idea where the time went, when can we get together?" plea.

Today it was the Hinkles, who'd called about five minutes after she'd picked up the kids from school. She already had a five o'clock, but she could squeeze them in at four, if she hurried.

Correction: if the *kids* hurried.

"Carrie! Lucas!" She jabbed her arms back into her sweater coat, quickly checked herself in the hall mirror to make sure what little lunch she'd gotten wasn't gracing her skirt and sweater. "You've gotta go to Nana's!"

Glass of milk in one hand, cookie in the other, Carrie's jaw dropped. "But we just got home!"

"I know, I know, but this is an emergency. And I've got like zero minutes to get you guys over there—Lucas? Where the heck *are* you?"

The toilet flushed, answering that question.

"Okay, guys," she said when Lucas emerged from the bathroom, "grab your backpacks if you've got homework and let's get out of here."

"Your job sucks," Carrie muttered.

"At the moment, I'm inclined to agree with you. Come *on*, Luc, geez!"

The frigid, sleety day had started out with pre-breakfast itchy-ickies and gone steadily downhill from there. That it should end in the current state of chaos came as no suprise. Mala shoved the grumbling, whining kids out the door, the dog back in, then herded them down the stairs and toward the car.

"C'n I please ride in the front?" came from the deep recesses of Lucas's parka hood.

"Luc, I've told you—"

"Pleeeeeassse? I'm not a baby!"

Shivering in the icy air, Mala yanked open her own door, scowled at her son over the hood. "It has nothing to do with—"

It was only ten blocks to her parents' house. By the time she won the argument with Lucas, she could have been there and back a dozen times.

"Okay, okay, fine. But just this once, you hear me? And buckle that seat belt. Oh, poop! I left my mobile in the house. Sit still, I'll be right back."

She grunted her way back up the stairs, unlocked the door, tromped around the house for a good half minute until she spotted the phone on the floor beside the dog's water dish— she didn't want to know—then flew back out of the house, stuffing her phone into her purse.

The weather had grown steadily colder and more miserable the farther north he'd driven. By the time he got back to Spruce Lake, a late season sleet storm reminded him that this far north, spring showed up when it damn well wanted to, not when the calendar dictated.

The streets had glazed over in spots, making driving treacherous even with good tires and nerves of steel. The Camaro's tires were okay—they'd managed just fine through the winter—but Eddie's nerves were something else again. After all, he was used to leaving.

Coming back, however, was a first.

He'd stayed in Albuquerque for a few days—after thirty-seven years, what else could he do?—until Lita had noticed his impatience and had goaded Rudy into letting his son go take care of his heart....

Just as Eddie turned onto Mala's street, three or four blocks from her house, the deluge let up enough for him to turn off the windshield wipers. The sight of Whitey in the driveway set his heart to thundering; the sight of the car backing out of the driveway drove it right up into his throat.

He let out a succinct curse as he watched the back end vanish in a puff of exhaust. If the streets'd been dry, he might've sped up to catch up with her, but he didn't dare try a trick like that in this weather, especially not with so many cars parked along-side the curb. Last thing he needed was to sideswipe somebody, lose time exchanging insurance information and what-all.

He saw her signal for a right at Lake Drive, cautiously turn the corner. Her folks lived that way—maybe that's where she was going. Eddie sped up as much as he dared, breathing a sigh of relief when he braked solidly at the stop sign, could see her heading straight over on Lake. Yep, that had to be where she was going. His heart whomping inside him like the bass on a boom box, he turned the corner, figuring he hadn't come all this way to go sit in some motel room and drive himself crazy while he waited until she got back home. When-ever that might be. Besides, he needed witnesses for what he was about to say, and he figured Carrie and Lucas and Bev Koleski would fit the bill just fine.

He was gonna tell her he loved her.

He was gonna ask her to marry him.

And at that last thought, the knot inside his chest he'd been coddling for most of his life suddenly unraveled, leaving in its place the first real sense of peace he could ever remember.

Only to be almost instantly annihilated as a pickup skidded, spun one hundred and eighty degrees and rammed its wonker back end into Mala's left front bumper, sending the puny little car flying off the road and into the trunk of some mother oak.

Chapter 15

Eddie screeched the Camaro to a halt twenty feet behind the Escort and erupted from the car, broken glass and bits of chrome crunching underfoot as he ran. His peripheral vision caught the truck's driver getting out, making his way over, but he was only aware of Mala, passed out over the wheel, bleeding some from cuts on her head and face. Eddie's gaze darted over to Lucas, strapped into the passenger seat, his stomach pitching when he saw the door partially crushed around his leg—

"Eddie!"

The instant Eddie yanked open the back door, Carrie flew into his arms, clearly in one piece but scared to death. Vaguely aware that people were beginning to clump around them, Eddie clung as hard to the little girl as she did to him, asked if Mala had her cell phone with her.

"I-in…her p-purse."

"Okay, baby? Let me set you down so I can get the phone—"

"I already called 9-1-1," somebody said. A woman, older, huddled inside a parka, worry crowding dark eyes. "Let me take the baby so you can check on 'em," she said, her offer trampled by the driver's horrified, "Oh, God, are they okay? I had no idea that ice was there—"

Eddie wrenched open Mala's door and lunged across her lap to get her purse, tucked beside her seat. Her breath fanned across his cheek, relieving him greatly, only then he looked over again at Lucas....

He tore the phone from the purse as he backed out of the car, called over to Carrie for her grandma's number. Over the sound of sirens wailing, onlookers murmuring, Carrie's tears, Eddie plowed through Bev Koleski's confusion, telling her to come, her granddaughter needed her—

"Mama!"

Eddie jerked around to find Mala had come to, that she was trying to move—

"Mala! Stay put, dammit!"

"Lucas!"

"He's still strapped in the car, honey." Eddie swallowed down his own fear, rancid and suffocating. "It's okay, looks like his hood kept him from gettin' cut by the broken glass..." He was rambling, anything to keep her from panicking, to keep him from losing it as well. "There—hear the sirens? Help's on its way, okay? You're all gonna be just fine...."

For the first time, Mala noticed Eddie's presence, which only seemed to add to her disorientation. "Eddie? What are you—? Where's Carrie...?" She tried to look over again at Lucas, only to cry out with pain.

Eddie crouched down beside her, grabbed her hand. "Stay still, baby, please. Carrie's okay, just shook up. I called your folks, they're on their way. The ambulance is just now gettin' here, you hear it? Everything's gonna be okay, honey...."

His heart tore in two at the tears slipping down Mala's bloodied cheeks, at the silent sobs she couldn't restrain, in spite of her obviously hurting so bad. "Lucas?" she whispered. "Lucas, talk to me, for God's sake, *talk to me!*"

"He's knocked out," Eddie shouted over the din of a half dozen vehicles roaring onto the scene. "But he's okay..."

He's gotta be, please, God...he's gotta be...

Emergency personnel suddenly swarmed the scene, all shouting to each other and moving with an urgent confidence that went a ways toward settling Eddie's nerves. Dispatch radios squawked as Eddie stood; somebody bumped him so that he stumbled backward, his heart banging inside his chest as he caught, through the crush of uniformed bodies, Mala talking to one of the rescue workers.

"...I never, ever let him sit up front..."

He started back toward her, but somebody yanked him back...his head snapped around as a generator or something thundered to life...he flinched against the lights, flashing, slashing through the late-afternoon grayness, off-sync and dizzying....

Carrie was back, trembling against him, coughing from the thick, diesel-scented exhaust...then she was in her grandfather's arms, nearly choking on her hysteria, going on about her mama and Lucas being hurt....

Eddie briefly met the older man's eyes, saw questions tangled with fear in their dark brown depths. Then Bev's face, still and pale beside her husband's.

"I was following her," Eddie said, feeling stupid, useless. "The truck skidded, sideswiped her—"

"Somebody said the little girl was in the car," a medic interrupted. "We really should check her out."

Carrie gripped her grandfather's neck even tighter, shaking her head, crying. Eddie cupped her fiery curls, linked his gaze with her terrified one. "It's okay, baby, go with the lady, she won't hurt you, your grandparents'll be right there with you...."

"Okay, she's out! Let's get to work on the boy!" he heard, immediately followed by Mala's, "I'm not leaving until I know my baby's okay!"

Eddie quickly kissed Carrie's forehead, took off toward the sound of Mala's voice. Her neck in a brace, her head motionless between two foam wedges, she'd been strapped on to a board and moved away from the car. But nobody had immobilized her mouth, which was arguing to beat the band.

"Sorry, ma'am," the attendant was saying. "You're hurt yourself, gotta get you to the hospital."

"I'm not going anywhere!"

"Mala, hush." Eddie stooped beside her, took her hand before she had a chance to find her voice again. "I'll stay with him," he said, only then somebody said something about "cutting him out" and Mala lost it for good.

"What the hell are they talking about?" she practically shrieked, her eyes wild with fear. *"No!"* she shrieked again when the attendants made to move the board. *"What are they going to do to my son?"*

"Now, ma'am, everything's gonna be fine—"

"Hey." Eddie reached out, snagged the attendant's arm. "I understand you're only doin' your job, but she's gonna be a basket case unless you get somebody over here to tell her what's goin' on."

The attendant shot him a dirty look, but not three seconds later, a firefighter was crouched on Mala's other side, somebody Mala knew, apparently, telling her that although Lucas' vitals looked good, his leg was caught, probably broken, and no, they wouldn't know the extent of the damage until they cut away the vehicle to get to him.

Even in the strobing lights, Eddie saw the color drain from Mala's face. "Oh, dear God...he'll be petrified! Don't you understand? I've got to stay! I can't let him go through that alone."

"Mala," the firefighter said, "there's nothing you can do in your condition."

"I told you," Eddie said, "I'll stay with him."

"Sir? I'm sorry, but I can't let you do that."

Eddie's head jerked up, saw in the kindly gray eyes across from him everything the man wasn't telling. His stomach pitched, then held firm. "And the only way I'm leaving," Eddie said through a strange and sudden calm, "is if one of y'all knocks me out and hauls me away."

Mala's hand tightened around his. "Warren?" she said to the guy. "Please? If it was Stacy...?"

After a moment, the man sighed, then nodded. "Okay. But you do exactly what we tell you, you got that? And the instant one of us tells you to move, you *move!*"

"Yes, sir. I got that just fine."

The firefighter got to his feet and strode away, barking orders to his crew as the medics finally lifted Mala into the ambulance, while Eddie saw a pair of rescuers lug what looked like a large lawnmower engine with rails attached to it over to the car, followed by somebody else holding the biggest pair of pliers Eddie'd ever seen.

"Wait! Eddie?"

"Lady, please…"

"One more second, then I'll shut up, I promise." Mala grabbed Eddie's hand again, tugged him toward her. "You sure you want to do this?"

He bent over, kissed the tip of her nose. "Never been more sure of anything in my life, darlin'. Like I said, only way I'm leavin' is if somebody carries me off." He skimmed a knuckle across her tear-soaked cheek. "Or tells me she changed her mind."

"Like hell," she whispered.

"Okay, buddy—can we *please* get her out of here now?"

Eddie gave her hand one last squeeze, then folded his arms across his chest as he watched them lift her onto a gurney, then into the ambulance where Carrie and an attendant waited; a second after that, Mala's folks said something about going on to the hospital. Eddie nodded, only to jump out of his skin when Bev reached up and hugged his neck so hard she nearly threw him off balance.

By the time they'd gone, Eddie realized the police had cleared everybody else away, that he was the only person left who wasn't a pro. Anxiety spiking his chest, Eddie walked over to the car, more than half scared of what he'd see. Both driver's-side doors had been popped off, the post between them severed; two firefighters were inside the car, working on Lucas even though he was still trapped. Eddie got close enough to see that the boy had come awake, and even though he could hear how the firefighters were trying to reassure him, he figured the kid could stand to hear a familar voice right about now.

"Please, sir—get back!" some guy shouted. Not the one

who'd told him he could stay, somebody else. "We've gotta work fast to get this sucker peeled back, get him outta there."

"Somebody—Warren?—told me I could stay with him," Eddie yelled back.

"You mean, in the car?"

"Yeah."

"Forget it, buddy, we can't take the risk, not with a civilian—"

"I'll take that chance!" Eddie roared over the awful, head-splitting noise. He glanced over, saw that Lucas had caught sight of him, his eyes wide with surprise and terror. The kid screamed; Eddie yanked his head back toward the firefighter. "You give him something for the pain?"

Sympathy shot from hazel eyes. "Sorry. But we can't, not until we know more."

"Oh, for God's sake—"

"Look, it kills us just as much as it does you to know he's hurting, we've all got kids of our own, but we don't dare—"

"Then at least let me stay with him, dammit!"

"Not if you're gonna go nuts on us, buster!"

Eddie gulped down a breath, held up his hands. "Sorry," he said, more steadily. "I'm fine, I swear. And I'll do whatever you say. Just, please…let me stay."

Seconds later, Eddie was bundled into a firefighter's coat and hat and told to crouch across the driver's seat while they worked on the roof. The minute he crawled in, somebody threw a heavy, musty-smelling blanket over both him and Lucas. Eddie grabbed the boy's tiny, trusting hand in his.

"You gotta stay real still, buddy, y'hear?"

"I'm scared, Eddie." He could barely hear the kid's whisper in the muffled darkness, over his own pounding heart. He tried to get closer, but the gearshift jabbed him in the ribs.

"Yeah. Me, too. I don't much like bein' in the dark." No reply. "How you feelin'?"

"My leg's stuck. An' it hurts. A whole lot. Where's Mama?"

"She got a little banged up, but she's gonna be okay. They took her and Carrie to the hospital already." After another few seconds of silence, Eddie asked, "You feel like cryin'?" The little hand squeezed his, making something squeeze around Eddie's heart at the same time. "It's okay, you know," he said. "If you want to—"

A godawful ripping sound exploded over their heads.

"What's that?"

"They're takin' off the roof, I reckon."

"Oh. Yeah. I forgot. They told me they had to do that before they can push out the part where my leg's stuck."

Eddie desperately tried to think of something comforting to say, couldn't come up with a damn thing. Somewhere in the back of his mind, he was aware that the air was thick and hot and metallic-smelling under the blanket, that his muscles were cramping up some in the awkward position. But that was nothing compared with what Lucas was going through, was it? And if he could, he'd gladly trade places with the boy, take on his pain.

They sat listening to the horrible noise for a minute or two, Lucas hanging on for dear life to Eddie's hand. But not crying. Not even a sniffle. Then: "Eddie?"

"Yeah?"

"Am I gonna die?"

A knife slicing through his gut wouldn't have hurt near as much. "No, Luc, you're not gonna die, where'd you get that idea?"

"My leg hurts really, really bad." The boy's breath was coming in short, shallow pants. "W-worse than it did."

"Hang on, buddy. It won't be much longer now." His mouth was so damn dry... "I broke my arm one time when I was a kid, it hurt like holy...the dickens."

"D-did you cry?"

"Probably. It was a long time ago. I don't remember."

"So, if I don't cry, does that mean I'm braver than you?"

Took Eddie a second to get his breath back after that one. "Yeah, big guy. It sure does. And you know something else?"

"W-what?"

"Next time somebody says you're a wuss, you tell 'em to come see me."

"Will you beat 'em up?"

"Nah. But I'll stand by and watch you do it."

He thought maybe he heard a tiny laugh, followed by a stifled wince. Then, "Eddie?"

"Yeah?"

The car shuddered as, with a shrieking, grinding sound, the roof got turned inside out. Damp, chilled air swamped him; somebody snatched the blanket off them, ordered Eddie to get out. As he backed away, keeping Lucas's gaze hooked in his, the kid said, "I knew you'd come back."

For the first time in probably thirty years, tears stung Eddie King's eyes.

Rubbing the muscles bunched up at the base of his skull, Eddie dragged into the E.R. waiting room nearly two hours later to run smack into Marty Koleski's glare. The older man stood up, tossing the magazine he clearly hadn't been reading onto the cluttered table bracing the corner seating unit. Worry pinching his jowly features, he crossed his arms over his open baseball jacket.

"Give me one good reason why I shouldn't punch your lights out right now."

"I'm here?"

"For how long?"

A tired smile tried to tug at Eddie's mouth. "Let's put it this way. Your daughter's last words to me before I left went along the lines of not botherin' to show my face around these parts again unless I was fixin' to stay." Eddie crossed *his* arms and met the older man's gaze dead-on. "How's that?"

After another interminable couple of seconds, Marty's face relaxed. Then he dropped back onto the corner chair, jerking his head toward the seat at right angles to his. With a heavy sigh, Eddie obliged. "Where's Bev?" he asked.

"In with Carrie. She got a couple cuts and stuff, they're patchin' her up. Haven't heard about Mala yet, but they didn't seem to think she was too bad off." He rubbed his palm against his pants leg, looking away. "Whaddya know…about Lucas?"

Eddie leaned forward, his hands knotted between his spread

knees. "His leg's pretty bad. Broken thigh bone, but…I don't know any more than that."

Silence. Then: "Poor little guy."

After another pause, Eddie said, "You ever see anybody get cut out of a car before?"

Marty glanced at him, shook his head. Then said, "Rough, huh?"

"Scary as hell. Once you see how they can peel back the roof like it was the top of a sardine can…you got any idea how much noise a car makes when it's being torn up like that? It feels like it's your head—"

Emotion clogged his throat. Eddie rubbed a hand over his face, almost flinching when he felt Marty's hand come to rest between his shoulder blades.

"Nothin' scarier than feeling helpless when your kid's hurtin'." He rubbed Eddie's back for a second, then said, "Lucas must've been scared out of his mind."

Eddie thought of the way the little boy had hung on to his hand the entire time, the trust implicit in that grasp. "I'm here to tell you, that boy's the bravest kid I've ever known."

"Lucas?"

A chuckle tried to get past Eddie's throat. "I never saw anything like it, the way he refused to cry. Even after I told him to go on ahead, it was okay—"

"Mr. Koleski?" Eddie looked up, noticed a dark-skinned, irrititatingly cheerful nurse in scrubs standing in front of them. He rose as well, shaking his head. "The name's King, ma'am. Eddie King."

"Oh. I thought…" Then she flapped aside whatever it was she'd been about to say. "Anyway, I just wanted to tell you Ms. Koleski's doing real well, we got her all trussed up good and tight so she'll be good as new in a few weeks. Her face isn't gonna look so good for a while yet, heaven knows, but the baby's just fine."

Eddie stilled. Then he and Marty both said, "The what?" at the same time.

"The…" The nurse's dark eyes zipped from one to the other, her grin fading as it obviously occurred to her that she was the only one standing there who knew what the hell she was talking about. "Uh-oh," she finished.

"You telling me Mala's *pregnant?*"

Looking like she'd rather be anywhere but right there at the moment, the nurse finally sighed and said, "Uh, yeah. About seven weeks along, from what we could tell."

"Where is she?"

"Down the hall, second room on the right—"

But he was already there by the time she finished the sentence.

The instant Eddie strode into her room, Mala searched his drawn face for answers. "How is he?" she got out on a strangled breath.

His thumbs hooked in his pockets, Eddie approached the foot of her bed. God, he looked awful, his hair a mess, his face and clothes smudged with dirt. "In surgery. He was conscious when they brought him in. It'll…be a while before they can tell us anything."

Us.

"You ride with him in the ambulance?"

"What do you think?"

She started to cry, even though it hurt like hell. Eddie carefully sat on the bed beside her, taking her hand in both of his, pressing it to his roughened cheek, his mouth. "You should have seen him, Miss Mala," he said with a gentle smile as he tucked her hand against his chest. She could feel his heartbeat, strong and steady. "Bravest little kid I've ever seen. He's gonna pull through this like a trouper, you just wait and see."

But, oblivious to her own pain, panic threatened to take her under. "Oh, God, Eddie, if anything happens to him…why'd I let him sit in the front of the car when I knew better, when I *knew* what could happen?"

"Mala, Mala…no, honey…" She saw her own anguish reflected in his expression, overlaid with something she'd never seen in any man's eyes before, not for her. "Don't you dare beat yourself up over this, you hear me?" He bent his head close to hers, whispered, "There's no better mama in the world than you, and don't you forget it."

"But what if he loses his leg?"

"He won't."

"You don't know that!"

Eddie's mouth drew down at the corners, even as his hand tightened around hers. "Then we'll deal with whatever happens," he said softly. "All right?"

She searched his eyes for the strength she simply didn't have at the moment, managed a tiny nod.

"And Carrie?"

"She's fine, honey. With your mama."

Mala tried to lift her hand to wipe her face, but winced with the effort. So Eddie did the honors, even holding the tissue over her nose so she could blow. That done, he pinned her with his gaze.

"Now. What's this about you being pregnant?"

She would have jerked if the contraption they'd wrapped her in had allowed for things like mobility. "They *told* you?"

"It slipped out."

"Oh, Lord." She let her eyes drift closed. How many crises could a brain handle at one time before it shorted out?

"How long have you known?" he asked, stroking her hand with his thumb.

"Twenty minutes?"

"You're kidding?"

Dear Lord, why was he making her talk? "No, Eddie…" Each word dragged from her throat. "I've always been irregular, it never entered my mind…especially since we always…" Her tongue slicked over her parched bottom lip. "They gave me a test, before they did anything. Routine." She forced open her eyes. "Why'd you come back?"

He reached up, gently brushed her messed up hair off her bandaged forehead. "Because I wised up."

"Yeah?"

"Yeah. Seems the idea of living without you and the kids…" One shoulder hitched. "I just can't imagine it, is all."

Another tear streaked down her cheek. "You can't, huh?"

''Nope. But seein' as your father knows about the baby—''

She groaned.

''—I figure I'd better make an honest woman out of you. And don't you even think of arguing with me, Miss Mala. I intend to marry you and that's that.''

She just did not have the strength or brainpower necessary to deal with this right now. So she let her eyes drift shut again, only to hear Eddie say, ''I went to see my father.''

Her eyes popped open again. ''You did?''

''Yep. And…you were right, he didn't know my mother was pregnant.''

''And…?''

A half smile played around his mouth. ''We'll see. He seems like a nice guy. It's just not easy lettin' go of a nearly forty-year-old habit.'' Then the smile dimmed. ''Would you have told me? About the baby?''

''Would you have sent me a forwarding address?''

A breath shot from his lungs. ''Good call.'' Then, still holding her hand, he laid his other hand on her tummy as a lopsided, incredulous grin snaked across his face. ''We really made a baby?''

''That's what they tell me.'' She contemplated his hand, protectively cradling the new life inside her, trying to sort out the thousand and one feelings churning through her brain. Then she lifted her gaze to the side of his face, her heart constricting at the wonder she saw there. ''But hey—I don't care if my father's toting a Howitzer…we don't have to get married just because I'm pregnant.''

Once again, his eyes zinged to hers, his brows raised in genuine astonishment. ''But I didn't know about the baby when I made up my mind to come back and ask you to marry me, did I? I love you, you aggravatin' woman—'' Then he stopped, as if realizing what he'd just said. Once again, he lifted her hand to his mouth. ''I *love* you, Mala,'' he whispered, tears cresting on his lower lashes. ''The baby's just a fringe benefit, far as I'm concerned.''

Even as she thought her heart would explode, she said, ''But we fight all the time.''

He shrugged. "Keeps the juices flowin'."

"And I get positively huge when I'm pregnant."

He just grinned.

"And you'll have to stick around for breakfast."

The grin softened. Then he leaned over, brushed a kiss across her lips. "I'll even cook. And after that night I spent cleaning up kid barf, I've already proven I can handle the 'or worse' part of things."

But even as his words made her smile, they also pushed Lucas's situation back to the forefront of her thought. She grabbed his hand, hope and fear suddenly strangling her. "Stay with me?" she said. "Until we hear about Lucas?"

That she hadn't yet agreed to marry him wasn't lost on either of them, she was sure. Especially when he gave her an understanding nod. Then he said, "Darlin', I'm never goin' anywhere, ever again," and for the first time since she was a little girl, she felt in her heart that everything was going to be all right.

So he stayed, and they talked, partly because they had a lot to talk about, partly because talking helped keep Mala from thinking so hard about Lucas. Kept Eddie from thinking about him so hard, too. And he thought about how good it felt, and right, having a woman to talk to, someone who'd keep her eyes focused on his the way she did while she was listening, and he knew somehow they'd always be able to talk this way. Even when they were scrappin'.

Carrie and her grandparents came in and out some, too—Mala tried to get Bev to take Carrie home, but the little girl fussed so badly about wanting to stay until she knew her brother was gonna be okay, everybody finally just relented.

Her family left them alone again, and Mala soon dozed off, her brow crinkled with worry. Eddie sat with her for a while longer, holding her hand, thinking he wanted to marry her so badly, to be part of her family, he ached with it. And he understood a little—he thought—that this wasn't about trying to fix things for anybody, but about just this: being there for the people you cared about.

And giving them the chance to return the favor. And as scared as Eddie was for that little boy who'd refused to cry, he felt the first real peace since he could remember.

After a bit, he figured he might as well take the opportunity to go get a cup of coffee, stretch his legs. Out in the waiting room, Carrie had zonked out with her head on her grandma's lap. Bev looked up, smiled.

"She asleep, too?" she asked as Eddie got his cup of coffee out of the nearby machine.

"Yeah." He ambled back over to a vacant seat next to Carrie, sank into it. "Where's Marty?"

"Went to get somethin' to eat. Geez, you look beat."

He shrugged, sipped his coffee.

"So. You gonna ask Mala to marry you?"

A smile pushed up his lips. "Already did. She hasn't exactly said yes yet."

"I swear," Bev said on a sigh, "that girl always has been the most hardheaded person on the face of the planet. Can't imagine where she gets it from."

Eddie hid his smile behind the rim of his coffee cup, only then remembering that this woman was going to be his mother-in-law. If he ever got through to her hardheaded daughter, that is.

He saw Bev look down at her granddaughter, skim a work-worn hand over those flame-red curls. "I wouldn't say nothin' to Mala for the world—" she looked up, her brows knotted behind her glasses "—but there's no guarantee they're gonna be able to fix Lucas up, is there?"

Eddie frowned down into his coffee, shook his head.

"And you're still willing to take this all on?"

He looked into Bev's amber eyes, solid and judgmental behind her glasses. "If it'd been Mala hurt that bad, would that've changed how you felt about her?"

Shock streaked across her face. "Of course not! She's my baby!"

"Well, I don't feel any different about Carrie and Lucas. Wasn't something I was lookin' for, God knows, but..." He leaned forward, the cup suspended between his knees. "I've never been so scared in my life as I was when I saw what-all they had to do to get Lucas out of that car, how much he was hurtin'." He reached over, brushed a curl from off Carrie's cheek. "But I've never been more sure in my life, either, that that's exactly where I was supposed to be."

Carrie stirred and yawned, then stumbled off of Bev's lap to crawl into Eddie's, where she promptly fell back to sleep. He shifted a bit to accomodate her sweet weight on his lap, tucked her head underneath his chin. "No matter what happens down the road," he said, "I figure maybe there's something these two and I can learn from each other." His eyes lifted again to Bev's. "And that I'll always be a richer man for that."

"Uh…folks?"

Eddie jerked awake, startling Carrie who let out a little yip like the pup might've done. He shot to his feet, Carrie in his arms, only then realizing the balding man in front of him was wearing scrubs…and a big grin.

"It's good news?" Marty said, just behind him, and the doctor nodded.

"Very. But I thought maybe you'd all like to be together when I tell Lucas's mom."

Less than a minute later, Eddie tiptoed into Mala's room and kissed her awake. Her eyes flew open as a small, "Oh!" popped out of her mouth; then she looked around, saw everybody standing there…saw the doctor.

"Lucas?"

"Is one tough little kid, Ms. Koleski. He pulled through just fine. And even though the leg's going to take longer to heal than a simple fracture would, *and* he's going to have to continue to be tough to get through his physical therapy, I see no reason why there should be any serious lasting effects from the accident."

Then she burst into tears, great heaving sobs that shook Eddie up at first, until he realized she was laughing at the same time. "Oh, God, I can't do this—it hurts too much! Oh, thank you, doctor—" she swiped her cheeks with the heel of her hand "—thank you so much. When can I see him?"

"Give him a little while to come around from the anesthesia, then I'll have someone wheel you up to pediatrics. I'm sure he'll be just as anxious to see you as you are to see him." The doctor turned to Eddie, smiling. "And you, too, Mr. King. In fact, the last thing he said before he went under was that I'd better fix his leg…because you promised to show him some football moves?"

Then everybody was talking at once and shaking the doctor's hand—or hugging the life out of him, in Bev's case—and Eddie realized he didn't feel like an outsider anymore. That he wasn't an outsider anymore. And never would be again. Well, unless he really screwed things up and Mala's father did come after him with that Howitzer.

Then the doctor left, the roar subsided, and all eyes turned to Mala.

"What?" she said.

"So you gonna marry this character or not?" Marty said.

With a gasp, Carrie scooted over to Mala, who smiled up into Eddie's eyes, her own filled with promises he hadn't allowed himself to believe in since he was a little boy. Then she said to Carrie, "Whaddya think? Should I?"

A headful of red curls enthusiastically bobbed.

Then Mala's smile turned downright wicked as she said with a shrug, "Oh, what the heck? Why not?"

This time, they all got so loud some old battle-ax nurse stuck her head in to tell them to keep it down, this was a *hospital,* for heaven's sake, only to yelp herself when Eddie grabbed her and started waltzing around the room, while his new family applauded and hooted with laughter.

And out of the corner of his eye, he caught his bride-to-be's dimpled smile.

Epilogue

They had to hold the Superbowl party at Steve and Sophie's this year because, as Eddie put it, there were just too dang many of them to fit inside the Koleski's tiny house anymore. And Mala had to admit, as she watched Eddie pump the air and high-five Steve when the Bears—not the Lions, but close enough—made a touchdown, their new daughter never even flinching from the safety of her father's other arm, that there were a *lot* of kids. And a *lot* of babies, by the time you counted Sophie and Steve's seven-month-old son, and little Prince Skye—Alek and Luanne were visiting again with their two…and Luanne was going to the bathroom with suspicious frequency—and Del and Galen's Sam, who had reached the lightning-fast toddling stage, and then Mala and Eddie's own dark-haired urchin, Abigail Terese, who'd already sprouted her first tooth last week, on her two-month birthday. Just what they needed, another precocious daughter.

Speaking of whom…guess who put her little sassy self in charge of Lucas's physical therapy sessions? Not that anyone would actually admit this to Carrie's face, but they all knew that Lucas's stunningly quick recovery had a lot to do with his

sister's goading. And he would never know how often Mala or
Eddie had found her in tears, those first few weeks after they
brought Lucas home from the hospital and everything was so
difficult for him. But when he'd wake up from a nightmare,
guess who was often first in her brother's room, cooing at him
and giving him a drink of water and telling him it was going
to be all right?

Of course, then she'd turn right around and torment him
during his physical therapy sessions, calling him a weenie
every time he'd say, "I can't" or "It's too hard." Many's the
time Mala was convinced Lucas's prime motivation for doing
whatever he was supposed to that day was based less on wanting to regain use of his leg than it was to just shut Carrie up.

Who, natch, would be the first to throw her arms around his
neck in congratulations every time he overcame his fears.

Whatever works, was all she had to say.

Mala wriggled her butt onto the sofa between her brother
and her husband, sighing when Eddie slipped his free arm
around her shoulder. Her oldest daughter was turning out to be
a Nice Person—even if Mala already sympathized with the man
crazy enough to marry her—Lucas had a backbone made of
far sterner stuff than even she could have imagined, and
Eddie…

She laid her head on his shoulder, toyed with Abby's chubby
little hand.

After the guy Galen had hired to run *Galen's, Too,* left after
less than a month, she again offered the job to Eddie. This
time, he grabbed. The hours were long, but that was okay. He
was happy. Content, Mala would guess. Wouldn't be long before he and Galen went into full partnership, she didn't imagine.

Mala and the kids had talked to Eddie's father over the
phone a lot, and several videos had made the trek between
Detroit and Albuquerque. Come spring, they were all going
down there for a visit—Eddie's idea, one she knew took a lot
of guts to implement. The kids couldn't wait: a *second* set of
grandparents to spoil them rotten? *Yes!!!*

During a commercial, Del crouched in front of Eddie to discuss an idea he had for the house remodel they'd been talking about for the past six months but hadn't yet gotten around to. They'd already unblocked the stairwell and shifted everybody around to accommodate this new little person, but now Eddie and Del were in hog heaven talking about family rooms and playrooms and real master baths with dual showerheads.

A blush warmed her cheeks. Then she chuckled.

For some time after their marriage, Mala found herself wondering what she was happier about: that this wonderful, loving man had found his way into her life, or that his finding them had helped heal his lonely heart. Except eventually she decided it didn't matter. All that mattered was that they were together…

Assorted bony elbows and knees jabbed into her as Carrie and Lucas—spitting nonstop loud, whiny insults at each other—wriggled both little skinny butts into the nonexistent space between their parents. The baby's arms flailed; then she settled back to sleep in the crook of her daddy's arm, her little rosebud mouth sucking away. Eddie looked over at Mala and winked.

…and would be together for the rest of their lives.

* * * * *

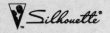

INTIMATE MOMENTS™

is proud to present a thrilling new miniseries
by award-winning author

INGRID WEAVER

Elite warriors who live—and love—
by their own code of honor.

Be swept into a world of romance, danger
and international intrigue as elite Delta Force
commandos risk their lives and their hearts
in the name of justice—and true love!

Available in February 2003:

EYE OF THE BEHOLDER (IM #1204)

After putting his life on the line to rescue beautiful
Glenna Hastings from the clutches of
an evil drug lord and landing in a hidden jungle prison,
can Master Sergeant Rafe Marek protect Glenna—from himself?

Continuing in April 2003:

SEVEN DAYS TO FOREVER (IM #1216)

Available at your favorite retail outlet.

INTIMATE MOMENTS

#1201 ONE OF THESE NIGHTS—Justine Davis
Redstone, Incorporated
Ian Gamble was on the verge of a billion-dollar invention, and someone
was willing to kill for it. To keep him safe, security agent Samantha
Beckett went undercover and became his secret bodyguard. Samantha
soon fell for the sexy scientist, but when her cover was blown, would
she be able to repair the damage in time to save his life—and her heart?

#1202 THE CINDERELLA MISSION—Catherine Mann
Family Secrets
Millionaire CIA agent Ethan Williams had his mission: find a missing
operative, and his new partner was none other than language specialist
Kelly Taylor. As he watched his bookish friend transform herself into a
sexy secret agent, Ethan faced long-buried feelings. He was willing to
risk his own life for the job, but how could he live with risking Kelly's?

#1203 WILDER DAYS—Linda Winstead Jones
After years apart, DEA agent Del Wilder was reunited with his high
school sweetheart, Victoria Lowell. A killer out for revenge was
hunting them, and Del vowed to protect Victoria and her daughter—
especially once he learned that he was the father. Would a sixteen-year-
old secret ruin their chance for family? Or could love survive the
second time around?

#1204 EYE OF THE BEHOLDER—Ingrid Weaver
Eagle Squadron
With a hijacker's gun to her throat, Glenna Hastings' only hope was
wounded Delta Force Master Sergeant Rafe Marek. As they were held
captive in a remote jungle compound, their fear exploded into passion.
Afterward, Rafe desperately wanted to be with Glenna. But could he
give her a bright future, or would he merely remind her of a dark,
terrifying past?

#1205 BURIED SECRETS—Evelyn Vaughn
Haunted by his wife's mysterious death, ex-cop Zack Lorenzo was
determined to defeat the black magic being practiced in the West Texas
desert. And Sheriff Josephine James was determined to help him—
whether he liked it or not. As they plunged into a world of sinister evil
and true love, they realized they held the most powerful weapon of
all....

#1206 WHO DO YOU TRUST?—Melissa James
Lissa Carroll loved Mitch McCluskey despite his mysterious ways. But
when she was approached with evidence claiming he was a kidnapper,
she wasn't sure what to believe. Searching for the truth, she learned that
Mitch was actually an Australian spy. Now he was forced to bring her
into his high-stakes world, or risk losing her love—or her life—
forever....

SIMCNM0103